Placement of Character

By Brian Polk

This is a work of fiction. All characters, names, ages, places, and occurrences are a product of the author's imagination. Any resemblance to people, living or dead, is a coincidence.

Thanks to Vanessa Gochnour, Nate Stone, and Colette Armstrong for their help as usual.

ISBN 978-0-9981120-9-1

Publishers:

Suspect Press
1280 Sherman St
Denver, CO 80203

YR Collective
C/O Brian Polk
P.O. Box 100263
Denver, CO 80250

Chapter 1

There are five words that always seem to elude a certain class and character in any given day and age. An utterance that Mason and Eileen Jarman and so many people like them yearn to hear. Seemingly normal folks pay large sums of money for self-help books and therapists just to be in the vicinity of an apparently merited anyone declaring a remark such as this. Seminars, sermons, and ceremonies full of pride and grandeur all promise eager audiences this splendid declaration. And yet, hearing these words never seems to soothe the soul, since they must be heard repeatedly to have any effect.

These prodigious five words? *There's nothing wrong with you.*

In a toxic stew of an environment where everything is wrong with everyone all the time, it is impossible to figure out exactly where to fit. It all seems to be rotting: Schools, television, ideas, land, air, water, minds, bodies, souls. With nothing full of life-affirming vigor or sincerity to combat the sheer anxiety of living the right kind of life, it's much easier to hand personal fates over to the seemingly distinguished authorities of existence—those religiously endowed, those politically powerful, and those promisers of material prosperity. But even the act of surrendering free will to the ones with all the answers doesn't guarantee a doubt-free reality. The fact that doubt remains an unavoidable part of life certainly worries a lot of people.

In fact it certainly worried the Jarmans, two unfortunate souls plagued with doubt and heavily burdened by the lack of knowledge that nothing was wrong with them. According to antiquated and dehumanizing monitors of societal success, both Jarmans were underachievers among peers. The pair eschewed home ownership, progeny, cars, and lucrative careers despite their respective ages of 36 and 34. And the fact that they didn't have any desire to lust after the fruits of their culture made them even more suitable for disdain.

They might have experienced the wrath of parental scorn and disappointment if either had any parents left. While they shared a mother, neither had met their fathers, and that was all the same since one was dead and the other in prison for unspeakable crimes. Even their mother had relocated to Texas when they were 14 and 12 respectively, and no one had heard from her since. The closest thing they could claim as a guardian was their maternal grandmother, who had raised them with her various suitors. However, she didn't speak to them anymore when she could avoid it. More than a decade ago, she saw the light of religious conversion and cut her grandchildren completely out of her life. She had no inkling that the young Jarmans were bad people prior to becoming a Born Again Christian, so praise the lord for that. There are few things greater than the smug sense of satisfaction a recent convert gets when she shuns activities and people she once enjoyed immensely.

But even the Jarmans hadn't spoken with one another in almost six months—the longest they'd gone since Eileen was born. This lack of communication wasn't the result of any religious conversion or animosity; it was simply because Eileen relocated to a roomy suburban home with her boyfriend while Mason remained in his two bedroom apartment in the city with a rotating roster of terrible roommates. When she first moved, they had planned to get in touch a few times a week, but life got in the way and weeks became months. The fact that they were about to be reunited evaded them both.

. . . .

Mason didn't know how to broach the subject of how uninteresting his friend Mark had become—or even if he should. Aside from artists, felons, and various derelicts, everyone becomes uninteresting in his or her thirties. Why should his childhood friend have been any different? Yet Mason hadn't accepted the invitation to dinner and drinks just to sip red wine and discuss the finer points of the cloth versus disposable diaper debate (for which he had no opinion). He came to drink excessively and expound on intellectual pursuits, new bands, new albums, fears, hopes, dreams, and the passion for life, which had thrived in Mason and Mark throughout their youths. Instead, all Mason encountered at this dinner party was a crying baby and two weary adults.

For the first time in the entirety of their friendship, Mason felt uncomfortable around Mark. They both had tattoos scrolling down their arms, but Mark wore a cardigan over his. Mason wasn't sure if the purpose of Mark's sweater was to cover his past or to look sharp, and Mason didn't want to ask since he was afraid of the answer. Mark generally dyed his hair blonde (or red or green); now it was naturally black like Mason's. He had removed all his piercings, including the gauges in his ears, and he even put on a few pounds. Mason's gauges were still in place, much like his Operation Ivy shirt, which he wore without irony. He also strictly maintained his weight—not for his vanity, he told himself, but for his health.

Mark's condo also looked and felt very different from the apartments of his mid-twenties. Framed artwork and respectable-looking furniture replaced gig flyers and couches with large rips in the cushions. Also gone were shelves of hundreds of records, books, and zines.

Mark confessed to his friend that he had sold most of his records and literature. His intellectual curiosity had also waned in recent years—he no longer listened to new music, or had any fears, hopes, or dreams outside of those he wished upon his expanding family. His passion, he mused with a sense of satisfaction on his face, was his own flesh and blood, which filled him with a purpose in life that hitherto had been nonexistent.

"I look at Marcus," Mark said about his child, "and it fills me with such joy and pride. Such hope." He paused as he beamed, staring deeply into his glass of wine. "I never really felt that before."

Mason's initial response would have been to scoff, but he didn't want to dampen his friend's obvious moment of elation—no doubt enhanced by the dopamine swimming in his brain from the first glass of booze he had consumed in months. But since social protocol begged a response, he sort of nodded and said, "Mmm."

"Having a kid is…" he said with a smile. "It's the best thing I've ever done. All those years of doing drugs and going to shows and playing in bands—that's great for being young, but it's hollow. There's no purpose to it, you know? Being a father, that's what gives life meaning."

As the conversation became more condescending, Mason was feeling much less generous with his responses. He sneered. "I still do drugs and go to shows and eventually I'll start another band. You think my life is meaningless?"

The smile vanished from Mark's face and he sighed. "Yeah, but... I mean... No, not for you."

Mason stared into his empty glass of wine. He had refilled it three times and now there was nothing left in the bottle. *Thank you for inviting me to your house for this nice evening of condescension*, he wanted to tell his friend, but he figured he'd try a more nuanced route first. "I don't understand why you would call me up and invite me over for dinner and drinks if all you were going to do is talk about how much better your life is than mine."

Before Mark had a chance to respond, his wife Sheila, who had excused herself to attend to the baby a few minutes before, ran down the stairs in a fit of white-hot rage. "How dare you come into our house with your cheap wine and crappy attitude and insult my husband!" she yelled.

All throughout the meal, Sheila hadn't drunk or contributed much to the conversation. Mason assumed her silence had something to do with his position on the couple's reunification after their last particularly nasty breakup (Mason was against it and Mark informed her of his opinion). While he wasn't incorrect about this specific assumption, she had plenty of solid reasons for loathing him. To begin with, in all the years that she and Mark dated, they never got along— especially not after Mason slept with Sheila's younger sister and never called her again. (To be fair, the sexual encounter was awkward and unfulfilling for them both.) Secondly, he was truant from the wedding, yet he attended the reception and, along with his sister, drank a substantial portion of the open bar tab. (The wedding took place in the morning at a "most indecent hour," as Mason put it, and an open bar was always a fantastic invitation in the presence of him and his sister.) Third, he didn't offer any response to the birth announcement, not even an email or call of congratulations. (Of course, even if he possessed any awareness about the custom of offering positive feedback in regards to the birth of a new human, there was no way he would have obliged, as he found the whole endeavor offensive.) And during the pregnancy, every time Mark went out with his old friend, he came back poisoned with bad ideas and booze. (Well, yeah.) And finally tonight, he attempted to change the subject every time Marcus was mentioned.

"This wine was $30," Mason said, clutching the bottle. "I could have gone way cheaper…"

"Who gives a damn?" she said. "You were the only one who drank it."

He was about to point out the fact that Mark did indeed have a glass and the offer was extended to her, so if she didn't have any, whose fault was that? Instead he said, "I'll be leaving now."

"Good," she screamed. "You're such a dumb asshole!"

"Sheila, that's enough," Mark said, placing his hand across her torso to restrain her as Mason gathered his sweatshirt and shoes.

"No, it's not enough," she said. "He's a loser from your past, from the former you, and he'll always be a loser. No car, no house, no kids, and for what? So he can keep being a teenager as an adult? Please!"

Mason tied his shoes as fast as he could while Mark attempted to contain his wife. A feeling of extreme anxiety came over him—one that he hadn't encountered since his grandmother's friend took him to church against his will as a young man. His grandma figured it would be a good experience for him. Of course, the church incident occurred long before she became born again.

"You're such a hipster loser," she scowled, breathing fire and contempt. "How could such a pathetic jerk-off like you look down on us? We have something to show for our lives: A home, a car, a career, a beautiful baby," she said, holding out a finger for each symbol of status. "You have nothing!"

He wanted to say, "At least I'm interesting," but he realized that was both debatable and not necessarily something that Sheila and new Mark would find impressive enough to award him a point in the debate. So he turned his back and walked out the door without saying goodbye.

Since both sides of the encounter considered themselves on higher moral ground, neither planned on apologizing.

Chapter 2

Buried in the back of Eileen's mind, a token of thought that was easy to ignore for two years, three months, and four days had become much more pronounced recently. At first this thought introduced itself as a murmur. Then it graduated to a whisper. Now it spoke in nagging tones, and Eileen had to confront it or surrender to anger and depression. The notion was this: She must leave her boyfriend Paul posthaste.

It wasn't as though Paul possessed the traits of an abusive or disloyal boyfriend. In fact, most of the time, he didn't seem to care if Eileen was present in his life or not—and therein lay the problem. The two shared no interests, had no mutual friends, and held very different worldviews. It was a relationship built on physical attraction, and even that began to wane, as Eileen increasingly preferred solo missions over coupling. The cultural dynamics were always difficult to navigate as well. Paul had no tattoos and always donned blue jeans and plain t-shirts; meanwhile, Eileen wore horn-rimmed glasses that hadn't been popular since the 1950s (or in Far Side Cartoons during the 1980s), had two full sleeves of tattoos, a nose ring, dyed jet black hair, and always wore band T-shirts (her favorites: The Cure, RVIVR, Citizen Fish, and the Ramones).

While he, too, maintained a healthy amount of doubt about the relationship, Paul was shy about broaching the subject. But similar to the manner in which seemingly normal people can be pushed to bouts of fury after they're cut off in traffic, he was still capable of reaching his own fit of rage if the conditions were right.

And the right conditions were beginning to take shape.

"What are you doing home so early?" Paul asked Eileen as she walked through the front door.

"It didn't work out," she said.

"What do you mean, 'It didn't work out?'"

"Well, I went into the building, rode the elevator up to the third floor, and when the doors opened I just kind of stood there," she said as Paul glared at her. "Then I had a premonition."

"A what? What's that mean?" asked Paul. He was beginning to lose control of himself.

"Like a vision," she said. "I had a vision of myself working a job I didn't like for a pathetic paycheck and it scared the hell out of me. So I waited for the elevator doors to close and I rode it back down. Then I drove around for awhile, got some tea, and came back home."

"It scared you?" Paul said incredulously.

"Yeah, you're always depressed and cranky from work, and I sure as hell don't want to be like that."

The job that Eileen had quit before she started was her first in three years. Since Paul brought home six figures as a pharmacist, she didn't really need to work. But somewhere between her boredom and feelings of inadequacy and his increasing weariness at having a sexless stay-at-home girlfriend, Paul came to an undeniable conclusion: Her unemployment had become a problem. So when Eileen told him she found a job, Paul was ecstatic. He had convinced himself that her dwindling libido was a result of her lack of both responsibility and physical mobility. Once she got out of the house more and her self-worth was restored, he reasoned, her sexual prowess would return as well. So when she came home six and a half hours too early, Paul's dreams of greater sexual frequency were dashed. And that, more than any of Eileen's other actions, made him as furious and disappointed as a social conservative receiving an invitation to his only son's gay wedding.

"But that's how it works," he yelled. "Everyone hates their job, and they do it anyway."

"But that's not how it should be," she said morosely.

Paul didn't know how to respond. His agitation rendered him speechless, and much like a recently cut off motorist, he was showing signs of extreme hostility. "Not how it should be?" he finally said, his voice shaking. "You know what your problem is?"

"Uh-," she managed to say before Paul cut her off.

"You're a hopeless idealist," he declared, a statement that surprised them both since he had never once spoken in accusatory tones. After a few seconds of stunned silence, Paul realized his venting granted him a sense of power, and he couldn't stop himself. "You always think of things the way they should be and not as they actually are."

"What's wrong with that?"

"Everything! You can't even keep a job for ten minutes."

"Yeah, well..." she began, but trailed off before she could make a point. She couldn't really think of anything to say in her defense, so she figured she'd desperately grasp at straws. "Your problem is that you don't care about the world; you just care about yourself."

"How can you say that? I care enough about you to pay for your entire lifestyle."

"Yeah," was the only thing Eileen could think to say. She had conceded the argument, now she was just hoping to minimize the damage.

"And you don't really care about the world either. You pretend to care about the world with your compassion and feminism and rants against fracking and all that, but it's all just so you can lord it over people. Your beliefs are just a way for you to make yourself feel superior to everyone else. 'Oh, I'm so interesting because I won't let my boyfriend get cable.' 'Oh, I'm so much better because I'm vegetarian and hate fur coats.' 'Oh, I'm so goddamn pure because I always tell everyone how much I hate living in the suburbs.' If you hate it so much, why don't you leave?"

"You're calling me a fraud," said Eileen. "And, wait a minute. Are you telling me I should leave the house? Are you kicking me out?"

Paul wasn't certain he meant to say that, and he was equally unsure if he should stay the course or quickly retract the statement. "Uh," in a matter of seconds, his mind went into overdrive as he weighed the pros and cons of the relationship. When it occurred to him that even her positive aspects had been reclassified as negative ones (for example, her physical beauty had moved from a pro to a con after their sex life dwindled into oblivion), he decided to stay the course. "Yes," he said confidentially. "You are a fraud, and I don't want you living here anymore."

Eileen was totally aghast, and Paul felt his stomach clench like a wrung out sponge. Neither knew what to do or say in this situation. "I wasn't expecting that," Eileen finally uttered, fighting back tears. She knew the sudden termination of this relationship would be a good thing for her, but she also didn't want it to happen like this. Of course, she couldn't possibly determine a favorable circumstance in which she wanted the relationship to end—no one really could. She just didn't know it could happen so abruptly, unceremoniously, and without warning.

"I wasn't either," Paul said.

Eileen turned and walked out the door. Paul wanted to stop her, but he knew he would never be able to take back the horrible things he just said. He let her go without so much as a whisper.

· · · ·

Eileen's first reaction was not to call her brother—far from it. Her first responses in the order they occurred to her were to cry, curse, get mad at herself for crying, curse some more, wonder what the hell she was going to do now while issuing further curses, and drive to get fast food burritos and soda. Immediately afterwards, the inevitable guilt that accompanies the consumption of high-caloric, low-nutritional food set in. Once that passed, she felt as though she should call her brother. And when he didn't answer, she left a message.

Mason had never fostered a reputation for answering his cell phone with anything resembling consistency. And anyone unlucky enough to have found themselves in the position of having to get in touch with him must also come to terms with some of his other communicative shortcomings. For example, he always failed to return texts or respond to (or even read) emails. If you wanted to get a hold of him, he always said, call his landline. Of course he never answered that phone or responded to (or even listened to) his phone messages. Since his cell phone was always set to vibrate, he didn't usually get any messages until he pulled out his phone to check the time, which didn't happen often.

Although Eileen had been trying for hours to reach her brother, Mason didn't get her six texts and three messages until he was walking home from New Mark and Sheila's house. Upon witnessing the chaos on the screen of his phone, he immediately called his sister without checking any of the messages or reading any of the texts, other than the last one, which read, "Where the fucking hell are you? Call me!!!"

"Mason, where the hell have you been?" Eileen asked without saying hello.

"Having a strange night," he said. "What's wrong with you?"

She sighed. "It's Paul," she said.

"Do I need to kick his ass?" he asked. This had always been Mason's response to any slightly negative relationship update from Eileen since she confided in him after the couple's first fight. It made Eileen laugh every time because his protectiveness made her feel less alone in the world, despite the fact that he had never really fought anyone before.

"No," she said with a smile. "We broke up."

Mason knew his response must be nuanced. He had to figure a way to offer his condolences without sounding both relieved and ecstatic. "Thank god for that," he said. So much for nuance.

"Hey," she said with a twinge of sarcasm in her voice. Mason had a knack for diffusing tense and somber situations. He always knew how to make his sister feel better. "I'm trying my best to feel bad about this."

"Sorry," he said. "I feel terrible, and I'm sorry." …*That this petty, boring little creep won't be a part of your life anymore.* He knew better than to say that last part.

"Thank you," she said. "A little sympathy, that's all I'm asking for."

"Come live with me," he said unceremoniously.

"Okay," she said. "You don't have to kick anyone out on my behalf, do you?"

"No, but even if I did, I would."

"Thank you."

Mason laughed. "You know you don't have to thank me. Even so, you're welcome."

"Where are you anyway?"

"I got kicked out of Mark's house and now I'm walking home."

"Mark Tormo?" She asked and Mason confirmed. "How the hell could anyone get kicked out of Mark Tormo's house? I've seen him get thrown out of every bar in Denver."

"What can I say? He's a new man."

"Hmm." She'd definitely have to see it to believe it.

"Where are you?"

"Across the street from your place," she said.

"Oh," he said. "How long have you been there?"

"You didn't check your messages, did you?"

"No, I did not."

"Right," she said, sighing and shaking her head. "A couple hours."

"Shit!" he exclaimed. "I'll be there in 15." He hung up the phone and started running.

Chapter 3

Mason's apartment stood at the corner of Lincoln and Kentucky in a large Victorian house that was cordoned off and converted into apartments in the 1920s, when Denver experienced a housing shortage due to population explosion. He lived in what was once the attic, so he had to walk up a flight of dilapidated, rotting wooden stairs that swayed to the left and right with each step. The landlord kept promising to repair them, but Mason figured she pledged the same to the last tenants and would repeat the offer to whoever came next. The inside of the house was both comfortable and spacious and looked as though its occupant didn't put a lot of thought into the *feng shui*—which was true. A couch here, a chair there, a nice used rug on the hardwood floor, a stereo, and a television—that was the extent of his decorating knowledge. Once everything was in place, Mason never gave it a second thought. It never would have occurred to him to "remodel" his meager possessions, so things appeared pretty much the same as they had the day he took up residence.

When Mason and Eileen settled in, they fixed themselves a couple of drinks and sat on the couch, staring at the reflections of one another on the screen of a blank television set. Since it was the polar opposite of her former living quarters, Eileen loved the apartment. She always felt comfortable here.

"So I'm dying to know," Eileen said, breaking the silence. "What did you do—what can anyone do for that matter—to get kicked out of fucking Mark Tormo's house?"

"Do you remember his wife Sheila?" Mason asked and Eileen nodded. "Well, she never liked me, for good reason. I never liked her either. But they just had a kid and that's all they talk about. It's just awful."

Eileen rolled her eyes. "Do you remember our old neighbor Lexi?" she inquired. Mason nodded. "It was the same thing. She asked me out to lunch a few months ago, and all she could talk about was, 'little Sammy smiled at this,' and, 'little Sammy made a poopy on that.' At one point, I was just like, 'Can we please have an adult conversation?'"

"This wasn't as bad as that. Or at least there was no baby talk. But, holy shit, did they lay down the superiority. Mark is proud of himself because he doesn't act like me anymore, and Sheila got pissed because I said something like, 'Thanks for inviting me over to talk about how much better your new life is than mine.'"

"Lexi did that to me too—made me feel like I was undeserving of any kind of meaningful life because I don't want kids."

The Jarman siblings both smiled in the relief of each other's company, basking in feelings of superiority that resulted from belittling those who belittled them. Most definitely an attitude derived from the ethos of punk rock, this coping mechanism allows social inferiors to defrock their perceived betters by devaluing their symbols of status they worked so hard to achieve. A nice car? Who needs it when one can just as easily—and much more frugally—catch a bus? Take out a mortgage? Why not sign a death contract? Have a kid?

With seven billion people on the earth and counting, what's the point?

While this manner of reasoning can provide the moral courage to make it through one's twenties, it begins to unravel during the hangover immediately following one's 31st birthday party. And that's when doubt rears its ugly head, and the pressure to become a well-adjusted adult sets in.

"What the hell are we going to do?" Mason asked.

"I'm not sure," Eileen replied. "Where are you working these days?"

"The government's paying me to sit on my ass," he said. "Well, kind of. I have to make five job contacts a week and record them in my work-search log…"

Her brow furrowed. "You're on unemployment?"

"Yeah, I got downsized from my job at the insurance office."

"Insurance office?" she said and Mason nodded. "Oh right, I forgot you were doing that. What did you do there again?"

"File documents, make spreadsheets, run errands for the bosses," he said. "Basically everything an intern does... In fact, they fired me so they could replace me with an unpaid intern. But they didn't contest my unemployment, so that was nice of them."

"That was nice," she agreed. "So what have you been doing?"

"Playing my guitar, trying to write songs, looking for jobs on the Internet, which really just means looking at porn and reading semi-interesting articles for hours," he admitted. "Oh, and brooding."

"Brooding?"

"Yeah, dwelling on sad shit."

"I know what fucking brooding means. I guess I've been

doing it too."

"It's underrated really."

She nodded.

"So what else have you been doing?" Mason asked.

"Other than brooding?" she said.

He smirked and nodded.

She dreaded his inquiry. She didn't want to admit that she was the recipient of the undue wealth and leisure Paul's occupation had afforded her. What had she been up to? Yoga, writing, exercising, staying up late, sleeping in, cooking, cleaning, reading poetry, drinking wine, brooding. While these weren't shameful pursuits, they didn't comprise a majority of her time. In fact, to accurately respond to Mason's question, she would have to say, *Mostly drinking and sleeping*, if she were being honest here.

"Mostly drinking and sleeping, if we're being honest here," she said.

"I forgot about drinking and sleeping," he said. "I've been doing that too. And of course, I have been trying to look for work to appease the people down at the unemployment office. Sometimes being unemployed is like working, which defeats the whole purpose, you know?"

She laughed. "Why don't you start another band?"

"I don't know if I'm ready."

"What do you mean?"

Mason stared at the blank TV screen for a few moments in silence. He invited his sister to remember how his last band, Tortured Metaphor, broke up on tour, its members refusing to speak to one another afterwards. "And I only ever played with Rich," he said about the band's bassist. "I'm not sure if I can even write songs without him. I'm trying, but I just don't have the confidence. I mean, I'll write a song, like song lyrics, and then I'll crumple them up and throw them away. I over-analyze everything. It sucks."

Eileen wanted to encourage her brother, or at least tell him to get over himself and just fucking do it already, but she wasn't exactly in the position to be offering advice on life at the moment. And she knew he would ask her about the zine she hadn't released since the '90s. So she changed the subject. "When do your benefits run out?"

"Oh, I don't know," he said, welcoming the new topic of conversation. "They last 26 weeks, and I'm two or so months in. I don't know how long I want it to last, though. I really don't like not working. In fact, I saw this thing on Craigslist, and I'm thinking about checking it out at some point next week."

"What kind of thing—like a job?"

"Yeah, it was under the gigs section. I'm not entirely clear on what it is, but it's called, hold on..." He fumbled around his pockets, looking for a slip of paper. "Here it is. It's this place called Lachesis."

"Lachesis?" She shook her head. "I've never heard of... What is that?"

"I don't know. I emailed the guy, and he just gave me an address."

"That's it? That's all you know about it?"

"No. Under the listing it said they needed 'talent,'" he stated, making quotes in the air. "And it also said something about being well read and open to new experiences."

"Uh oh," said Eileen.

"What?"

"Any time anyone ever asked if I was 'open to new experiences,' it was because they were trying to get me to do a threesome."

"Yeah, I don't think this is like that."

"I'm sure it's not. But it never hurts to prepare yourself for what you might be getting into."

He smirked and shook his head.

She smiled as she raised her glass. "Thank you for being so accepting of me, your fucking loser little sister."

"You're not a loser," he said in a semi-serious tone that acknowledged his obligatory reply to her sudden self-pity.

"Yes I am," she contested.

"Eileen," Mason said in a more earnest tone, "I'm going to tell you something that you might not believe at first, but it's the truth."

"What," she said with a smirk.

"There's nothing wrong with you."

She scoffed at both the sudden weightiness of the conversation and the fact that it was mystifying to hear someone who communicated solely in smart-assed comments to say something so genuine. "What are you, fucking listening to the Grateful Dead? Are you going to read me my horoscope?"

"What?" he said, defensively.

"Of course there is," she countered. "Plenty of things are wrong with me."

"If that's what you want to think," said Mason.

"What about you?" she said and he shrugged and shook his head, as if to say, *What about me?* "Don't give me that shit. There's nothing wrong with you, either."

"Hmm," Mason uttered, realizing how awkward it feels to be on the receiving end of the statement. He thought about it for a few seconds. "I hope you're right," he said.

"Of course I'm not right. You're awkward without alcohol and anxious all the time. You never want to be anywhere because you're always worried about where else you could be. Don't get me wrong, there's a lot right with you—in fact, you're mostly right..."

Mason smiled, rose from his side of the couch and

embraced his sister. "I'm so glad you're here," he said.

"Me too," she said, hugging him back. And for the first time in as long as he could remember, he didn't want to be anywhere else.

Chapter 4

Mason typed Lachesis' address into his phone's GPS and it led him to a marijuana shop. He checked the slip of paper in his pocket and his phone several times, and walked up and down the block to see if there was a suite number he missed, but he couldn't find any discrepancies in the information he possessed. Once again he looked up toward the building's facade and read the sign, "Budtenders' MMJ and Rec"—no mention of Lachesis.

When he entered the building, a tall, muscular gentleman demanded his ID. Upon determining its legitimacy, he returned it and nodded Mason through the door to the merchandise. He figured he'd save his confusion for one of the budtenders, since this beast of a man before him was most likely hired for his sheer strength and not for his ability to provide answers. Besides, his body language made it clear that he hadn't even a passing interest in chit chat.

Mason walked through the door and marveled at the vast array of choices the local pot smoker has at his behest, now that legalization had established itself throughout Colorado. He didn't remember the last time he'd smoked pot, but he'd been meaning to procure at least a bowl or two since the option was open to him. He figured he would be making history, or at least contributing to a healthy tax base.

"Welcome to Budtenders," said the amicable clerk who appeared as though she had been sampling the wares. "Is there something I can help you with on this fine spring day?"

It was a perfect April day in Denver—68 degrees and sunny, without even a hint of a breeze.

"Two things, really," said Mason. "First, what's the least amount I can buy?"

"A gram."

"Alright, how much is that?"

"It depends what you want."

"I don't want anything too intense."

"So you probably want some indica," she said. "Everything to the left up here is indica," she motioned to a shelf with about fifteen jars of pristine-looking buds.

"Okay," Mason replied. "So what's that mean?"

"Well, there's indica and there's sativa. The sativas are over there," she said, pointing.

"Is that so?"

"Indica will mellow you out and sativa will pick you up. Think of it like 'indica' is 'in da couch.'"

"Alright, I will," Mason said. "I'll take one gram of indica."

"Which one?"

"Oh, I don't know," he said. "Surprise me."

She strongly recommended Master Kush, and since Mason didn't know what the hell that meant, she didn't exactly have to twist his arm. She handed him a brown paper bag containing a prescription bottle full of about a joint's worth of legal, taxable marijuana, and he handed her the money. Mason relished the exhilaration of lawfully acquiring a substance for which millions of people had gone to jail across the globe. It was a whole hell of a lot of ado about such a little plant.

"And the other thing I came here for," he said. "Or at least, this is the address... I mean, maybe it's the address." He took a deep breath. "Have you ever heard of something called Lachesis?"

Her brow furrowed. "Who wants to know?" she wondered.

"My name is Mason and I emailed back and forth with a guy named Ted. It's about the job posting on Craigslist."

"And you think you have what it takes, huh?"

"I don't know much about it, to tell you the truth."

"Alright," she said with a flirtatious kind of smirk. Then she yelled, "Hey Ron!"

"Ted," he corrected her. "I spoke with Ted."

"I know. Ron is Ted's brother. He'll take you to Ted."

"I see," he said, and as soon as he did, a skinny, balding man with an unlit cigarette in his mouth, a wan complexion, and various stains on what used to be a white shirt lurched forth through an open doorway that was obscured by a curtain.

"What?" the man demanded.

"This guy here wants to see Ted," she said.

"How you know Ted?" he spoke in words so breakneck, Mason's brain spent a few seconds deciphering them.

"I don't," Mason finally said, attempting not to appear flummoxed. "I'm responding to an ad posted on Craigslist… it's something called Lachesis."

His eyes turned to slits, his head cocked, and he carefully surveyed Mason. "You're cool, right?" he asked after a pregnant pause.

"Cooler than you'd ever believe," Mason said in an uncharacteristic bout of self-assuredness.

"That was the right answer," said Ron. "Follow me."

He turned and Mason followed him through the curtain and back into a room beset with stacks of haphazardly arranged papers, folders, and books. Ron rushed over to the desk in the corner, picked up a sticky note near the phone, read it, and said, "God damn it, that fuckin'..." He gnashed his teeth, slammed the note back down, charged through a corridor, and jogged up a flight of stairs to the second floor as Mason ran to keep up with him. Then Ron walked down a short hall, knocked on the door, didn't wait for a response, and opened it. "Ted, this guy's here to see you," he said.

"What's he want?" Ted said, speaking about Mason as though he wasn't there. He stood near the entrance of the room, quiet and awkward. Ted took his smoldering cigar out of his mouth and squinted his eyes at the sun pouring through the window in an attempt to catch a glimpse of the intruder. Slouching in a large leather chair, he was surrounded by even more clutter than Ron had in his room downstairs. And even though the windows clearly opened, Ted seemed unfazed in a room besieged by a cloud of tobacco smoke. He was as skinny and disheveled as his cohort, except he managed his balding by clinging to wisps of hair that he combed across his head in a misguided attempt at vanity.

"Lachesis," said Ron.

He looked up at Mason and coughed violently for a few moments. When he collected himself, he said, "You're one of the guys that sent an email?"

"Yes," he said.

Ted motioned for him to sit down as Ron fled the office, slamming the door behind him. Mason nervously took a seat while Ted attempted to regain his composure after another fit of coughs. "What's your name again?" Ted wondered.

"Mason Jarman."

Ted laughed and then coughed for what seemed like minutes. "Like a mason jar?" He said.

Mason rolled his eyes and sighed. He spent his whole life

on the receiving end of taunts of this exact nature. What exasperated him the most was the sheer lack of imagination by which people made the old "mason jar" joke.

"Yes like a mason jar, but with a man on the end of it," he said. "Use it as a mnemonic device, and not as a tired joke." He mumbled that last part, but Ted still heard him.

Since Ted's last name is Redbone, he sympathized with him enough to steady his demeanor. A staunch capitalist in the age of the Cold War, he used to threaten to fight anyone who called him Ted the Red. (They also referred to him Ted the Red Bonehead, but he didn't threaten anyone for calling him that. He beat the shit out of them outright.)

"Well okay, Mr. Mason Jar with a man at the end," he said once he settled down. "Do you know what Lachesis is all about?"

"Other than looking for candidates who are well read and open to new experiences, no, I don't."

"Have you ever heard the expression, 'Art imitates life?'"

Mason furrowed his brow. "I thought it was, 'Life imitates art.'"

"It's both. It's a mess of life imitating art and art imitating life with all the lines blurred."

"You lost me here, Ted."

"Basically, we find characters in stories for you to play. Then you play the characters and collect your pay at the end."

"So it's like acting."

"In a way, yes."

"In what way is it not?"

"You're not on a stage, for one thing. And there ain't any audiences."

"So who would I be acting to?"

"You really just follow the narration on the one-sheet. It's fiction, and you're the character."

"That doesn't make any sense," said Mason.

"Let me explain it to you the same way I explain it to all the newbies," Ted said, fighting back the urge to cough. "Stories all happen one way or another. You got your non-fiction—biographies, war stories, and the like—and they're all about real people, so of course they happened, am I right? Well then you got your fiction, and everyone thinks fiction is made up, but it ain't. Well it is and it ain't. Let me put it another way, these stories need people and Lachesis gives them the people. It's character placement. And of course there's another way to put it—we pay cash at the end of each story, so if you have any doubts about the business, I can assure you, cash don't bounce."

Mason thought about it. "So who pays you?"

"Publishing houses, literary magazines, and sometimes authors—they pay us. We give you a percentage of that. It starts out small, 10%. Then it can get as high as 20-25%." Mason didn't respond, so Ted took that as a cue to keep talking. "This late in the afternoon, I usually have all the positions filled, but you happen to be in luck. I got a job you can start right now—a short story that's going to run in the *New Bedford Review*. It's a supporting role to a guy named Ronald. You show up and comfort the leading man after his wife left him. You think you could do that?"

"Sure," Mason said. "...So, uh, let me see if I understand this. I'm supposed to act out a story for the benefit of the writer? Does he watch us and write down what we're doing or something?"

"Don't worry about that. Just work on becoming the character. Here," he said, handing Mason a sheet of paper. "That's the one-sheet. It includes the synopsis and outline. It's the only time an author of fiction imagines scenarios out of thin air. When you start to work on novels, you get a new one every day. But since this is a short story, you only get one. Now get yourself familiar with the character and then get yourself to the place listed on the back. That's where the story takes place."

"This is all so surreal."

"If you do a good job, I'll pay you a starting fee of $50 for an afternoon's work. How's that sound?"

"That sounds good," said Mason.

"Good, now get your ass down there and we'll see you when you're done."

Mason left the office in a daze. If it weren't for the sheer boredom of unemployment, the meeting would have instilled in him a deep sense of distrust and disbelief. A man so haphazardly composed with such fantastic claims sacrificed all his credibility and subsequently deserved no benefits of any doubts. But of course Mason had nothing better to do, and since he was just as subservient to his curiosity as anyone else, he figured he'd make an afternoon out of it.

Chapter 5

The setting listed on the back of the one-sheet was about a twenty minute walk from the shop, a bar called Danny's Mixed Cocktails. Unsure of whether or not he needed to report to anyone, he shrugged and walked through the front door, hopeful that whatever awaited him on the other side would recognize him.

"Dale," someone shouted in his general direction. Mason looked behind him to see if anyone else had followed. "Over here, Dale," he said again.

The realization occurred a second later—Mason was Dale, he read it on the one-sheet. It was time to act the part. "Ronald," Mason said, "how's it going?"

"I wish I could say, 'good,' my man. But I can't."

"Why? What happened?"

"She left me, man," Ronald said. "Jamie's gone."

Mason glanced around the bar, not sure whether or not he was supposed to be following a script. Was there a narrator for which he should be listening? After an uncomfortable pause—during which Ronald, to his credit, never broke character—Mason figured he would commence conversing in the manner of the man named Dale on his one-sheet. "I'm so sorry to hear that, my friend."

"You're sorry," he said. "I'm the one who's sorry. She took

the cat, the kids. I don't know what to do." With pain in his eyes, he looked to Mason. "What am I going to do, Dale?"

Mason never had cats or kids under his care, so he never grew fond of or attached to either. Consequently, he had no words with which to comfort Ronald, as Dale or otherwise.

"I don't know," he said. "What even happened?"

"Fucking Jamie 'borrowed' my phone," he said, making quotes in the air. "And... Remember that girl Stacey?"

"The one you were getting comfortable with behind her back?" Mason guessed.

"The very same," he said with a smile. "So Jamie 'borrowed' my phone and searched everything—my texts, my emails, all my pictures."

"What'd she find?"

"Everything," Ronald confessed. "Texts about meeting up, emails about meeting up, pictures of us meeting up and fucking."

Mason laughed.

"It's not funny Dale," he said.

"I'm sorry," Mason said as Dale. "It's just, you kind of brought this on yourself, you know?"

Ronald nodded and exhaled at the same time. "I need another drink," he said. "What are you drinking?"

He tried to imagine what Dale might drink and opted instead to order what Mason drank. "A vodka soda," he said.

Ronald ordered a round, and the two stared at the television in silence until the bartender returned with two glasses. The protagonist put them on his tab. "How long have we been friends?" Ronald asked after taking his first swallow.

A sense of panic inundated Mason as he tried his best to appear as though he were contemplating his question. The one-sheet made absolutely no mention of the span of their friendship. He tried to think like a writer of a short story, but how did they think? He wondered how they came up with details such as these. Did they just make it up as they went along? Could Mason do that now? "Oh man," he said, taking a mouthful of his drink. "A long time."

"You bet your ass, a long time," he said, as Mason smiled. Maybe Ronald didn't know either. "And in that time, have I ever done you wrong?"

Mason's brow furrowed. He thought about making up a story of Ronald doing Dale wrong, but thought better of it. "No," said Mason, shaking his head.

"I haven't, have I?" said Ronald. "I do one bad thing to one person and all the sudden my marriage turns to shit…"

Authors sure can use a lot of swear words in their stories for the New Bedford Review, Mason thought. "It's fucked, man," Mason decided to say in support of a literary journal that didn't censor its content.

"It's totally fucked," Ronald agreed.

"Fucking fucked."

"You couldn't be more right."

The two nodded in unison. "Well, except for one thing…" Mason said.

"What's that?"

"Is this the first time cheating on her, or the first time you got caught?" Mason asked.

"Um," Ronald said, and then glared down at his beer in silence for what seemed an eternity. Then he began counting with his fingers. "This is probably the fifteenth time I've cheated on her," he admitted finally.

"Fifteen times and you never got caught," he said. "Until now."

"Until now," Ronald confirmed.

"So it's not really one bad thing; it's fifteen, isn't it?" Mason said to Ronald's nods. "Let me ask you this: Did you cheat fifteen times, or with fifteen girls?"

He sighed. "Girls."

"So you probably cheated multiple times with multiple women?"

"Shit," Ronald said at the epiphany that was becoming crystal clear for the first time. He couldn't paint himself as both a victim and an occasionally wayward saint if he was neither. Sure she "borrowed" his phone, but he looked through hers from time to time when it was charging in the laundry room. And sure she caught him cheating this one time, but it was only because he had grown too careless and aloof to cover his tracks. "Dale?"

"Yes?"

"This may be my fault," Ronald confessed.

"If we're connecting the dots," Mason said, "that's a conclusion we might come to."

"God damn it," he said, and then he guzzled the rest of his drink and arose in haste from his barstool. He threw $20 down on the bar.

"Are you leaving?" Mason asked.

"I gotta go talk to Jamie," he said as he passed Mason towards the bar's exit. "Thanks Dale," he yelled behind him.

Mason scanned his surroundings, wondering if the scene had concluded. As he sat at the bar, he silently hoped his performance was adequate. Erring on the side of caution, he bided his time by ordering another couple of drinks in case Ronald needed further guidance, but no one bothered him again. Once he was sure his character had finished furthering all necessary plot developments for the story, he paid his tab and left a couple of dollars for tip before heading out.

· · · ·

"Excellent work," Ted said when Mason returned to his office later that afternoon.

"That was good?" Mason asked.

"Perfect," he said. "I'm reading the notes from the scene right now. You got talent, you know that?"

"Well thank you," he said. "So you're reading something from the scene we just did?"

"Yep, just got the email in the time it took you to make it back."

"That's crazy you got it already," Mason said.

"The business happens fast these days," he said. "Not like it used to be. Before email, they used to fax the notes. Before that, they had to wait for them to come in the mail. That's back when it took a lot longer to get paid. Now characters expect to get paid the same day, which is good for you, not necessarily great for us."

Mason nodded. "So is it any good—the story, I mean?"

"It's your standard 'dirtbag male epiphany' story," he said. "*The New Bedford* is one of these new edgy erotic lit journals out of New England. After your scene, the male protagonist finds his wife and apologizes. They go home, send the kids to bed early, and spend all night screwing, or whatever. Like *50 Shades of Grey* but with decent writing."

Edgy erotic lit journals? Mason had no clue such a concept existed. And the part about screwing all night? "Wait a minute," he said. "What's the part about screwing all night? Do the characters actually have sex?"

"Well yeah."

"Can you get me in on one of those?"

"Those parts go to union members most the time."

"Union? How do you join the union?"

"You have to be asked to join," Ted said. It was clearly not his favorite subject to discuss. "Anyway pal, you did good today."

"Thanks. I just hope the story turns out well."

"That's one thing you learn quickly about the business—it doesn't matter if the story's shit. All that matters is if you do a good job, understood?"

"Sure," agreed Mason.

"Here," he said, counting out bills and handing them to Mason. "That's $50—not bad for an afternoon's work, huh?"

"Not at all," he said with a smile on his face.

"Here's a coupon for 10% off if you want to spend any money at Budtenders."

Mason thanked him.

"Come back on Thursday, early, around eight. I might have another short story that needs a strong male character and I think you'd be perfect. It pays a lot more, but it is more work. Just make sure you come to the back door. The dispensary doesn't open until nine."

Mason agreed and then thought of his sister. "The story doesn't need a strong female character, does it?"

Ted shook his head. "No, there is no female part for this one. Why, you know someone?"

"My sister would be really good at this," he said.

"Have her come talk to me," he said. "I have to tell you though, we don't get many requests for strong female characters. Nothing against your sister, that's just the business."

"Well, I'll tell her still," he said. "She could be different characters, I'm sure."

"Like I said, have her talk to me."

Mason stood up to leave. "Thanks Ted."

Ted nodded. "See you Thursday."

Chapter 6

Three suitcases, packed with room to spare. That was Eileen's worldly belongings—even less than she owned when she had first arrived. Sure, she bought things—in fact, she completely redecorated Paul's house—but she procured most all her effects with credit cards he gave her. And he made it very clear in their discussion last night that, aside from clothes and her cell phone, she wasn't to remove anything from the residence that she hadn't purchased with her own earnings.

She couldn't help but lament her outright refusals to his myriad marriage proposals. At least a divorce at this point would grant her some leverage. She suspected his hard-line stance on matters of finance was retribution for rejecting him for so long.

For the grand relocation, Paul let her use what until very recently had been "her" car for the last time. As circumstances changed, so too would her ownership status when it came to the car, the cabin in Glenwood Springs, the house, and access to finances. The official transfer of ownership hadn't been arranged just yet, but Paul planned on canceling all her credit cards, removing her name from the bank account, and changing the locks on the house soon. If she didn't return the car by 9 o'clock that night, he warned her, he would report it stolen.

Mason was supposed to help her with the move, but apparently he found reason to celebrate and didn't come home last night. As was his *modus operandi*, he didn't answer his phone all morning either. When he finally got around to returning her calls (and texts), her trio of bags were already packed.

"Mason, where the hell have you been?" she said as she answered the phone. He was beginning to suspect this was how she was going to respond to his calls from now on.

"I went on a bender and ended up at this girl Trish's house," he said.

Eileen sighed. "You told me—you promised me—that you would help me move, not get drunk and screw some girl you picked up at the bar."

"I didn't mean to," he said. "Well I meant to go get drunk and I definitely meant to have sex with Trish—holy shit is she crazy—but I honestly didn't mean to stand you up. I'm sorry."

She was about to tell him to fuck off, but then she sighed. "Oh, that's alright," she said finally. "I'm not really mad at you. I'm just pissed at this situation."

"I'm sorry," he said again.

"Don't worry about it. I guess when you're faced with a choice to get drunk and screw a crazy girl or help someone move, you gotta go drunk and crazy."

"Yeah," he said. "How's it going over there?"

"Fine, I'm done. Are you back at the house?"

"Yeah, why?"

"I'll let you take me out for some food and drinks to make up for bailing on me."

"I can do that," said Mason. "I have to talk to you about that job thing I went to yesterday anyway."

"Oh yeah, Latch Key, or something like that."

"Yeah," he said with a laugh.

"Well alright," she said. "I'll be there soon."

· · · ·

"There's something not right with me," Eileen told Mason over drinks at the Syn-Think, a hole in the wall vegan restaurant and bar on Broadway. It was dimly lit, its bathroom covered in graffiti, and most important of all, there was no television. "I'm not a very well-adjusted person."

"No, you are not," Mason playfully said, shaking his head. "No siree Bob. No indeed-ee-doo."

"That's enough… Jesus, someone got laid last night," she said with a smile and a little bit of envy. "And anyway, like you're any better."

"Nope," he said. "I'm totally fucking hopeless."

She smiled again and then considered the implications in his statement. After a few moments of silent contemplation, she said, "Does that ever bother you—that hope seems to be in such short supply these days?"

Mason sighed. He imagined new Mark and Sheila—especially Sheila—and their complete and total lack of respect for him, and how their opinion was a microcosm of the value system of society at large. Then he thought about his grandma and how her religious conviction made her certain that he was doomed beyond any doubt. Did that bother him? Of course it bothered him, but here was his little sister reaching out to him, in dire need of any kind of role model. And since he was all she had at the moment, he didn't want to appear weak in the face of adversity.

"A little," said Mason. *A lot*, he thought.

"What do you do about it?"

"Lie in the fetal position and cry."

"No seriously. You have to have some kind of coping mechanism."

"Alcohol," he said. "And having sex with crazy girls."

"That's it? What about your friends—what happened to them?"

"I still have plenty of friends I see at the bar, or whatever. But I don't really have any close friends anymore. They moved, or they don't speak to me anymore, or I don't speak to them anymore, or they had kids and don't want to associate with an aging punk rocker who has no ambitions."

"Oh Mason, that's so sad."

"I'm sorry. I didn't mean to..." he began to say, but his concentration was hijacked when he caught sight of a man grooming himself at the table next to him. "...bum... you...out." He glared at the man. "Is that guy fucking clipping his fingernails at the bar?"

Eileen quickly turned to look. "He totally is," she said, and then turned back around to face Mason. "Who does that?"

"That's unhygienic," Mason said. "You know, there was this guy at the insurance place that would clip his nails at meetings. Everyone would be sitting there with their coffee and donuts and he'd be there, clipping away. And it wasn't like there was even a trash can he was clipping into. He was just flinging them on the floor. Who does *that*?"

"Fucking weirdoes. Did one of his nails ever shoot into anyone's coffee?"

Mason laughed. "No, but that would have been amazing if it did."

Relieved at the distraction the nail clipper provided, Mason took advantage of the opportunity to change the subject from hopelessness to something a bit lighter. "So this Lachesis place," he said. "It's pretty far out there."

"How so?"

"Well, you've heard the expression, 'Art imitates life,' right?"

"I think it's the other way around—life imitates art far more than art imitates life. It's an Oscar Wilde thing."

"You know what? Never mind."

"You brought it up."

"Okay, forget about that. The thing I'm doing—it's like acting," Mason explained, "but there's no audience. In fact you really just act out scenes for the purposes of fiction." Eileen's face glazed over, so he continued. "Okay, so you know how non-fiction is real." Eileen nodded. "Well fiction is real too, in that, the characters take on the action. So we're becoming characters in a story that will one day be published."

"You know what?" Eileen said, wide-eyed. "I've heard of this. This woman in my yoga class tried to explain it to me, but she's one of those new agey chicks, so I thought she was full of shit. She's into crystals and shit, so, you know, whoosh," she made a gesture, "there goes her credibility."

"She wasn't full of shit about this," said Mason. "Or maybe she was, I don't know. I still have my doubts about what exactly is going on there. But I did get paid in cash."

"In cash? That seems kind of sketchy."

"Yeah, but it's also a pot shop, so they only deal in cash" he maintained, realizing as he said it that he wasn't doing much to dispel the apparent unsavoriness of the situation.

Eileen laughed. "A pot shop paying you to act out fictional situations—that seems like an elaborate prank."

"Even if it is a prank, the cash they paid me didn't bounce."

"Hmm," she muttered, obviously impressed. "So I guess it doesn't even matter if it's real or not."

"Nope," he said, shaking his head. "I tried to get the guy to hook you up with some work."

Eileen winced at the mention of the word "work." Even when she managed to maintain a job, she was always a hair's breadth away from getting fired. She couldn't imagine going through the motions of pretending to care about someone else's business again, getting castigated for lack of promptness, and cursing the sheer injustice of her scant salary. In her mind, no job could ever compensate for the amount of agony it caused.

"I don't know about that," she said.

"You mean you don't want to work?"

"No, I don't want to work." When Mason scoffed, she said, "You see that's what's wrong with me."

"What?"

"Last week you told me that nothing was wrong with me. That's one thing that's wrong with me—I don't want to work."

"Hmm," said Mason. He realized his theory on the state of his sister's disposition might be a bit oversimplified. Her unwillingness to work was most certainly a character flaw. Come to think of it, Eileen had many flaws: sloppy drunkenness, chronic tardiness, and occasional insecurities—just to scratch the surface. Since these shortcomings negatively affected other people, they weren't superficial: They were bona fide personal failings. And Mason realized he shared some of the very same failings, which meant there was plenty wrong with him as well. "I guess we're all fucked up," he said finally.

"Amen to that," Eileen said, raising her glass to his. The two finished their drinks at precisely the same moment.

Any meaningful dialogue tapered off after they ordered their next round of drinks. Then the pair devolved into their usual topics of conversation: sex, drugs, punk rock, bodily discharges, dick/vagina jokes, and the occasional high-brow literary criticism. These imperfect souls enjoyed each other's company—not to mention the company of a few of their old drinking buddies and casual acquaintances as they sauntered into the watering hole and joined them at their table. Eventually the gracious staff of the establishment threw the whole lot of them out at two in the morning. That was when most everyone paired off for the evening's coitus.

Chapter 7

Mason would have overslept if it hadn't been for Jill—or Jasmine, or Julie. The nice woman he made love to the previous night had a name, but Mason didn't remember it, which was all the same since she didn't remember his. Whatever her handle, she had arisen around seven in the morning and was in the middle of an early morning escape—or an undetected vanishing act, more accurately. But then her leg inadvertently wrapped around the cord to the alarm clock and knocked it to the floor with a thud. Mason stirred, looked over at the woman and asked why she was leaving so soon.

"I have yoga at eight," she said as she put the clock back on the nightstand.

"Wait," said Mason groggily. "What day is it?"

"Thursday."

"Oh shit," he said. "I have somewhere to be at eight." He rolled out of bed and ran to the bathroom.

"Nice meeting you," she yelled over her shoulder as she showed herself to the door.

. . . .

Mason hadn't prepared himself for the scene that greeted

him at Lachesis that morning. Instead of a one-on-one conversation with Ted, there were twenty people crammed into the back room. Before he went through the door, a man with a clipboard recorded his information—name (Mason), character preference (strong male lead or support) and genre request (romance or erotic fiction)—gave him a number, and told him to wait inside.

There weren't many seemingly well adjusted folks in the place—Mason included—which made sense since most characters in novels are irascible and neurotic, and therefore interesting. The only time people want to read about uninteresting characters is when interesting things happen to them. Accordingly, most everyone in attendance was either earthy, quirky, or off-kilter, to say the least.

Half an hour went by before his number was called, and Mason spent that time wondering if all the strange behavior in society could be attributed to characters trapped in bad plots. Perhaps there were no bad people, just bad stories. However, he quickly abandoned the supposition when he thought about historical cruelty and all the sadists who perpetuated it. Surmising barbarians were simply actors who had no control over free will would let way too many assholes off the hook.

"Number 24," a man with a flat cap bellowed. "That's me," Mason said, holding up his ticket as he walked across the room.

"It says you requested romance or erotic fiction," the man said. Mason nodded. "You're not union pal, there's no way you're ever going to get one of those. And anyway it says here that Ted's already got something for you." He handed Mason a one-sheet.

"Thank you," said Mason, clutching the sheet in his hands. He wandered to the opposite side of the room to pore over his assignment and figure out who he would be today. Apparently he was a man named Rufus who'd inherited his father's candlestick shop, Candlestick Larry's, after the old man died under mysterious circumstances. He needed to arrive at the storefront on South Broadway (almost to Englewood) to open by 9 a.m. There was a key to the shop attached to the back of the paper. He folded the sheet, placed it in his back pocket, and hurried to catch the 0 bus.

· · · ·

When he arrived at the Candlestick Larry's, he couldn't help but puzzle over its very existence. He also found it difficult to imagine modern readers expanding their willful suspension of disbelief to allow for the actuality of a place that sells candlesticks. A candle shop, maybe, but not an entire retail outlet dedicated to holders of candles. Any respectable household with disposable income might justify the acquisition of two candlesticks in a decade, tops. With no repeat customers and very little demand for a commodity hardly anyone uses anymore, a shop like this would not last long in real life.

Although these glaring failures of reason permeated Mason's mind, they were fleeting once he recalled the payment awaiting him at the end of the day. He shrugged it off, unlocked the door, and went inside as if it were a normal part of his morning routine. The layout of the storefront also seriously tested the average readers' ability to willingly suspend disbelief. A couple of candles and holders lined the wall of the display cases that faced the street, but other than that there were no candlesticks in the front room. He walked through the "staff only" door to the back and discovered the mother lode of candlesticks segregated into two separate sections. One read "Crystal," and the other "Silver," with various sizes charted out on each of the compartment's shelves. There was a glass window next to the staff door reminiscent of a ticket booth where Mason would be conducting business. He wondered what kind of candlestick he would be selling that required the protection of a glass barrier between him and the customers. He didn't think much of it as he located the restroom and the back exit to the alley. He put his sweatshirt on the coat hanger in the back, and then opened for business.

To his surprise, Candlestick Larry's was busy almost immediately. And after helping several customers throughout the morning, Mason began to notice something amiss: This was not the candlestick-buying demographic he had imagined. He supposed he'd be helping elderly women, young hipsters, and maybe the personal assistants of the ultra wealthy. Instead, his customers were mostly single young men—some returning multiple times in the span of a few hours.

"Didn't I see you earlier?" asked Mason—who was acting as Rufus—of a patron he knew was on his third visit. The man had to be in his early forties, disheveled, and with large black bags under his eyes.

"Yeah, man," he said with a look of condescension. He kept sniffing and running his finger under his nose. "Give me two more silver candlesticks."

Rufus characteristically shrugged. "Alright," he said as he turned his back to retrieve his order. "What are you having a party tonight or something?" He asked when he returned to the front desk.

"I'm partying right now, bro," he said with a laugh and another set of sniffs and wipes across the nose. He put down his cash on the counter and scurried out of the store.

Mason broke character as he cocked an eyebrow and headed back to the storage room to investigate. He picked up a silver candlestick and peered over it from top to bottom. Nothing seemed out of the ordinary. As he was placing it back on the shelf, he noticed a slight line of separation between the base and the stem. Intrigued, he twisted the stick to determine whether or not it would detach. Sure enough, it screwed apart, and Mason was holding two parts of the same candlestick. As he glanced up the body of the stem, he noticed a bag, which he pulled out with two fingers. When he unraveled it, he made an audible gasp and threw it on the shelf. Mason took a long hard look at the white powdery substance within the thin clear plastic as it seemingly stared back at him. His eyes widened. He felt a pang in his chest.

The realization came down upon him as though he was trapped in the basement of an imploding building. The pot shop, the unkempt businessmen in stained shirts, the preposterous notion that fiction could ever be real—it all made sense. He'd been had, propped up by unscrupulous drug lords to sell cocaine out of candlesticks.

The first story must have been nothing more than a ruse to gain his trust, and then they lured him here with a fake story and the promise of money. That was why there weren't any seemingly well adjusted folks at the shop that morning. They must have all been drug dealers too.

As Mason was putting all this together in his head, he heard the bell from the front door ring. He quickly slid the bag back into the candlestick and headed to his booth. When he took a seat, he saw two police officers, one of which was inspecting the candlesticks in the display case.

"Um," Mason said. Both the officers looked at him and Mason instantly regretted drawing any attention to himself.

"Is your name Rufus?" one of the officers asked.

"I suppose it is," he said.

"Are you the owner of this establishment?" the other officer wondered.

"No I just work here," he said. "But the owner's in back. Do you want me to get him?"

"If you would," said the other officer.

"I'll be right back." Mason turned around and yelled at the empty back room, "Hey Larry, there's some people here to see you." Then he casually walked towards the exit, grabbed his sweatshirt, and slowly opened the door. When his feet met the pavement in the alley, he ran as fast as he could.

Once he arrived at what he deemed a safe place, he pulled out his phone and called his sister, but she didn't pick up, which was strange because she always answered her phone. With nothing else to do, he walked into the nearest bar and ordered himself a drink.

Chapter 8

Eileen didn't answer her phone when Mason called because she was having coffee with Paul. Although she vowed never to see him again, her ex-lover sounded desperate on the phone, and her curiosity and boredom begged a break in her routine of doing nothing. She also hoped he missed her in spite of herself.

"Sorry to call you here like this," Paul said as he stood up to take off his coat. "I know you're probably busy."

"Paul, you know I'm not busy," said Eileen.

"Well I don't know your schedule," he said defensively.

"Keep your cool, Paul. I don't have to be here, and I can easily leave if you're going to be all judgmental and shit."

"I'm not being..." he stopped himself and took a deep breath. "Listen, I called you here because I miss you, and I want you back." Eileen broke eye contact to pick up her vibrating phone. "Do you have to get that?" he asked.

"It's my brother," Eileen said, hitting the lock button to reject the call. "I can always call him back. I mean, how much trouble could he be in, right?" They both laughed.

"So what do you think?" he asked. "Do you miss me too?"

"It hasn't even been a week, Paul. How much can you miss someone in that time?"

"Well, I miss you a lot," he admitted. "And I'm sorry I said those things to you. So when you're ready to come back, I'm ready to have you."

Eileen looked incredulous. "You think that's how this works? That you can come in here and grant me a pass back into your life? What am I supposed to say? 'Thank you, Paul, my liege.'"

"Come on Eileen," Paul said and then immediately winced.

Much like Mason contending with sealable food storage container jokes his entire life, Eileen endured her fair share of snide allusions to the Dexys Midnight Runners' song she had grown to hate. Paul knew this, for on their third date, he played the song on the jukebox at the bar they frequented. She sat on the patio in protest, despite the negative five degree temperature on that dark, brutally cold February evening. It was only begrudgingly that she allowed Paul to talk her into coming back to her bar stool. She didn't have much of a sense of humor when someone else intentionally brought the song to her attention just to get a rise out of her. She referred to it as musical terrorism.

"I'm sorry, I can't believe I just said that," he added.

"Whatever," she said. She now had the upper hand in the argument.

Paul sighed heavily. "Listen, I'm the one who provided for you in this relationship, and I'm the one who broke it off with you. So what I'm saying is, I'm willing to provide for you again, and I'm calling it back on. But I do have some conditions for this time around."

"Conditions?" she said with a laugh. "Okay, Paul. Name your *conditions*." Eileen couldn't decide what she liked less about her former lover: His condescension or his obtuseness.

"Would you just listen before you judge?" Paul said

frustratingly. "You always do that. You always judge me before I even finish talking. Just listen. Please." Eileen shrugged. "First of all, you need to be more intimate. We need to have more sex. This once-every-couple-months schedule we were on doesn't do it for me. Two, you have to do something around the house. You can't just sit at home all day and not cook or clean. And third, you have to tell me you love me back. I always tell you I love you and you never say, 'I love you too.'"

Her eyes narrowed as she thought about his commands. "Okay, let me respond to those one at a time. First of all, there's no way I can meet the first one, Paul. And since this is the first time you brought it up, let me tell you why we stopped having sex." She considered walking out at that moment, but she knew she would regret not informing him about how wrong he was about everything. There were a lot of different ways she could say this, but since he had his opportunity to be mean when they broke up, it was her chance to be mean now. "You just got to be so damn vanilla in bed—missionary or me on top and that's it. Do you know how boring that is?"

"What should I have done?" Paul asked defensively. He always hated talking about sex. "You never told me you liked it any other way."

"Yes, I did. You just never listened. You acted the same way every time I listened to my sexy podcasts. You just turned them off."

"So what? I don't like podcasts about sex, big deal."

"It is a big deal! The fact that I can't talk to you about sex is a big deal. I can't say what I want around you without you getting freaked out."

"Okay," he said. "What kinky sex act should I have done to you?"

"See, the fact that you even put it like that is a huge fucking turn off."

"Okay, so what do you want?"

"I want to be able to tell you my kinks. What if I wanted you to pull my hair?" Paul winced. "Or rim me?" He double winced. "Or put a dress on and beg me to peg you with a strap-on?"

"No fucking way."

"You're such an amateur," she said. "But whatever, that's okay. It's the way you are, which is why we're sexually incompatible." He started to pout. "Let's move on, shall we? You insulted my cleaning, but I cleaned plenty. I decorated the house, I vacuumed, and I cooked every now and again. I admit, I always sucked at cooking, especially when you demand meat at every meal. I don't know how to cook meat. I've been vegetarian since I was ten."

"Yeah well, a guy can't live on vegetables alone."

"Sure they can. Mason's been vegan since he was twenty-five."

"Mason's not a man."

"You say anything bad about my brother again and I'll have your balls," she said. Paul scoffed, but dared not say another word. "What's the last bullshit demand of yours? To say I love you? You know, when I said I loved you earlier in the relationship, I meant it. If I said it now, it would just be words."

Neither of them said anything for what seemed an eternity. The silence was full of awkwardness and melancholy, but mostly, it had the indisputable feeling of finality. "So that's it." Paul finally muttered.

"That's it," she said.

"You're such a fucking waste of time," he said as he hastily picked up his coat and turned to walk away.

"Seriously?" yelled Eileen to his back. "That's how you want to end this?"

She wasn't sure if he heard her or not. Either way, it wasn't her problem anymore.

. . . .

By the time Mason worked up the nerve to head back to Lachesis, he had also worked up quite the buzz. In fact, he was what Harold, his grandmother's pre-Christian lover, used to call "jiggered and happy as a loon." The back door of Budtenders was open, so Mason stumbled in. Ron greeted him with crossed arms.

"Well if it ain't the prodigal son," he said.

"Where's Ted?" Mason slurred.

"He's in his office," he said. "You look like a damned drunken hobo."

"Ah," Mason said with a wave of his hand.

He relied heavily on the railing as he haphazardly scaled the steps. Since he felt his footing slip, he closed his left eye in an attempt to focus his efforts. By the time he made it to the door, he nearly fell through it.

"What the fuck, Ted?" he yelled as he pointed at him.

Ted was in the middle of a meeting. The two people who sat facing his desk whipped their heads around to catch a glimpse of the commotion. Mason squinted at them and realized they were the cops who came to the shop earlier, only now they were wearing street clothes.

"I should say the same to you!" Ted said.

"Who the hell are these guys?" Mason asked.

"This is Eric and Martin," he said, gesturing at each man. "You bumped into them earlier at the shop." Mason looked confused, so Ted continued. "They're characters like you."

"Yeah, and you weren't supposed to run away like that," said Eric.

"Eric," said Ted, "let me handle this." Eric apologized. "Mason," he continued, "you weren't supposed to leave, but it doesn't matter. The author is going to use it as a plot twist. It actually makes for a better story in my opinion. The author wanted you to get killed with a revolver in a candlestick shop. I think it's a Clue reference. Remember that game?" Eric and Martin nodded.

"They were going to kill me?"

"With a prop gun."

"Like the one that killed Brandon Lee?"

"No, these are completely different. They don't even look like real guns. They look like cap guns."

"Why didn't you tell me I was going to be selling drugs?" Mason asked.

"First of all, they weren't even real drugs," he said.

"Why should I believe you?"

"Look at these guys," he said. "They ain't real cops!"

"Well why didn't you tell me I would be selling fake drugs? Then I wouldn't have freaked out and ruined the scene."

"We don't give characters too much information going into the scenes," he said. "In this story your dead dad set up the shop and never told you it was a front for drug running before he died because he wanted to give you plausible deniability. He got killed by lead pipe, by the way. Another Clue reference." He shook his head. "Here, take this." He handed Mason a stack of papers.

"What's this?"

"That's the printout of the notes for the story up until you ran away."

Mason flipped through the pages, but he was too inebriated to make sense of them. "What about the drugs? I could have been arrested."

Ted shook his head and said, "No one's ever been nailed."

"That doesn't mean anything. I could have been the first."

"You worry too much," he said. "Here." He handed Mason an envelope. "It's $75."

Mason snatched the envelope from Ted's hand. Although he still felt used, he also felt the elation of receiving a large cash payment. "Thanks for this," he slurred, holding up the envelope.

"You're welcome," he said. "You're also welcome to come back any time. You do good work, and I got enough jobs coming my way to keep you busy."

"Yeah, we'll see," sneered Mason.

"I suppose we will," Ted said with a laugh.

Chapter 9

"Who the hell are you?" Mason said to a young man in a Broncos hat, Nike shoes, and a collared shirt.

"Who the hell are *you*?" the young man replied.

"I live here."

"Oh, well then brah, I just banged your roommate," he said, pointing both his index fingers at Mason.

"Well isn't that charming?"

"Charming?" the man said as he put his shoes on. "What are you, gay?"

Mason chuckled derisively. "Hmm," he mumbled.

"Hmm," he mocked him in a high pitched voice as he walked towards the door.

"Looks like you're leaving."

"Looks like I am, pretty boy," he said as he shut the door behind him.

Eileen emerged from her room a short while after the macho man left. Her hair was disheveled and she had bags under her eyes.

"Please tell me he had the biggest cock west of the Mississippi," Mason said.

"Who, Dickey?"

Mason laughed. "What a perfect name for a douche-bag." When Eileen didn't defend him, Mason continued in a mocking tone, "'Oh that guy? Don't mind him, he's a just a little dickey.'"

"He's not..." she began to say. "Okay he's a bit dickey—although I think he's just confused and really conflicted. But he did have a huge cock, *and* he let me stick four fingers up his, well, you know."

"Let you?"

"More like demanded it," she admitted with a laugh. "I found the guy on Tinder. I just bought a strap-on and I needed someone to use it on. Oh, and let me tell you. If you're ever a girl looking to use her new strap-on, go on Tinder. There's an entire marketplace of dudes looking to get pegged."

"I'll keep that in mind."

"So anyway, I'm getting ready to peg him, right? And he asked me if I have any gay porn, which is weird, because most guys that like to get pegged are straight—otherwise they'd just go for other dudes, you know? Gay guys want cock, not a plastic strap on. Anyway... where was I?"

"He was asking you about gay porn."

"Oh yeah, so I tell him I don't have any, and then he pulls out his phone and watches gay porn while I'm nailing him with my strap-on."

"Eileen," Mason said. "That is a lot of detail."

"Oh Mason, don't go getting all suburban on me."

He sighed. "It's just the visual I'm getting is... unsettling, I guess. But whatever, what else did you do to poor old Dickey?"

"Okay, get this. As soon as he came, he made me promise never to tell anyone."

"Yeah, that makes sense. He called me gay."

She smiled. "That's because you probably awakened the latent homosexual urges that I had only recently confirmed."

They both laughed. "I feel sorry for those tough sports guys who are all insecure about being attracted to other hulking manly men," Mason said. "It's like they're taught to admire the perfect form of the male athlete right up to the point of sexuality—and then a thick line is drawn in the sand. But you just can't fetishize something like that without sexualizing it to some extent."

"Yeah," she said. "Remember that guy Rich I dated in high school? The big football guy?" Mason nodded. "We used to have threesomes with other guys all the time, and he was always way more into the guys than he was into me. I saw his profile online the other day. He's married with three kids now."

"Really? I wonder how that works."

"Oh, I don't know—repression, porn, strap-ons. A healthy combination of all three."

Mason laughed. "Imagine if grandma ever heard the way we talked."

Eileen looked confused. "What made you think of her?"

"You said Rich was married with kids. That's what grandma always wants for us."

"Oh, I see." Eileen said. "Yeah, she'd shit herself. She'd take a great big Christian dump in her pearly whites."

"If it weren't for her and people like your little boy toy, I'd forget that there are even such things as homophobes."

"Yeah, me too."

Since it was a rainy/snowy Colorado springtime morning, the siblings felt no remorse in cleaning the apartment. (Had it been sunny and warm, they would have resolved to spend the day in the park.) Mason scrubbed the kitchen counters and brought the recycling down to the purple bins in the alley, while Eileen put a Bikini Kill album on the turntable so she could righteously scour the bathroom and rearrange the scant furniture and posters on the wall. Once the living quarters appeared in an acceptable condition, they made breakfast—scrambled tofu, potatoes, and toast.

"So Paul and I are done for good," Eileen said as they ate at the modest dining room table.

"I thought that was old news," Mason said.

"It was, but we met up the other day and had a talk. He wanted me back and then gave me all these demands. It didn't end well."

"I see," he said as his chewing slowed and he became immersed in concentration. "So is that why Dickey was here? You were all vulnerable and then you brought the bi-curious homophobe home for some homo-erotic action?"

"Well I'd be lying if I claimed one didn't lead to the other. Though I did meet Dickey the day after."

Mason and Eileen had always been earnest and forthright in their discussions about sex. Having lost their virginities a couple months apart at 15 and 13 respectively, they only had one another—and equally misinformed friends—with which to share information. In a pre-Internet age with a post-menopausal guardian who only slept with four different men in her life—not to mention a public school sex education class focusing solely on the biology of procreation and little else—their support system for the topic was extremely limited. So while the subject matter of their conversations may have seemed vulgar to others, this exchange of knowledge, guidance, and particulars was how they emerged from the fresh-faced pleasure and often awkwardness of teenage experimentation to the sexual maturity, and by extension, emotional maturity of their 30s.

"What about you?" Eileen asked. "Have you met up with anyone recently?"

"A few days ago I had a one-nighter. That was right before I had a terrible time at Lachesis," he said.

"Terrible time? What happened?"

Mason explained the candlestick situation, the drugs, the cops who turned out to be characters like him, the $75 in cash at the end of it all. He expounded his doubts about the very premise that fiction needs a real life counterpart. And he posited that Lachesis didn't exactly exude professionalism or even legitimacy. "I think I'm done with the place," he said. "I have a really bad feeling about it."

"Really? I was just going to ask you to get me some work," Eileen said.

"You were?" said Mason. His brow furrowed. "You know that guy Ted I was telling you about? He briefly mentioned a union. I wonder if I can find it. And maybe I can go and ask some questions. Ask them about Lachesis. Ask them how hard it is to become a member."

"It's worth a shot," Eileen said.

Her enthusiasm surprised Mason. "So, why do you want to work anyway?"

"Rent's not going to pay itself around here."

"Are you planning on staying long?"

"Is that okay?"

"Of course. We just haven't talked about it or anything."

"We can talk about it now," she said. "I would like very much to stay here for the foreseeable future."

"Well alright," he said.

"Do you need to put me on the lease or anything?"

"No, my roommate, or I guess ex-roommate, Sam, signed the first lease a few years back and I never changed it. I think I've been on a month-to-month for two years or so," he said. "So no, you don't need to sign any lease."

"Thanks Mason," she said. "See, you've given me a place

to live, and now all you have to do is find me a job. It's like you're my life coach."

Mason laughed. "You know how fucked you'd be to have me as a life coach?"

"I was being facetious," she said with a laugh. "I'd never let a loser like you help me decide my fate."

Mason laughed. "That's... thanks for that."

· · · ·

Mason figured he'd get to business Monday morning, but he had lost the ability to properly identify days of the week. His unemployment had made it virtually impossible for him to remember things like dates.

On his way to the union local, he was fairly certain it was a weekday, judging by the sheer amount of traffic and pedestrians who appeared as though they were on their way to important places. The words that greeted him on the facade of the building were reassuring. They read in part, "Local 2557, Characters Guild West."

When he walked through the doors, he found himself alone in a large building. There was an empty desk in the front, several chairs facing a podium in a large assembly room in the building's center, and a hallway that appeared as though it led to bathrooms.

"Hello," Mason bellowed. No one answered, so he walked through the assembly room and down the hall. "Hello," he said again.

"Hello?" responded someone. It sounded as if the voice came from behind a doorway at the end of the hallway. Mason walked towards the door and knocked on it. "Come in," the voice instructed.

"Hey," Mason said. "Sorry for the interruption."

"It's okay, I wasn't doing anything," he said and then burst into laughter. The man appeared to be in his mid-50s with a head full of graying hair, huge bushy eyebrows, and a large, round nose. He had a presence that seemed to own the room, and he beamed at the sight of Mason. "The name's George, George Levin."

"Mason Jarman," he said, as he shook the man's hand.

"A pleasure," George said. "Please, sit," he motioned to a chair opposite his desk.

"I'm very sorry to take up your time like this," Mason said. "I'm just curious about the union."

"Please," he said, "don't apologize. I'm here eight hours a day. I could use some company. Besides, a young guy like you wants to come in here and talk about the union. I'll tell you everything you want to know—maybe even some things you don't want to know." He let out a series of guffaws.

"Well, thank you. I certainly appreciate it." Mason leaned back in his chair. "So this is the union for characters, right?"

"Yes sir. Local 2557—we've been representing characters in novels, novellas, short stories, and other prose at this location since 1972."

"So this profession does exist?"

"Well of course it does, dummy," he said, laughing and slapping his desk. He remained doubled over for an awfully long time. When he eventually recovered, he said, "I kid. I kid. Seriously though, if this wasn't a legitimate profession, I wouldn't be sitting at this desk, now would I?" Mason shook his head. "Granted, we're not as big as we were in the 1920s, '30s, '40s thanks to the radio and TV, but we've still got numbers. Two million members west of the Mississippi—mostly in California, because that's where the stories take place. But you have your stories in Denver too. Thank you Mr. Kerouac and Cassady for getting that ball rolling. Of course the Beats mainly played themselves in their novels. They didn't rely on character placement very much."

"Do many westerns take place in this state?"

"Not anymore," he said. "They all moved up to Wyoming—partly because they have more open spaces but mainly because the union's so weak up there."

"That figures," Mason said. "How do period pieces work?"

"Similar to the movies," he said. "Costumes, sets, the whole shebang. Fictional productions always try to keep a low profile—mainly to avoid leaks."

"Sure," said Mason. "Let me ask you this, how do you get into the union?"

"Are you a character?"

"In more ways than one," said Mason, who chuckled at his joke while George laughed uproariously.

When he recuperated, he excused himself, took a deep breath, patted his eyes with a handkerchief, and said, "In order to prove your eligibility, you have to bring us two pay stubs from your employer from within the last three months. There's also an initiation fee of $75. After that, dues are $50 a month."

"To tell you the truth, I've only been on two jobs and they paid me in cash."

"Who's 'they?'"

"This place called Lachesis," Mason said.

The life went out of George's face. "Ted Redbone," he said with guile.

"You've heard of him?"

"That man, and his ilk, are the bane of my existence. They're all anti-union blowhards—right wingers who got into the liquor and marijuana industries and then weaseled their way into the character placement business by using unskilled characters and paying them a pittance of what they charge the industry. You could easily take what he's paying you, double it, and add benefits if you were a union man!" George was shouting. Subtlety wasn't exactly his strong suit. "There are no contracts, no guarantees. He could stiff you any time he damn well pleased!"

"I thought it was strange getting paid in cash, but then again, he runs a pot shop and they only deal in cash."

"That's the thing with the marijuana business. You get guys like him that were already dealing on the shady side of the market and make it so they can only take cash. Most of them operate on the one-fourth principle, meaning they don't report every fourth sale so they can cheat on their taxes." George just assumed that last part, but it sounded good and reinforced the point he was trying to make.

"So what you're telling me is that I'm not eligible because I did character work through Lachesis."

"Yes," said George. "Unfortunately, you need experience through a more reputable placement agency."

"Can you recommend one?"

"There are waiting lists for all the legitimate agencies in town. I could get you onto one of those if you can produce three references."

"How long until I get work?"

"It could be weeks," he said, "but it could also be months."

"You see, that's what makes a guy like Ted so appealing, isn't it?"

"Desperation, impatience, ignorance?" George was shouting again. "That's why you're willing to work for Ted? You see, this is what's wrong with America. There's a certain class of people that's so willing to take cut rate pay and no dignity that it lowers all of our pay and dignity. It's immoral. It's disgusting. It's…"

"Okay, George, calm down," said Mason. "I didn't say I was

going to work for Ted again. I just meant, that's why people do it."

George tried to regain his composure. He slowed his breathing and clutched the desk as though he was keeping it from flying across the room. "Fine," he said.

"Let me get your contact information and I'll produce three references. Sound good?"

"Sure, sure," he said. Steadily, he produced a business card and handed it to Mason. "And go ahead and write down your information for me too."

"Thank you for your time Mr. Levin," he said as he scribbled his name and number on the back of some scratch paper. "This visit has been most enlightening."

"You're welcome, Mason," he said, wiping sweat from his brow with the handkerchief. "Don't work for Ted, and we'll make a union man out of you yet."

"That'd be great," he said with a smile.

Chapter 10

Mason was never good at waiting. When a scant couple of weeks passed and he hadn't heard a thing from any of the agencies, he considered heading back to Lachesis. But since he didn't want to jeopardize his potential union membership, and since he still harbored reservations about the unsavoriness of the whole operation, he continued his routine schedule of unemployment activities—mainly pissing away entire afternoons on the Internet and hanging out with Eileen.

Then one morning when his bank account hovered precariously near the zero dollar mark and Eileen didn't come home the evening prior, Mason headed out in the general direction of Lachesis. He resolved to pass by and see how he felt. If he sensed any kind of skepticism or dread, he would just keep walking—resolving to wait on the legitimate character placement establishments and hold out for his unemployment checks. If, on the other hand, he remained as cool as a cucumber at the prospect of another rendezvous with Mr. Redbone, he would inquire about another job.

Once he made it to Budtenders, Mason quickly realized his plan was ill conceived—since both apprehension and enticement coursed through his veins. He paced back and forth in front of the building for a few minutes, weighing the pros and cons in his head before throwing caution to the wind and heading around back. He could use the money, he decided, and hopefully this lapse of integrity wouldn't get back to George.

When Ron led Mason into the office, he found Ted tearing into his lunch. With a napkin tucked into his collar, Ted held a hunk of fried chicken in each hand, devouring the flesh with more ferociousness than a pack of starved, ravenous hell beasts. He made grunting and smacking noises as grease ran down his chin onto the napkin. Mason instantly realized he had made a mistake.

"Mason," he said between hulking bites of meat. "What brings you here?"

"Well," he said, trying to mask his disgust, "I'm interested in another gig."

Ted replied with indistinguishable noises that sounded like a husky man drowning in lard.

"I'm sorry, could you please repeat that?" said Mason.

Ted held up his finger as he chewed thoroughly and swallowed. "Something just came in that starts tomorrow. It's a novella for a publishing house that deals primarily in horror. The working title is *Wrong Turn in Susurrant*."

"Horror, huh? Do I have to sell drugs?"

"No, no drugs."

"What about fake drugs?"

"No, there's no drugs at all."

"I don't have to kill anyone, do I?" Mason asked. Ted shook his head. "Okay I know the first two didn't have any contracts, but could we sign a contract for this one?"

Ted froze. "I don't do contracts."

"Not a contact per se, just a guarantee that you're going to pay me."

"Have I stiffed you yet?"

"Well no, but I'm getting offers from other agencies, and they all have contracts and guarantees."

"What agencies?"

"C&F's Character Placement, Beforehand Characters."

"You're talking to them, huh?" he said and Mason nodded. "Alright, I'll give you a guarantee, but it's going to cost you ten percent of the money I was going to pay you."

"Fine," he said.

Mason and Ted drew up the paperwork securing him $500 for a week's work—or $100 a day—less a $50 fee for drawing up a guarantee in the first place. The total payment would be determined by the author of the story (for example, he wouldn't receive the full $450 in case his character was killed off early in a twist of the plot). He knew as a union member he would stand to make twice that and benefits, but an under-the-table shot at $450 when he was already on unemployment wouldn't hurt anything—especially since, as Eileen said, rent wasn't going to pay itself.

· · · ·

Early the next morning at Lachesis, Mason met his co-character in the novella—an intelligent, well-spoken woman named Sophia Cruz, who, for the part, had to cover up the tattoo on her right arm, trade her glasses for contacts, and act ditzy despite the fact that she was well-read and quick-witted. Her fictional name was Kelly. Mason would be playing the part of Brett, a former college football player turned insurance salesman. For his role, Mason also had to cover up his tattoos, take out his plugs, and act tough and dense. He also had to pretend he liked sports, which was something he wouldn't even deign to do when he worked with insurance salesmen, most of whom he despised.

The Mile High Character Prop Depot (dubbed "the Prop Stop" by the regulars) supplied them with a red sports car that Mason felt ridiculous driving. He hoped his sister didn't catch a glimpse of him behind the wheel and kept an eye out for her just in case. Still, he tried his best to stay in character, if only to demonstrate his capabilities to the others in the industry.

The one-sheet divided the couple's activities in blocks of a few hours, with the first one dedicated to setting the plot trajectory and establishing characters while driving around the city and gathering supplies. They would head out to a secluded campsite in Susurrant, Colorado where they would have to contend with a psychopath of Chaffee County legend.

• • • •

The story began with a coarse narration. Mason acting as Brett said, "What do you do when you get a couple days off work, the kids are with the ex, and your new girlfriend wants to head to the mountains for a ride on a non-stop sex train? [Chuckles] You pack up your things and get the hell out of town—that's what you do."

The car quickly jerked into the parking lot of Brett's condo, a stylish three-bedroom dwelling procured by Beforehand, one of the other character placement agencies involved with the project. He emerged from the driver seat and ran inside, while Kelly took her time departing the vehicle. The interior of his dwelling appeared unkempt with empty beer cans and dirty plates strewn over his couch and coffee table. Stacks of *Maxim* partially obscured photographs of his two children.

"Yuck," Kelly said when she walked through the door. "How do you live in this filth?"

Across the room in a frenzy, Brett haphazardly tossed clothes and toiletries into an unzipped bag. "The maid is on vacation this week," he said. "And the kids were here yesterday. They always make a mess."

"Yeah well, if you ever want me to spend time over here..." she trailed off.

"Yeah?" he asked on his way to the bathroom.

"You're like, gonna have to clean."

Brett opened a drawer underneath the bathroom counter, grabbed two boxes of condoms, and threw them in the bag. He opened another drawer and added a pair of handcuffs and various other sex toys designed to increase his pleasure. "I told you, the maid's on vacation," he yelled through the wall.

"Did you remember to get pickles when you were at the store?" she asked.

"Yes," he said, exasperated. "You told me a hundred times. Your family has a tradition of roasting pickles over a fire instead of marshmallows. I got the big jar."

"Good, because I can't go camping without pickles." She wandered around the apartment, staring at the few pictures he had displayed on the otherwise bare white walls. "What kind of tent are you bringing?"

"Damn it," he said, dropping his deodorant. "Tent? I don't know. I picked one up on the way home from that sporting goods store on Colorado Boulevard."

"How many people does it fit?"

"One. Or two if they're on top of each other," he said with a wink.

"Oh Brett," she said, vivaciously.

"Just kidding, it's a big one. Come on," he said, taking her by the wrist and leading her to the car. "We got to go to the liquor store and the pot shop, and then we're out for the weekend."

The two sped down a few blocks before whipping into the parking lot of the Liquor Mart. "You coming or staying in the car?" Brett asked.

"Staying," she said. "Can you leave the keys?" Brett had already taken the keys out of the ignition and closed the door, so he sighed and tossed them through the opened window at Kelly, where they landed with a thud in her lap. "Thanks," she said sarcastically to herself.

Brett headed straight for the light beer and wine coolers and loaded his cart with a case of each. He was about to head straight for the cashier when, in spite of his professionalism, he allowed Mason to pick up a fifth of vodka and a case of soda. Maybe Brett would get drunk enough to do vodka shots, Mason reasoned, so why couldn't he purchase additional booze and still maintain a sense of professional integrity—especially if he still characteristically acted like a dick to the cashier?

"Anything else?" the cashier asked after ringing up his items.

"If I wanted anything else, I would've put it in my cart," Brett said like a dick. The rest of the transaction occurred without another word.

Brett opened the trunk, placed the beer, wine, and soda in an iced cooler, and stashed the vodka in his backpack. Then he walked across the street to a dispensary. Since the novella took place in Colorado, readers expected to read about pot to some extent. So he picked up an eighth of a sativa/indica blend and a small package of brownies for Kelly.

When he returned to the car, Kelly was transfixed by her phone. "Brett," she said. "I just googled Susurrant, Colorado."

Brett nodded aloofly—more of an indication that social regulations required him to offer some sort of response and less of an acknowledgement of her statement. She continued, "It used to be an old mining town and now it's mostly abandoned. That's kind of creepy," she paused for dramatic effect. "And it says there was this miner, Franklin Builder, who fell 70 feet down a mine shaft to his death on July 25, 1902. And the few locals that are left swear that his ghost still haunts the hills around town."

"No!" Brett said, with feigned terror.

"Shut up, this stuff is spooky."

"Ooo, spooky," Brett said mockingly as he made jazz hands.

"I'm trying to get in the mood for camping, you big jerk."

"I don't like to think about that kind of stuff when I'm camping," he said.

"Why? Are you ascared of ghosts?"

"No, I'm not. I just don't like to get that crap stuck in my head so that every time I hear a noise, I'm jumping out of my skin."

"Don't worry, big bad Brett," she said in a lovey dovey voice. "I'll protect you!"

"Shut up," he said as he accelerated to demonstrate his increased annoyance.

The first day's activities listed on the one-sheet ended when the couple reached Santa Fe Drive. So once Brett took a left onto the street, he once again became Mason and Kelly became Sophia, and they weren't driving to Susurrant, Colorado; they could go whatever they wanted.

Chapter 11

With the visor mirror, Sophia immediately removed her contacts and put on her glasses. She also made her hair into a ponytail, squirmed out of her pink, name brand sweatshirt, and lit a cigarette.

"I am so glad that's over," she said.

"Yeah," Mason said. "Brett's an asshole. I really don't like being an asshole."

"I hate playing a ditzy chick," she said. "But you can't get any character work as a woman if you can't act dumb and you aren't in a union."

They let out a collective sigh as Mason drove south. Once he was in sight of the highway, he snapped out of his post-work trance and pulled into the parking lot of a diner. When the car was in park, he removed his long-sleeve shirt and replaced his plugs. He turned towards Sophia and said, "So what do you want to do now?"

"Oh I don't know," she said. "Get a drink. Maybe have sex later."

Mason's eyes widened. "With me?" he stuttered, then immediately cleared his throat. In a more collected tone, he said, "Do you want to do those things with me?"

Sophia laughed. "Yes, with you."

Mason quickly sped to the B-Street Bar on Bayaud and

Broadway. It was a dignified dive with a decent jukebox, promotional posters of vintage B-movies lining the walls, a decent patio, and on most nights either a swing or rockabilly band. On a clement spring evening such as this, Mason figured he could always converse with Sophia on the patio if she didn't want to dance.

She ordered the house red and he ordered a vodka soda, and they sat at the bar, taking in a couple of the musical act's songs, politely clapping at the end of each number. Neither were drunk enough to want to dance. Before the band launched into another tune, Sophia placed her arm on Mason's shoulder and said, "Let's go outside."

When the two sat down at a patio table, Sophia lit a cigarette and offered one to Mason. "I don't smoke," he said. She shrugged and put the pack in her purse.

"I probably shouldn't either," she said. "But I'm not going to quit, so what are you going to do?" She took a long drag and then flicked the ash over the patio railing.

Eying the rest of the smokers, they sat in silence just long enough to make it uncomfortable. Mason did his best to break the awkwardness, but ended up vomiting a sludge of half-words with no decipherable meaning. With the realization that she had a lot of comfort to lose in his social drowning, she threw him a figurative lifebuoy. "So Mason," she said, "how'd you get to be such a character?"

He laughed. "That's... good. Did you just come up with it?"

"I've been doing character work since I was 12. My dad used to say it to me when I would come home from a job."

"So you were a child character?"

"Pre-teen. My younger sister was a child character."

"Did it fuck her up? You know, like how child actors get fucked up?"

"No. Yes... Actually, I don't know. She got into acid—like really into acid—when she was in high school and college. I think she was tripping every day for a while. She quit doing drugs years ago, but then she discovered mysticism and joined this weird cult that she eventually got kicked out of because she wouldn't let the elders impregnate her or something weird and creepy like that. The last time I saw her, she changed her name to Starbeam and was dating a white guy who called himself Mighty Bear," she trailed off and Mason could see the sadness in her eyes. When Sophia met his stare, she immediately focused her attention back to the present. "But see, I don't know if all that shit is because her childhood character experience, or if she was damaged before that—or even after that, but damaged by something else that wasn't that, you know?"

"Yeah, I get it," he said.

"What about you?" she asked. "How did you get into the character placement racket?"

"I'm new at it. I just answered an ad on Craigslist."

"Is that Lachesis place that I met you at any good?"

"I don't know," he admitted. "But I haven't heard good things."

"Neither have I. That's why I was asking."

"So you don't work for Lachesis?"

"No, I work for Beforehand. They're the ones who sent me to Lachesis to meet you."

"So are you union?"

"No, freelance. I was union when I was younger, but I don't want a steady job now. I just want to work whenever I want to. I live in a collective house in Five Points so rent's only $500 a month."

"That's nice."

Sophia laughed. "So are you a man of few words, or just

incredibly awkward?"

"Oh the latter, for sure." They both smiled. "If you don't work full time," he said, "what else do you do?"

"What else *don't* I do?" she asked. "I read, take my room-mate's dog for walks, ride my bike, paint—even though I'm not really good at it. I cook, write columns; my goal is to one day have a sex and relationship advice column, but for now I just have a blog no one reads."

"Sounds like you're busy," Mason said with a sense of envy. He seemed to recall a time when his life brimmed with excitement, hope, and potential, before the crash of adulthood introduced a seemingly endless cavalcade of limitations—including responsibilities, weariness, and broken hearted regrets.

"Definitely," she said. "I have to be compelled to live life, otherwise I might as well be a mystic and refer to myself as Sunray Child." Mason laughed. "What do you do?" she asked.

Mason expounded upon his unemployment, his sister, and his work at Lachesis. About halfway through his expla-nation he realized he was beginning to sound as uninterest-ing as his old friend, new Mark. "I guess it's all kind of boring, when I say it out loud like that."

Sophia nodded. "Pretty pit-i-ful," she said, careful to enunciate each syllable. "Are you good at anything? I mean, do you have any hobbies? I mean, what are you doing with yourself, Mason?"

He laughed at her bluntness. "Mainly just drinking and sleeping," he said. "I guess that's it. I mean, I used to do cool stuff. I used to be in a band and we used to put out records and tour."

"Alright," she said, perking up. "That's cool. Very respect-able."

"Yeah, but we broke up five years ago and I haven't played in a band since."

"Well that's stupid."

Mason nodded. He knew he had no good reason not to be in a band, and he lamented that fact. After his last musical endeavor dissolved, a series of circumstances occurred that prevented him from starting a new one. At first, he was just too exhausted from constant touring, bickering, alcohol and drug use, and the crushing disappointment that followed the cessation of an eight-year creative enterprise that came close to supporting itself, but never quite made enough money. And once he recovered from the turmoil, he just couldn't imagine starting from the beginning again, coping with the ill-at-ease feelings and doubt that came from reapplying an old skill set towards something new, or worrying incessantly about whether his songwriting skills were still in sync with a new generation's sensibilities. Then when he finally began to overcome those obstacles, he made several attempts to play with other musicians, but none of those attempts graduated past a few practices, either because the others lacked sincerity and only wanted to play music in theory, or because no musical chemistry developed. Eventually, he washed his hands of the whole undertaking altogether.

"So what, you're just going to drink and sleep and stay on unemployment the rest of your life? You have to try harder than that. You just have to."

"My unemployment won't last forever," he said.

"What do you want to do?" she asked.

"I know myself well enough to know that I don't want kids or a big house or even a lot of money."

"Ew, gross. Who said they wanted any of that?"

"I'm just saying," he said, and grew silent in contemplation.

"I think maybe I focus too much on the stuff I don't want and not enough on the stuff I do want."

"Seems likely," she said. "So are you like this serious pessimistic depressive?"

"I don't know about a serious one—more like an amateur."

She laughed. "Even an amateur pessimistic depressive would have found a band by this point. You're the real deal—like a tortured artist without the art."

"Yeah, well..." Mason trailed off. He had nothing to say in his defense. And with that the pair had bled the conversation dry. He couldn't think of a new topic and she was attempting to figure out a way to ditch him without it leading to unbearable awkwardness the next day at work.

"Hey," said a voice from the patio, breaking the silence. "Weren't you the lead singer of Tortured Metaphor?"

"Yeah," said Mason smiling.

"Oh my God, I loved you guys," she said.

Mason thanked her.

"I'm Cindy." She leaned forward and shook Mason's hand vigorously.

"Mason," he said, half-heartedly pointing to himself with the thumb of his free hand.

"I have your record!"

"Cool, which one?

"Um, I think it's the first one. It's blue and grey and has a dog with a gasmask on the cover."

"That's *Humanity's Not Humane*. It was our first one."

"I haven't listened to it in years," she said. "What's that song? 'There's no race, just accidents,'" she sang.

"No, it's 'There's no fate, only accidents. No future, only happenstance.'"

"Yeah, yeah. I love that song."

"Well thank you," Mason said.

She doted over him and his band's music and intro-duced him to her boyfriend, who was obviously annoyed at the prospect of meeting the man upon whom his lover was lavishing so much attention. The boyfriend smoked his cigarette with silent fury and offered only a head nod as his sole introduction.

When the couple extinguished their cigarettes at the boyfriend's insistence and retired back into the bar, Sophia and Mason returned to their lack of conversation, only now she saw him with a whole new perspective—not as a loser who was too craven to start a new band, but as a guy with a cool past. She wasn't enamored with his former celebrity, as insignificant as it may have been. What she saw in him now was his talent. Obviously he could write and play songs other people found endearing, and not everyone could do that. It intrigued her.

"No fate, only accidents," she said. "That's clever."

"Yeah, it's actually a bastardization of a Napoleon quote, but I didn't know that back when I was in my young 20s. That was in the early 2000s and we sure as hell didn't have Internet in our shitty little punk house. And it's not like I was reading books on Napoleon."

"How did you figure out it wasn't, um, for lack of a better term, original?"

"A few years after the album came out, I was in a library somewhere on tour, wasting time on the Internet. I had an inkling that the quote was too obvious not to have been said before, so I googled it. Sure enough, Napoleon Bonaparte beat me to it by couple centuries."

"Oh well, at least no one called you out on it."

"You know what's funny? We even played a show in France in 2007 and no one said anything. Of course we never had a big following there and our lyrics were in English. So it's not like we were plastering it on buses in Paris or anything. We were always obscure everywhere we went."

"Hey," she said slapping her hand on the table and frightening Mason, "have you ever been on the roof in this place?"

He shook his head. "There isn't a roof. I mean, there's a roof, but not a bar on the roof. There's a bar on the second floor."

"No, not to the upstairs bar. I'm talking about the actual roof. You want to go up?" she asked. Then she started singing The Drifter's song, "Up on the Roof" which she discovered in her late teens when she dated a 32-year-old with a huge soul record collection.

Mason shrugged. "Okay," he said.

He quickly finished his drink as Sophia stood from the table. She clutched his hand in hers and rushed him to the bar upstairs, which was really a replica of the main bar with pool tables and different B-movie posters lining the interior. Unleashing his hand, she rushed into the women's restroom without him, as he stood around, trying his best to establish an air of aplomb and not appear awkward—both of which he failed at miserably.

A few seconds after a short, dark-haired woman departed the restroom, Sophia popped her head out and whispered, "Come on."

Mason glanced around him and made a break for it. She shuffled him over to one of the stalls and locked the door. "They're going to think we're doing blow in here," he said.

"Do you have any?" she asked. He shook his head. "Too bad, too bad," she said as she opened the window. "Okay, you're going to want to stand on the toilet seat like this, grab the top of the windowsill like this, and then kind of throw yourself up until you're sitting in the window." Her head was out the window and all Mason could see was her torso and feet. "Then stand and kind of jump and pull yourself up at the same time." And with that she was gone.

Mason followed her instructions and joined her. By the time he made it up, she was already on the other side looking down Broadway.

"I love this shit," she said, letting cigarette smoke lazily flow from her mouth in a slow, relaxed exhale.

"It's nice," Mason said. "How the hell do we get down?"

"Don't think about that," she said annoyed. "We just got here."

"Yeah, well…" He trailed off and she looked at him pityingly.

"Jesus, are you always like this?"

"Like what?"

"Do you always ruin the moment for yourself by thinking about what you're going to do when it's over?"

Was he really so transparent? "Yes," he admitted sheepishly.

"So that's how you go through life? Letting the future paralyze you so that you can't sit still?"

"Alright, we don't have to dwell on it. I'm a big wiener, is that what you want to hear?"

"Oh my god, yes! Wiener! That's great. Thanks for not saying 'pussy.'"

"I don't say that word."

"Well I'm proud of you… for that," she said. "When it's time to go down, you see that railing over there? That leads to the fire escape. You still have to drop down a floor, but it doesn't hurt if you do it right."

"Why didn't we just take that way up?"

"Because I don't have enough upper body strength to do a pull up, and that's the only way to get on the ladder that leads to the fire escape. Going down I have no problem." Once he appeared content with her elucidations on roof scaling, he sat down next to her. "Take a deep breath Mason," she said, holding his hand.

He tried his best to relax and behold the scenery, but his personality kept getting in the way. *What's so great about seeing city lights and cars from this height?* he wondered. Still, he tried to push the anxiety out of his head.

All of his inner demons were rendered moot, however, when he felt a hand working its way into his pants. He felt Sophia's lips on his face, and all of the sudden, all was right with the world. Before he could make sense of the events, his pants were around his ankles and he was on the receiving end of unexpected oral sex. At that very moment he beheld the beauty of city lights and tranquility of watching the cars pass. *So this is what it's like not to be crazy*, he thought. *Now if only I can figure out a way to feel like this all the time…*

A few minutes later, the couple climbed down the ladder, ordered another round of drinks at the bar, and then danced until two in the morning.

Chapter 12

Eileen heard her brother come home late last night, but her drunkenness and the fact that he seemed to be with someone else prevented her from sharing the news of a very interesting text she had received while he was gone. In fact, the text was the catalyst to her intoxication. So once noon rolled around, she figured she had allowed enough recovery time for the two of them to have a sober conversation.

"Mason," she said as she knocked on this door. "You awake?"

"Yeah," he shouted, "but..."

Eileen didn't wait long enough for him to finish the sentence, so when she opened the door, she witnessed him and Sophia having sex. She was riding him reverse cowgirl style, her chest facing the door—so Eileen had a lot to see.

"Oh shit," Eileen said, turning her head.

"I was just about to say, '...but don't come in,'" Mason said.

"Is that your sister?" Sophia asked.

"Yes," said Eileen as she turned to shut the door.

"I'd ask you to join if it weren't, you know, incestuous," Sophia said, but Eileen was already out of the room. "She looks a lot like you," she said to Mason.

"Could we please talk about something else?" Mason pleaded.

"I could just focus on moaning."

"That would be apropos."

After fifteen minutes of solid moaning, the pair emerged from the bedroom, glazed and triumphant from sexual jubilation. Eileen had just finished making breakfast.

"Sorry you had to see that, Eileen," Mason said.

"Well at least I got to look at her and not you," she said with a laugh. "I made enough for everyone, so grab a plate and help yourself."

"Thank you," said Sophia. "I'm Sophia, by the way. You've already met my tits, so you might as well meet the rest of me."

Eileen laughed. "So, should I shake your hand or shake your tits?" she asked.

"I'll let you decide," she said.

Eileen shook her hand.

The three of them sat down on the couch and huddled around the coffee table to eat and exchange pleasantries. Eileen delighted in Sophia's social ease and apparent lack of a single misplaced word.

"This is delicious," Sophia said. "What the hell is it?"

"Green chile over potatoes, black beans, and quinoa with some nutritional yeast mixed in," she said.

"I could eat this every morning," Sophia said.

"Mason does," said Eileen. "That's where I got the idea for it." She turned toward him. "By the way, I need to talk to you before you leave."

"Like in private?" he wondered. Eileen nodded.

"You can talk about it in front of me," Sophia offered. "I don't mind—unless it's something really weird. And then I insist."

Eileen looked toward Mason and he shrugged. "Okay," she said. "Fucking grandma texted me yesterday."

Mason's jaw dropped. After several moments of stunned silence, he said, "I... I'm not sure what I'm more shocked about, the fact that she got in touch with you or the fact that she has a cell phone."

"Both are equally frightening," Eileen said.

"How did she get your number?" he asked.

"I don't know exactly, but the last time I talked to her was when I first moved in with Paul. He had a landline—still does actually. Maybe she called him and he gave her my number."

"Did you text back?"

"No. I don't know what to say."

Mason's brow furrowed. "I guess I wouldn't know what to say either... Wait a minute. How did you know it was her?"

"She called me Leeny, first of all."

"Hmm," he said. "Well if it's not her, whoever it is did their homework. What did the text say?"

"Leeny, call me. This is your grandmother."

"That's just so weird..."

"I hate to interrupt," Sophia said, glancing at her phone. "But we have to be at work in an hour and I have to stop by my house first."

"Oh, if you guys have to go..."

"Yeah, we probably should," he said, gathering up the dishes to bring to the sink.

"Thank you so much for breakfast," said Sophia. "It was damned delicious."

"We'll talk about this later," he said. Eileen nodded.

Once the door slammed behind them, Eileen found herself in an empty apartment, staring at her phone. Her grandma listed her number at the end of the text in a blunder of technological redundancy appropriate for someone her age. Mason was right—if it wasn't her, someone had done her homework.

After a few hours of pacing the apartment, mindlessly surfing the web, and otherwise profoundly dreading the sound of her grandma's voice, Eileen poured herself a tall glass of vodka and cranberry juice and quickly dialed the phone number before she could lose the nerve.

"God bless, this is Elizabeth," her grandmother said when she answered the phone.

Eileen laughed in derision. "Hey grandma, it's Eileen." Her grandma offered only an ostentatiously audible sigh to air her disappointment. "Good to hear from you too, Grandma Betsy," Eileen continued.

"It's Elizabeth, child."

"Didn't used to be."

"I'm not who I used to be."

"That sounds great and all," she said dryly, "but what did you text me for?"

"First and foremost I wanted to see if you've accepted the Lord Jesus Christ into your heart."

"Nope."

"I figured as much. I spoke with your former partner in sin, Paul," she said. Mystery solved on where she acquired her number. "I was relieved to hear you're not still living in sin with him."

"Great."

"Are you still gallivanting around with your homosexual lesbians?"

"Homosexual lesbians?" Eileen said. "That's a little redundant. And you used to like some of my girlfriends. Remember Karen? You gals were in the same bowling league."

Back in the mid-to-late '90s, Eileen went through a hardcore riot grrrl phase where she listened to nothing but

Bikini Kill (and later, Le Tigre), L7, and The Gits. She even bought her grandma the Heavens to Betsy CD, *Calculated*, and it quickly became her favorite. Eileen also had a zine that she ran for two years called, *Grrrl Reaction*, a digest of articles, poetry, and band reviews relating to the riot grrrl movement. During that period, she dated a procession of young, angry punk rock women, the longest lasting of which, Karen Crowley, grew to be one of her grandmother's good friends. In fact, Betsy dyed her hair green just to match Karen's. If only the countercultural '90s Betsy could see the future Elizabeth.

"I'm not a sinner anymore, Eileen. Bowling alleys are dens of iniquity and your friend Karen is going straight to hell."

"I'm sure she appreciates the judgment. Can we get to the point?"

"Hold on, Leeny," she said. It was strange for Eileen to hear her grandma use such a handle of affection now that she was so prim and proper. "What about your brother? Is he still drifting across the country with a van full of sinners?"

Everyone was a sinner to Elizabeth, except for her pastor and congregation. "No he's not in a band anymore. Hasn't been for several years."

"Good, has he settled into a steady career and met a nice young woman?"

Eileen laughed. "No grandma, we're still both huge disappointments in your tidy little world of the saved and the damned…" After a pregnant pause, she continued. "Now will you please tell me the point of this call of judgment?" She chuckled. "This is a literal judgment call."

"Your great uncle Ernest has been diagnosed with terminal cancer," she said. "He only has a month or two to live."

"Unkie Ernest?" That was Eileen's name for him since she was three years old. "Oh, no. That's terrible news. I'm so sorry."

"He's 80 and living in sin with a woman he's not married to," she said with disdain. If Eileen had a dime for every time grandma used the word sin…

It seemed unfair to Eileen to diminish this grave diagnosis with such a hypercritical statement, but she knew not to mention it. Instead, she said, "Can we go see him?"

"He's back at his house now. He would probably like it if you called him."

"Of course."

"There's more," Elizabeth said. "Since the cancer's terminal, he's giving his estate away. His son Darren told me to tell you that he's giving you and Mason some money."

"Really? How much?"

"Darren will be in touch. God bless you and Mason. Good bye."

And that's how the first conversation between Eileen and her grandmother in almost four years concluded. It would probably be another four years until they spoke again. The gallimaufry of emotions that remained in Eileen's head confounded and dizzied her. She made herself another drink, finished it in a matter of minutes, and made another one. Soon enough, she was sprawled out on the couch, somewhere between heavily buzzed and drunk, yearning for a time when her grandma brimmed with respect, love, and a penchant for fun.

Bearing witness to such a grand shift in her grandmother's personality had emotionally traumatized Eileen. It was as though her grandma had died—or as if a completely different soul commandeered her bodily vessel and destroyed the personality that had once resided there. But since her grandmother's life hadn't actually ended, there was no funeral; there was also no closure and no real occasion to mourn her loss. The lack of communication between them was a result of Eileen's reticence as much as it was her grandma's. Every time Eileen spoke with her, she felt like she was processing her death once again

Eileen succumbed to dejection and tears for a good forty-five minutes before Darren called. When she saw his name light up the screen of her cell phone, her mood lightened, and she wiped away the tears in preparation to appear as though she hadn't just emotionally unraveled.

"Hello," Eileen said with sadness in her voice.

"Eileen," said Darren, "are you okay?"

"Not really," she said. "There's just a lot going on, you know. I'm so sorry about your father."

"Thank you," he said. Darren was a generation removed from the Jarmans and much less of a square peg. He didn't have an ear for music or a taste for alcohol, and he was religious—which set him apart from his father as well. But he still had a lot of respect for Mason and Eileen.

"Uncle Ernest and I had a wonderful relationship," she sniveled.

"We're definitely all going to miss him."

"Yeah," she said. "And to make things just a little crappier, I also just had an upsetting talk with my grandmother. That's another reason why it sounds like I've been crying."

"Me too. I mean, I haven't been crying, but I spoke with her when my dad was in the hospital and she called him a sinner for living with his girlfriend. She called me an idolater because I'm Catholic. She didn't have kind words for you or Mason either."

Eileen sighed deeply. "She's become intolerable."

"I'm sorry, I know you used to be a close-knit family. It's a shame what happened."

"Yeah well, Mason and I are still very close. I just moved in with him again."

"That's so good to hear," he said. After the two exchanged more pleasantries and caught up on some family gossip, Darren explained the situation, detailing how the Jarman siblings fit into the great distribution of Ernest's wealth. "So my father is very fond of you especially, but also of Mason. And he has a lot more money than I would have assumed. Anyway, he's giving you and Mason somewhere in the neighborhood $10,000 each."

"Holy shit," she said. The brooding immensity of life that had weighed down her soul during the past few months diminished incalculably. While money didn't solve every problem, it certainly eased some immediate threats. The good news almost made the communication with her grandma an acceptable price of admission.

Almost.

After Eileen's subdued elation abated enough to concentrate, Darren explained the details. The check would be mailed later this week and should be there by the beginning of next week. If Ernest felt well enough, Darren would drive him to Denver from his home in Pueblo over the weekend. They would be happy to see Eileen and Mason, if they could make it.

Before ending the call, Eileen confirmed the particulars of the rendezvous and once again offered her condolences. Then she grappled with the alternating emotions of muted elation and melancholy that emanated from situations such as this.

Chapter 13

Mason and Sophia were having difficulty getting back into character. They wanted to get to know each other better, but they had to get back to being Brett and Kelly. Once they turned onto Santa Fe Drive, they assumed their fictional personalities and began addressing one another as the names in the story.

"How far is Susurrant?" Kelly asked.

"I don't know," Brett said, "a few hours."

"You know how to set up a tent, right?"

"You know, I don't think Brett would talk much during the ride," he said.

Wide-eyed, Sophia didn't know how to respond. In all her years of character placement, she had never heard anyone compromise the fourth wall like that. "Um," she said, "is referring to yourself in third person a nervous tick of yours?"

"Yeah, sure. Listen Kelly, let's just let the narration take us to Susurrant. In the interest of avoiding unnecessary dialogue, the prose can magically whisk us to our destination in a matter of a sentence or two."

"Brett," said Kelly. "Why are you talking like that?"

"You think this thing's on?" Brett said, grabbing the digital recorder left in the ashtray.

"I don't think we're supposed to touch that."

He tossed it back down. "Why don't you just sit back and enjoy the ride, babe?"

"Okay," she said with a feigned smile.

After a few hours of winding highways and scenic views, the couple pulled into downtown Susurrant, which consisted of two square blocks, including a post office, gas station, and diner. The car skidded to a stop at the gas station and Brett got out to pump gas. Kelly checked her makeup and wandered into the store to use the bathroom and buy some kind of crispy, ultra-salty snack. When he went to unscrew the cap to the gas tank, he caught the sight of a black glove on the ground. He smirked at the gas station characters and their utter sloppiness with props and then kicked the glove under the car, since that's what Brett would do.

"Front tires look a bit low," said one of the ominous-looking locals to Brett as he waited for the tank to fill.

"They're fine," said Brett, rolling his eyes at the hackneyed storyline unfolding before him.

"Are they?" the man said with a grin. "This here's the last stop for miles before wilderness takes over. If you get a couple of flats out there, you're outta luck."

"Is that when Old Man Frank Builder is gonna get us?"

"So you know about Franklin?"

"I've heard a thing or two."

"Now I don't venture into the woods much myself, but all of my friends over yonder have their stories," he said pointing towards the road Brett was about to drive down.

Brett stared at the man, trying to get a glimpse at the person behind the character he was playing. "Between me and my girlfriend, who do you think survives?" Brett said.

The man's eyes widened. "Pardon?"

"In this story, who do you think is going to get hacked to bits first, me or my girlfriend over there?" he motioned to Kelly, who was buying a bag of potato chips from the cashier.

His face tightened and he leaned close enough to kiss Brett. "Listen here, buddy," he whispered in forceful tones. "This is not the way the story's supposed to go. Stick to the one-sheet."

"What kinds of stories do your friends over yonder tell you?" Brett said.

"Well," he said, getting back into character, "they say city-folk go into the woods and they don't never come back."

"That's a shame," said Brett. "Hey, do they have, like, a lot full of used cars that city-folk leave in the woods? You know, since they don't never come back?"

He looked at Brett in contempt, as though he were sizing him up for a physical confrontation. Just when things were at their most tense, he turned in haste and walked away, muttering about the lack of integrity of non-union characters.

"What did that guy want?" asked Kelly when she returned from the store.

"He was talking about the gender-bending alien raves that happen in the woods outside of Susurrant every full moon. Apparently this place is pretty hip intergalactically."

Her jaw dropped. "What's gotten into you, Brett?"

"Just get in the car, Kelly. I'm going to go pay for the gas."

The road to the campsite was unpaved, and Brett's car began to slide and fishtail on the gravel. Undeterred, Brett's ego kept his right foot on the gas as the couple sped through the backcountry roads to the campsite about forty minutes out of town.

"Maybe you should slow down," Kelly suggested.

"Maybe you shouldn't worry so much, babe," said Brett. "Even if something happens to the car, I have Triple-A. I got it all under control."

Relieved he was back on the one-sheet, Kelly didn't say anything else. At the moment, she was just supposed to appear increasingly worried.

And she had every reason to agonize over his driving. First of all, he clearly turned off the main road for a short-cut that was probably going to add twenty minutes to their travel time. Secondly, he drove increasingly faster through the narrow road, which was often obscured by low hanging branches and overgrown brush.

As the car careened around a blind curve, they came upon a fallen tree in the road. Brett slammed on the breaks and violently turned the wheel in an attempt to avoid it, but it was too late. The vehicle plowed into the protruding branches of the tree and slashed the two front tires. Brett let out a string of obscenities and Kelly screamed.

When the dust settled, Brett got out of the car to assess the damage. As he glared at the front wheels, Kelly rolled down her window. "Is everything okay?" she asked.

Brett shook his head. "It looks like we're down two tires." Kelly smiled smugly at him. "Oh, don't look at me like that," he shouted. "I'm calling Triple-A."

He looked at his phone. "Shit," he said. "There's no service."

Kelly pulled out her phone. "Mine won't work either... What are we going to do?"

"Don't panic. We have a tent. We have food and booze. We'll be fine."

"How are we going to get back?"

"Well, we'll camp at that clearing over there," he pointed about twenty yards up the road. "Then if we see a car, we'll flag them down and ask for a ride back to town."

Kelly smiled. "Well," she said with a shrug, "it's not quite what we planned, but at least we're still camping, and that's kind of like what we came here to do anyway."

Once the couple made several trips between the clearing and the car to retrieve everything, Brett set up the tent as Kelly gathered firewood. After transforming the clearing into a respectable campsite, they built a fire and rested their backs against a large boulder. Brett opened the cooler, handed a wine cooler to Kelly, and took a beer. Upon his first taste, Brett became Mason, who absolutely hated the taste of beer so much that he couldn't even pretend to enjoy it.

"I fucking hate the taste of beer," Mason said.

"But Brett, you love the taste of beer," said Kelly.

He took another mouthful and grimaced.

At that moment, Kelly looked at her phone and became Sophia. "We've actually been done with the day's activities since we opened the drinks," Sophia said. "Let's go back to Denver."

About fifteen minutes after the scene reached its scheduled ending, a truck pulled into the campground to take Mason and Sophia back to Susurrant where they would borrow a vehicle from the Horror Camp car lot, a division of the Four Corner Character Prop Department—or at least, that was what Mick, the bearded, chain-smoking driver told them. And that was just the beginning of his monologue. Aside from a couple of casual "hellos," the passengers didn't utter a solitary word as Bearded Mick regaled them with the following subjects: This year's below-normal snowpack, how the former owner of the Susurrant Saloon had to die before they let him back in the bar (which happened in late 2010), the difference between Scotch whisky and bourbon, the advantage of cultivating marijuana legally after running an elicit growing operation for 25 years, how owning a hot tub didn't necessarily mean you'd get laid any more than you do now, his failed attempt to learn Scottish Gaelic, and his love of getting drunk on Scottish Whisky, smoking his home grown weed, and sitting in his hot tub during a snowstorm.

Mason and Sophia were relieved not to speak to one another. He knew his unprofessionalism perturbed her, since she had spent the better part of her life in character placement and couldn't bear to witness someone disrespect the esteem of the industry. And she recognized that her intense physical attraction to Mason might be on the wane, since it was difficult to fawn over someone who wasn't very good at his job. Sophia was beginning to realize this was one of the reasons not to become romantically entangled with people she worked with.

Once Bearded Mick dropped them off at their loaner car—a bright yellow clunker from the early 1980s—they didn't have a backwoods orator easing the tension, and as such, the car buzzed with the restlessness of a looming conversational confrontation.

Chapter 14

Some circumstances require instant reconciliation—situations like foot-in-the-mouth utterances, occasions of jealousy in romantic relationships, and asking for forgiveness immediately following grossly inappropriate flatulence (funeral gas, for example). The car ride back to Denver was not one of those situations. Both Mason and Sophia had no interest in discussing the day's developments. Besides any necessary discussion regarding the specifics of the trip—bathroom stops, car temperature, music selection, et cetera—the couple didn't have much to discuss.

It wasn't until he pulled in front of Sophia's house that he even thought to turn on his phone: Six missed calls and a collection of texts from Eileen. Since he didn't feel like pulling over to investigate their nature, he figured he would just speak with her when he made it home ten minutes later.

"Where the hell have you been?" Eileen offered her standard greeting when Mason walked through the door.

"Working," he said.

"Did you get any of my messages?"

"I saw them when I dropped Sophia off, but I haven't looked at them yet."

She sighed in exasperation. "Alright, I have good news and bad news."

"Bad, always do bad first."

"Uncle Ernest has terminal cancer."

"That is bad..." he said. He couldn't think of much else to add to that. In deference to the situation, he paused in contemplation before speaking again. "Well… I mean, I guess it could be worse. He is in his 80s. And no one can say he hasn't lived a full life."

"Oh, for sure..." Even though she could hardly wait to tell him about the money, she had enough class not to mention something so trivial in the same breath as her uncle's condition.

"Okay, what's the good news?"

"He's giving a lot of his money away before he dies, and we're getting some."

"How much?"

"Something like ten thousand a piece."

He took a few moments to process the information. And then he chuckled in spite of himself. "So I guess rent really is going to pay itself."

"I thought the exact same thing!" Eileen explained the details of both the arrangement and their scheduled rendezvous with Ernest and Darren over the weekend.

With his enthusiasm for his current character placement work already diminishing, Mason went to his room to find the guarantee he signed with Ted. He hoped there was an easy way to shirk his obligations, but once he found the document—under a pile of concert fliers and receipts—right there in plain English, it read, "While the undersigned character is under the employ of Lachesis, he/she must meet all obligations mutually agreed upon by both parties. Failure to complete these obligations to the satisfaction of management will result in the immediate termination of contract." A breach of the guarantee was the least of his worries. With ten grand on the way, he didn't need the money. In fact, he could only think of one reason to continue with the project: Sophia. Still, he wondered if the writer of the story could kill his character so he didn't have to stick around until the conclusion. Could characters contact the author of the stories in which they appeared? He didn't even know the writer's name, much less his or her number. He supposed it was privileged information, or its listing would've appeared on the one-sheet.

Mason once again rifled through the mess of papers, this time uncovering the business card from George, the union representative. He considered giving the boisterous practitioner of labor rights a call, but he didn't want to admit he was working for Lachesis again. So he called Ted, but he was out—or at least, that's what Ron told him. After a few hastily exchanged logistics between the two, Mason asked him if he didn't mind answering his inquiry.

"Only if you answer one of mine," Ron said cryptically.

"Okay," Mason said. After what felt to him like a long and awkward pause, he continued, "I guess I'll go first. Can I contact the author of the story that I'm a character in?"

"Do you want to keep your balls?"

"I do."

"Then hell no. Writers and characters don't speak to each other, you got that? It just don't happen in this business."

"Okay, I won't."

"Ready for my question?" he asked.

"Yeah sure."

"Why is it you can make eye contact with people all day long and it's fine? It ain't no problem. But if you make eye contact with someone through a mirror, all of a sudden it's weird?"

Mason thought about it. "You know, I was on the light

rail a few nights ago and I totally made eye contact with someone through the reflection on the window. We stared at each other for like a second and then looked away real quick. It *was* weird. Very unpleasant."

"That's what I'm saying. There's a mirror on the door in the office and I was daydreaming—not even paying attention, just staring into space. And all of a sudden I'm looking at this young, attractive female who's there for character work, and she's staring right at me. And we did that thing. We looked away real quick."

Mason laughed. "It happens."

"You're telling me. It's not even the first time it's happened. Those poor young girls must think I'm some kind of pervert... You know, I got to get rid of that fucking mirror."

Alarmed and blindsided by Ron's suddenly talkative mood—most likely the result of emptying a few candlesticks of actual uppers—Mason laughed and offered a few pleasantries and strategic voice inflections he hoped would bring an expeditious end to the conversation. Before Ron would let him hang up the phone, however, he repeated his warning not to contact the author. The repercussions would be dire if he did. Mason once again heeded his words of caution and ended the needlessly long call with a sigh of relief.

• • • •

The next few days with Sophia and character placement were uneventful. Mason closely followed the daily one-sheet in an attempt to win back the affection that had begun to fade in the face of his unprofessionalism and disregard for the craft. He could sense his efforts had a positive effect after the first day when Sophia invited him to her house after several grueling hours of characterization.

The two rekindled their romance very unceremoniously by tearing off each other's clothes the second they were behind closed doors. However, the sex was very different—the kind that occurred after an argument or adversity. Hitherto this moment, their intimacy had been propelled by an element of newness and exoticism—merely an exercise in pure lust. Now it contained the foundations of lasting adoration, since some mutual respect had been established.

Their revitalized passion enhanced the authenticity of the story when on the last day of work they found themselves in the midst of a sex scene, which the two were able to act out with stunning credibility. The only difference between the character sex and their real-life copulation was related to the specific segment. Seconds before he climaxed, he had to abruptly stop and investigate a suspicious sound outside.

Over Kelly's protestations, Brett threw on some clothes, wrapped himself in a raincoat, and left the tent. Seconds later, a vicious torrent of rain mixed with violent wind and thunder inundated the campground. Kelly recoiled in fear as she attempted to listen for Brett's footsteps, but the calamity of the storm made it impossible to discern any other noise. The bright flickering of rapidly materializing lightning made shadowy outlines on the sides of the tent, which Kelly assumed were tree branches swaying in the wind. As she peered closer, however, the dancing silhouettes appeared more human than botanical. It looked as though two men were fiercely struggling with one another in a battle of strength. She cowered, grinding her body into the floor of the tent, as if proximity to the ground offered more protection than sitting upright. Just when she couldn't be any more petrified, the loudest crash of thunder she had ever heard clamored across the woods and Kelly fainted.

Chapter 15

Once Mason and Sophia made it back to Denver, they went to B-Street Bar to celebrate. Mason was relieved he fulfilled his end of the guarantee and didn't have to rely on any more character placement gigs with shady agencies— at least not for a long while.

"Who were you fighting outside the tent at the end of the story?" asked Sophia when the couple sat down.

"I don't know," Mason admitted. "And I don't think we're supposed to know. I think that's part of the mystery. Though, I'm sure it's supposed to be the spirit of Franklin Builder."

"It was definitely a suspenseful way to end a story."

After the first couple of drinks, and a wide range of mutually flattering compliments on each other's performances, Sophia excused herself to use the restroom. Since it was the 21st century, when pocket computers had long since eradicated any trace of boredom, Mason took advantage of the next couple minutes of solitude and pulled out his phone. Once again he failed to respond to a text from his sister and once again she sent a profusion of follow-ups, the last of which read, "Are you dead?" To which he responded: "No, still kickin.'"

When Sophia returned from the restroom, his phone rang and he excused himself to take it outside.

"Eileen!" Mason answered the phone in high spirits, high on spirits.

"Where the hell..." she trailed off. "Oh, who the fuck cares where you've been? What's happening?"

"We finally finished our characterizations for that story."

"That's cool. Where are you now?"

"B-Street."

"You know we have to meet Uncle Ernest and Darren tomorrow."

"Oh yeah. What time?"

"Around noon. You going to make it?"

"Of course I'm going to make it."

"No, I mean, are you going to show up reeking of booze on two hours of sleep with bloodshot eyes and a headache the size of Aurora?"

"Oh... Maybe."

"Mason, this may be the last time we're ever going to see Uncle Ernest. He's the last link we have to the family. Once he's gone, it's just you and me."

"I know..."

"You need to come home tonight so we can go together."

Mason agreed and ended the call. When he took his stool at the bar, Sophia looked up from her phone and greeted him with a kiss.

"When I get you home tonight," she said, "I'm going to put on a little fashion show for you. Have you ever been arrested and strip searched by a sexy, horny cop before?" Mason shook his head. "I've got some handcuffs and a baton and..."

"Alright alright," he said. "Hold on... I have to go home tonight. My great uncle is terminally ill and tomorrow may be the last time I'll ever get to see him."

"Seriously? Did you just find all that out now on the phone?"

"No, I found out earlier this week. But Eileen wants me to be home tonight so she doesn't have to track me down tomorrow morning. I'm sorry as hell to have to say this, but I can't let you arrest me tonight. I will take a rain check though. I didn't know you had a sexy cop outfit."

"I have a lot of sexy outfits."

"Hopefully I'll get acquainted with all of them at some point. But right now would you want to finish these drinks and go home with me?"

"Definitely," she said.

When they arrived at Mason's house, they spent some time conversing with Eileen, who was up watching a reality show about veterinarians on DVD. Once she went to bed, the couple retired to Mason's room, where they cuddled and shared their thoughts about life and death, which eventually segued into a conversation regarding the status of their relationship.

"What about us? Do you see us as a part of your future?" Mason asked after Sophia mentioned not wanting to die alone.

"It's kind of early to tell, isn't it?"

"I suppose so. Do you ever see us as boyfriend/girlfriend?"

"I don't really do the whole boyfriend/girlfriend thing. I date people, but I'm not a monogamous person. I hurt a lot of feelings in every relationship I've been in that was monogamous. And every time it was because of cheating."

"I see."

"What about you? Are you a strictly monogamous kind of guy?"

He hadn't thought about what he'd want out of his next long-term romantic partner. In fact, he more or less gave up looking for one months ago. All of his previous relationships were monogamous by default, since that was just what people assumed would happen when two bodies coupled in this culture.

"I always have been," he said. "I've never even thought about it being different."

"You've never cheated on anyone?"

"On my second girlfriend, I did. Nora was her name."

"Wait, Nora was the girlfriend or the affair?"

"The girlfriend. I can't even remember the other girl's name. I met her in Rapid City when we were on tour."

"So you nailed someone on the road? You're such a rock star," she said. Mason chuckled. "Let me ask you something. Did you love your girlfriend any less after you cheated on her?"

He thought about it. "No, not really. I sure felt guilty as hell though."

"That's the whole thing about open relationships—you do away with the guilt."

He shrugged. "That all sounds good on paper and all. But that's not how... real life just doesn't work like that."

"But it does if you're open and honest with yourself and your partner. You're still going to get jealous, and all the things that suck about relationships still suck, but when it works out, it really works out great."

Mason asked a few more questions and Sophia provided a few more answers. How many open relationships had she experienced? Two, if she counted the first one that began monogamously. Obviously these things didn't work out if neither of hers did, right? None of Masons worked out either and all were supposed to be monogamous. What did she enjoy about them? Freedom, nonstop sexual excitement, and the absolute lack of guilt.

"I know you're only selling me on the *idea* of this, right?" he asked. "You're not trying to say that you and I should actually be in an open relationship, are you?"

"Maybe. What would you say if I was?"

"I would say, 'Let me mull it over.' It seems like a brave new world. I'm not so sure I can be that swingin.'"

"So you, Mason Jarman, former singer of Tortured Metaphor, cheater on girlfriends, touring adulterer—you don't think you're swingin' enough to be in an open relationship?"

"I mean, I'm pretty hip and liberal when it comes to everything else. I'm just a bit sexually reserved, I guess."

"Conservative," she said. "The word you're looking for is 'conservative' not 'reserved.'"

"No, no, no, I am not conservative in any capacity."

"Except for this one."

Mason turned his head and glanced at the clock. It was three in the morning. "Let's go to bed," he said.

"Wait, hold on," she said. "I'm not ready for bed yet."

"What do you want to do?"

"Tell me one thing about you that I wouldn't know by looking at you."

"Um," he thought about it. All he wanted to do was go to sleep, but he knew she wasn't going to let him. He had to think of something. "Oh, I played Arthur Denton in my high school's presentation of *Little Shop of Horrors.*"

She laughed. "A theater guy, huh? I like that…" She put her arm on his chest. "Arthur Denton—which guy is that?"

"He's the masochistic patient that takes pleasure in the pain he gets from going to the dentist. Bill Murray plays him in the movie."

"Okay, I remember him in that movie."

"Alright, now your turn. Tell me one thing about you."

"I was a center forward on my high school soccer team."

"So you were a jock, huh?"

"I bet you were a jock too."

"Look at me. Do I look like a jock?

"Did you skateboard?" she asked. Mason nodded. "Then you were a skate jock."

"Skate jock? That's not a thing. By the way, my British friend Matt Padgett would throw a fit if you used the word soccer around him. It's football."

"Oh, who cares what your wanker friend thinks? He's a daft prat, or whatever the hell they say over there."

"'Daft prat,'" he repeated. "The British sure know how to insult people."

"Yeah, they do," she said.

"Alright, well this daft prat is going to bed."

They said their goodnights and fell asleep in one another's arms. When he awoke the next morning, she was gone, and his sister was yelling at him to get ready.

Chapter 16

Eileen was able to usher Mason out the door and onto the bus in time to arrive at Citizen Cafe by noon. Eager brunch-goers formed a line out the door as they waited for tables. Mason, exhausted by the events of last night and grumpy from the twenty minute bus ride, was gearing up to complain loudly about his need for and lack of coffee.

"We're never going to get a fucking table here. Whose fucking idea was it to come here anyway?" he fucking said.

Eileen, herself drowsy, was in no mood whatsoever to put up with her brother's shit, and was about to say so when she spotted Darren through one of the restaurant's windows. "Shut up, they already found a seat."

Mason wanted to respond to her demand of his silence, but once Darren and Uncle Ernest noticed the Jarmans, they began to wave and his mood couldn't help but improve instantly. He didn't want family members he saw so infrequently to be privy to his petty little tantrums. He wanted them to imagine him as a full-grown man with a strong and steady emotional state that remained immune to the vicissitudes of life.

They got to the table as the busser was filling waters. Mason tried to order a coffee from him and was informed that his server would be over to the table momentarily. This didn't thrill the cranky Jarman, who thankfully had his sister to calm him down by whispering under her breath, "Lighten up, you damned wiener." Her suggestion made him laugh and he sat down with a smirk, which didn't quite match the smile on the face of his uncle, who beamed at the sight of Mason and his sister.

Ernest waited for either Jarman to say hello, but since they seemed more concerned with coffee and bickering in hushed tones, he decided to go first. "As I live and breathe, look who it is!"

"Unkie Ernest!" said Eileen. She was almost sad to see him, since he didn't exactly appear healthy. The cancer had withered his once proud physique and he looked fragile and weak. But he still had brown, piercing eyes, a proud nose, and a demeanor that exuded confidence.

"Get off your asses and come give me a hug," he said.

They sat right back up and placed him in the center of a nice warm Jarman sandwich. He wrapped his aged hands around their wrists and closed his eyes. His smile reached the borders of his face. It seemed like it wanted to get bigger, but simply ran out of room.

"Okay," he said when he opened his eyes, "take a seat and let's get some breakfast. I'm starving."

Mason finally got his coffee and stopped being such a damned wiener, Eileen ordered a Bloody Mary, Ernest procured a glass of whiskey and water, and Darren stuck with just water and no ice because he was sensible like that.

Once the appropriate introductions and small talk were out of the way, Ernest initiated the discussion on the current state of his health.

"As you know, I'm dying," he said.

"Yeah, Elizabeth told me," Eileen said.

He shook his head. "You mean Betsy…"

"I wish that's what I meant."

"Yeah well, let's not waste any time talking about that," Ernest said. "There's no need to get upset about something that none of us can change. And frankly it's not going to change, so what's there to worry about?" No one at the table had a good answer to the question, and since it was meant to be rhetorical anyway, he continued. "This may be the last time you see me, so let's get down to brass tacks. You already spoke to Darren about the gift I'm giving each of you. But instead of writing two checks and mailing them, I brought two envelopes full of cash. That way, you don't have to go to the bank and it won't affect your taxes." He handed the envelopes to the Jarmans. "Furthermore, I'm putting each of you in my will. Darren is the executor of the estate, so he'll see to it that you receive your inheritances."

"That's incredibly generous," Mason said. "You know you don't have to do that. I mean, you shouldn't feel obligated or anything."

"Mason, a dead man can't spend money. Besides, it's not like your grandma is going to leave you anything."

"Well don't you have a hot new girlfriend? Shouldn't you give her a cut?"

"Give her a cut? What, did I rob a bank?" Ernest explained the arrangement he and his girlfriend Jenny had made. She would keep the house because he didn't want to force her to move—even though she didn't really need the money. When her ex-husband died, she gained a pension and an impressive estate.

After the particulars of the will were sorted, Eileen could feel tears welling up in her eyes. The last of her blood relatives with any interest in her and her brother stood before them with mere months to live. That's not to say Darren had no interest, but he was more avuncular and couldn't relate to them on the level that Ernest could.

"How much longer did the doctors give you?" she asked.

"Not long. I won't live to see another month."

"How do you know? What if we get you some marijuana and Chinese medicine and, and, I don't know, yoga?"

"I'm taking my own life."

"What?" she raised her voice. "You can't, you can't..."

Mason reached over and held her hand in a gesture to both comfort her and quell her emotions. "Eileen, don't," he pleaded.

She took her napkin up to her eyes to wipe away the tears. She didn't want to make a scene, but she was having difficulty soothing such a fiercely emotional response.

"But why?" she said.

He took a deep breath as he carefully contemplated what to say next. When he did finally speak, he enunciated every word in a calm and collected manner. "When I watched Sharon slowly suffer and decay into oblivion from her cancer, I made a solemn vow that I would never let that happen to me. And now that I have cancer, I aim to honor that vow." Sharon was his fourth wife.

"I can respect that," said Mason.

"Thank you Mason... Listen Eileen, it will be fine." He took her hands in his. "You know the first thing I bought when the doctors told me I was dying?" Eileen shook her head. "A bottle of whiskey and a joint." He laughed and Eileen smiled. "When I bought the whiskey, I thought of you. Do you remember when I was staying with you and Betsy, and that girl with the green hair was there too—what was her name?"

Eileen snuffled, "Karen."

"Karen, that's right. Remember Betsy drank too much wine and went to bed after dinner, and we stayed up 'til all hours of the night, drinking and listening to records?" She nodded. "Remember what you told me when I offered you a beer?"

"Beer's for wimps. I drink whiskey."

He laughed. "Yes! You were what, 18, 19 years old? I remember thinking that was some impressive shit." Everyone at the table had a laugh. "So when I heard my prognosis, I drove straight to the liquor store and I went right to the beer aisle, like I normally do. But this time all I could think was, 'Beer's for wimps. I drink whiskey.' So then I walked over to the whiskey aisle and got myself a bottle."

The story made Eileen feel much better. Of course, Mason had to dampen her relative emotional ease with his lack of tact by asking, "So why'd you get the joint?"

He laughed. "Two reasons. One, because grass is legal in Colorado and I wanted to be a part of that. And two, because I wanted to get stoned." Once again the table erupted with laughter.

"So tell us," Mason said, "have you become wiser in the face of death?"

"Mason, don't!" Eileen pleaded.

"It's okay, Eileen. It's a fair question. I can't say I've gained any IQ points, but my perspective has certainly changed." Ernest matter-of-factly elucidated his current state of mind, which he admitted was always threatening to veer into bitterness and resentment if he didn't attempt with every fiber in his being to remain positive. "When people put me on the spot—and you'd be surprised how many people put me on the spot—they expect me to be the Dalai Lama. But I don't have much in the way of life-affirming advice..."

"So you don't, I don't know, think any differently about your life?" Mason wondered.

"My own life—now *that* I do think differently about," he

said with wide eyes. "I'm totally and completely in awe at all the fun I got to have. It's unreal. I accomplished everything I set out to do." He regaled them with stories of smoking pot with Allen Ginsberg, playing guitar in jazz and rock and roll bands, getting kicked out at the Trocadero, seeing Ella Fitzgerald and Dave Brubeck at Red Rocks in the early '60s and The Doors at The Dog on New Year's in '67. And he drank enough booze to sink a cruise ship, he said. After a considerable silence, he added, "There is one thing about dying that I cherish above all else."

"What's that?" Eileen asked.

"I don't have to worry about bullshit manners anymore. Now if I don't like someone, I don't have to pretend to like them. And if I want to leave a social gathering early, I just leave. I don't even say goodbye anymore. It's great."

When the server brought their meals, the conversation tapered off as everyone concentrated on eating. After Darren finished his potatoes and before he started on his biscuits and gravy, he realized he was at a stopping point meal-wise and could subsequently state the sentiment he had been saving for an opportune time. "Hey Mason, we were listening to your CD in the car."

"Which one?"

"I think it was the second one. What was that called?"

"*Athletic Apocalypse.*"

He laughed. "Yeah, that's it. Did you call it that because you didn't exactly get along with the muscle heads?"

"More or less."

"I like it. Nice and full of angst."

"Thanks," said Mason. "Are you still playing in Rock Lingo, Uncle Ernest?"

Rock Lingo was a band Ernest and two of his aging musician buddies formed in the mid 1990s. They played covers and original numbers, mostly around Pueblo and Colorado Springs, but they had been up to Denver, down to New Mexico, and out to Gunnison and Durango a few times. Although they did a few protest tunes from the '70s, they focused mainly on '50s and '60s rock, country, and rockabilly.

"No, we disbanded a year or so ago. We just got too damn old to play."

His answer dulled the mood at the table, so Mason told an off color joke about Jesus giving a motel owner three nails and asking to put him up for the night. It worked, and the laughter returned.

When everyone at the table finished dining, they ordered another round of drinks and retold stories they've all heard a hundred times. Did they remember when Mason had to call Ernest for bail money in Montana after he tried to break into what he thought was the house where the rest of his band was staying, but was actually the residence of an elderly couple who thought he was a burglar? Of course they did; they've been hearing it since the early 2000s. How about the one where Eileen lost her car after a night of tripping mushrooms and spent hours searching for it the next day? She eventually found it in her own garage. She was so out of this world, she didn't remember giving the keys to her sober friend Matt, who agreed to drive the car home in exchange for cab money to his own apartment. That was one of Uncle Ernest's favorites.

After the bill was paid, Ernest, Eileen, and Mason stood outside waiting for Darren to pull the car around. Ernest looked over to Mason and said, "When you two sat down for breakfast this morning, Eileen said, 'Stop being such a damned wiener.'"

"Yeah," Mason said.

"That's it. Those are my wise words. Stop being such

a damned wiener. All of life's woes are the result of being afraid. All regret comes from being afraid. You're not playing music now, are you?" Mason shook his head. "Well stop it. And you're not writing right now are you?" Eileen shook her head. "Are you happy?" Mason shrugged. "What about you?" Eileen also shrugged. "Well stop it, the both of you. If you're not happy, you're being afraid, and you need to change that. Tattoo it on your forehead if you need to. Don't be safe. Take chances. Stop being damned wieners."

Chapter 17

Darren pulled to the curb to pick everyone up, and Eileen helped her uncle into the car. Since it was only a five minute drive, he offered the Jarman siblings a ride home, which they graciously accepted. Tortured Metaphor was still playing on the car stereo when they opened the door. It was the first time in years that Mason had heard his band, and the memories came flooding back.

At first, he smiled at the nostalgia. And then he felt a sensation that had eluded him for the better part of a decade— almost like a sense of gratification for the moment. It was definitely not something he experienced as a 36 year old going through the motions of existence, expecting nothing and feeling the same. No, the music reminded him of a time when his ambitions inspired him to follow his dreams, when he wasn't so jaded and insecure of happiness. Back then, he had faith and confidence in his ability to bask in the excitement that came from the uncertainty of each new day, and he had the gumption and spirit to endure events as they unfolded.

It was an energy that was absent from his life now. Through a string of disappointments, he had allowed that spark to extinguish. Consequently, he was trapped in a low level, spirit-deadening lifestyle that led to unfulfillment and apprehension. In fact, he dreaded everything he used to take pleasure in: Jobs, relationships, writing music, buying new records from bands he enjoyed. Why did he dread these things? One word: Bitterness.

He just didn't have the good sense to do himself any favors. He slogged around in defeat and awoke each morning burdened by the sense of trepidation about anything that might give him even the slightest twinge of displeasure. It was a cowardly way to live, and he knew that, yet he lacked the motivation to remedy the situation.

But something happened as he heard his 26 year old self singing on the CD. He realized his fear of immediate disappointment was the only guarantee of continued long-term disappointment, and that maybe FDR was right when he spoke of fearing only fear itself. It wasn't a mind-blowing epiphany, he knew, and it would require a lot of willpower and patience to put it into everyday practice. But this was also the first time he gave credence to the notion that his incessant brooding might be his own damn fault. Maybe the galaxies hadn't aligned against him in some intergalactic conspiracy of bad luck.

When the vehicle slowed at a stoplight, Mason glanced toward the front seat and saw that his uncle had caught a glimpse of him in the visor mirror. It was almost as if Ernest had been in his head with him, and the two smirked knowingly at one another. Then Ernest looked back towards Eileen, who squinted as she watched the scenery pass by from her window once the car accelerated again.

Eileen was having some thoughts of her own on the state of her life, though hers were a bit more convoluted than Mason's. She couldn't remember exactly when she stopped writing, but it had to have been shortly after she broke up with Karen. Not until she began dating men again did she stop releasing her zine—that much she knew for sure. How was all of this connected, she wondered? Did men drain her creativity? Did Karen inspire it? And how was it that a person could ask herself so many questions for which she had no answers? How could a mind be so unknowable to itself? It perplexed her until she realized she could probably tell her inner monologue to quite down at some point so she could get some work done. It's a technique most artists use to get out of the way of their thoughts and get back to their craft.

When they arrived at the apartment, Uncle Ernest invited them to a party a few weeks later at his house in Pueblo. It would be a celebration of his life and the very last time they would see him alive. After a tearful goodbye, the Jarman siblings watched Darren's car head toward the highway.

"I'll get my computer," said Eileen. "You get your guitar. We have work to do."

. . . .

With ten grand apiece, the Jarmans ordinarily would have gone on the mother of all binges, but they were so involved with their pursuits that they spent the rest of the weekend behind closed doors.

As he worked on riffs and arranged them into rough drafts of songs, Mason wondered what Sophia would think of them. He sent her a text on Saturday evening, but she didn't respond to it.

So he solicited an opinion from his sister, who had set up a workstation at the dining room table. Eileen enjoyed the new material, she said, but she reserved full judgment until he paired it with lyrics. Then she showed Mason her new story, and while he had a few copy edits and content suggestions, he found her writing promising.

On Monday morning, he finally heard from Sophia again. Her call jolted him awake at 8:30 in the morning. His answer when he picked up the phone: "Why?"

"What do you mean why? Is this a bad time to call?" she asked. He sort of grumbled a response, so she skipped the pleasantries and got down to business. "Did you hear from Lachesis?"

"No, but I was going to go up there today. They owe me $450."

"Well the author of *Wrong Turn in Susurrant* wants to turn his novella into a novel, and his publishing house is going to pony up the funds. Beforehand is going to extend my contract another week. I'm surprised they haven't called you yet."

"Hold on," Mason looked at his phone. Six missed calls. "It looks like they did."

"So call them. We could be at work this afternoon."

"I don't know."

"What do you mean, you don't know?"

"I don't think I'm into it, you know? I just... Maybe I'm not cut out for this kind of thing. You know how I wasn't very good. I kept messing up the directions on the one-sheet. I suck. There I said it."

"You weren't that bad. Besides, I really want to see you again. I just got back from Lawrence last night. I was breaking up with my boyfriend."

"You had a boyfriend this whole time?"

"It was an open, long distance relationship, and it wasn't working out."

"Okay, so what does that mean? Are we like a thing now?"

"We're still hanging out, Mason, and I want to hang out with you."

"Alright," he said. "Let me call them and I'll call you back." He ended the call and let his phone fall on his chest.

Of all the ill-timed propositions he had ever received, this had to be up there with the time in 11th grade when Jade Kopischke asked him if he wanted to make out at the Youth Brigade show the day after he agreed to be Abigail Lagrand's boyfriend. Or when he was broke on tour (having spent his $5 per diem on Advil and a bag of chips after a particularly hard night of partying), and he received an email extending him the opportunity to replace Bad Religion's guitar tech on its European tour—an offer he had to decline since he still had two weeks of shows to play. Or when two different ex-girlfriends called him with two separate pleas of sex during the recovery period from hernia surgery when his orgasms were intensely painful.

Needless to say, he didn't need the money, but he could use the love—or at the very least, the sex. But the last thing he needed was the work. For five or so minutes he dwelled on his predicament, and he realized there were far worse situations in which he could have found himself. Besides, maybe this was a chance to put his newly resolved bravery into action.

Chapter 18

Eileen was still sleeping the morning Mason returned the call from Lachesis. She had spent almost the entirety of the previous night mulling over life and her place in it. She was at the age where most of her peers were trading booze and one night stands for children, but since she didn't want any part of that, a terrible case of mid-30s angst gripped her. With her social media page plastered with pictures of acquaintances' newly-born children, she yearned to fill her life with something meaningful—a purpose greater than mere survival.

She needed to reanimate her identity as a feminist—or, failing that, a person with convictions. But she couldn't imagine how to begin the process of—for lack of a better phrase—rewriting the lead character in her own story. But people did it all the time. She remembered Mason's friend Liam who reinvented himself every other week in high school. A few of the phases he went through, as far as she could remember, were goth, punk, straight-edge punk, drunk punk, drug user, raver, addict, AA leader, and finally yoga instructor. Of course, identity changes were less common in adulthood, but not inconceivable. If her grandma could become a Born Again Christian in her late 60s, she could radicalize herself once more.

Her ex-girlfriend Karen helped cultivate her identity as a riot grrrl, but was she essential to it? Eileen nixed the idea, not because she could probably figure out how to reinvent her past persona alone, but because she wasn't sure she even aspired to it.

Still, she felt she needed to contact her former lover, if for no other reason than to hear her laugh again. In moments of uncertainty, she always found comfort in imagining conversations with former lovers and friends she hadn't talked to in years.

Though it seemed almost pointless to check, Eileen didn't find a profile for Karen on social media. So she spent the better part of a few hours on search engines and library databases but didn't find a listing. She scoured her current email accounts in search of old emails Karen may have sent, but none were active during the late '90s.

After she was about to concede defeat, she remembered the Hotmail account she set up for her zine, which she hadn't checked in at least a year or so. She had to request a new password, but eventually she was greeted with page after page of spam emails. She tediously checked boxes and mass deleted hundreds of them in bulk. Finally an email from nine months prior piqued her interest. The sender was named Karen Crowley-Gasovic and the subject was in all caps: "EILEEN HOW THE HECK ARE YA?" She clicked on it and the message read:

> Eileen, I know you probably don't check this account much anymore. You probably haven't done a zine in years, amiright? I mean who the heck does print publications anymore? Anyway, I was moving and came across a box of old fliers, tapes, and zines and I found some old copies of *Grrrl Reaction*. They

literally sent chills down my spine!!! We need to get in touch, lady. My number's in my nifty signature at the bottom of the page. Anyway, call or email soon. I need to hear from my gal!

P.S. I hope you're not still hurt about how things ended. I was the worst breaker-upper on the planet back then, and I very much regret what happened. I hope you're well.

For reasons she couldn't begin to explain, Eileen cried when she came to the end of the email. A bizarre set of emotions gripped her all at once—relief in Karen's existence, bewilderment at her obvious marriage, and melancholy at how things had ended (basically Karen mailed a breakup letter just before leaving to spend three months in Europe). Eileen picked up her phone in excitement and enthusiastically entered her pass code, but as she hit her phone icon, she glanced at the time. Back in the '90s, she could have called Karen at 3 in the morning, but that was then. Now that she had a hyphenated name, she probably had a totally different life. Maybe she even had kids.

She put her phone back on the nightstand, rolled over, and went to sleep. She would try to call Karen at an hour polite society might consider decent.

• • • •

Mason didn't even have time to shower and shave before he found himself at Lachesis once again. Judging by the lack of commotion in the back room of Budtenders' MMJ and Rec, he missed the Monday morning rush. As he made his way to Ted's office, he caught a glimpse of the back of Ron's head as he sat in his office chair. He must have discarded the mirror at some point because no uncomfortable eye contact was made.

"Mason, the man of the hour," Ted said as he drank coffee from a styrofoam cup, his smile revealing variously discolored teeth.

"I honored my contract," said Mason.

"Yes you did. I have your money somewhere..." Ted muttered as he opened and closed a few desk drawers. "Ah ha! Here you go." He handed him an envelope, which Mason counted immediately. It contained all $450 in cash. "You ready to turn this novella into a novel?"

He halfheartedly nodded.

"You got a little bit of action on this one, huh?" he asked with a wink.

He squinted. "I'm not in the position to reveal any particulars about the plot."

Ted stared blankly at him. "A professional, I see. I suppose you want to sign another guarantee."

Mason smiled at his rhyme. "I'd take another guarantee, yes. I mean, I don't really need the stress."

"If you go out there and half-ass it, it would stress me out!" he said, ignoring the sheer wit of Mason's rhyming comeback. "I got a reputation here."

Mason's assured him that he wouldn't harm the esteem of Lachesis and its high-minded business practices. The two agreed to terms identical to the last contract: He would receive $90 a day, up to $450 for the week unless the author of the story decided to kill his character in a twist of plot. He shook his hand, walked out the door, and called Sophia. "Let's rock and roll," he said.

Mason and Sophia convened at her house and embarked to Susurrant after a passionate make-out session in her bedroom. During the commute, he tried his best to maintain any semblance of motivation for the project. But after some careful introspection, courtesy of her drifting off to sleep outside of Bailey, he knew he was headed straight into the middle of a situation in which he had no business.

It was worse than his touring days when he was driving to play a Monday night show in a city where his band had no following. At least back then, he knew playing bad shows was just paying dues—a small step on a low rung on the ladder to sustainability as a functioning tour band. Sure, that Monday night in Sioux Falls might garner 15 paying audience members, but those 15 would enjoy the show, buy the records, and tell their friends. The next time around, there would be 50 kids in the audience. Besides, even a bad show still meant he got to play his songs on his guitar with his band halfway across the continent. How many people got to say that?

Now he was driving to a nearly deserted mountain town for a job he didn't respect or need. He was doing it for the girl, of course, but he had no confidence in his abilities as a character, and so he worried about alienating her with a lackluster performance. Couple the lack of faith in his talent with his festering apathy and he figured he had himself a recipe for disaster.

A decade of performing in rock and roll prepared him for moments like these, however. And he knew once he had his guitar in hand—literally or figuratively—it was time to play. The crowd had paid their money and now they expected a show.

Chapter 19

They arrived in Susurrant that evening and wasted no time taking their places for the scene that was about to commence. Sophia zipped herself up in the tent and became a frightened Kelly. Mason paced around the campsite near his last confrontation—with what they assumed was the spirit of Builder—and became an embattled Brett. The evening's rain had even created a setting similar to the one that concluded Part I of the story.

In the calamity of the storm and through the darkness of night, his visibility diminished profoundly—down to a few yards in front of his face, at most. Just when he determined the campsite clear of danger, an unseen force struck him on the side and knocked him down into the mud. He rolled over in an attempt to ascertain what or who it was, but he couldn't make out any distinct shapes. As he struggled to get up, another force pushed him to the ground again. Anger and frustration replaced any kind of fear in him and he charged in the direction of his assumed attacker. But he didn't come into contact with anything and almost fell again from his sheer velocity. At that moment a furious bout of lightning illuminated the campground and Brett witnessed an old, weary miner with a weatherworn black prospector's hat. They charged each other and engaged in combat for several seconds. The miner overpowered him, knocked him to ground, and kicked him in the stomach.

Brett lay in the fetal position, watching the miner retrieve his shovel from where he had laid it against a tree. He carried the shovel with a determined expression on his face and raised it with both hands over his shoulders. Just as he was about to administer the death blow, a man dressed in black burst on the scene and tackled him, the shovel falling to the ground. Brett tried to determine what was happening, but rain and mud clouded his vision. There was a struggle; that much he knew. But that's all he could see.

Before he had a sense of what was happening, he found himself on a motorcycle, traveling with the man through the darkness and rain. Brett asked him where they were going, but he didn't respond. Then he inquired about his girlfriend back at the campground and received no reply. His impatience growing, he shouted at the man, pleaded with him to return to the campground so he could tend to his partner.

A minute or so into his tantrum, the man slowed the motorcycle to a stop, and speaking very firmly and deliberately said, "Kelly, she's okay. She'll sleep until morning. Mr. Builder... the miner, is incapacitated. If you come with me, we'll talk."

His words calmed Brett. "Okay," he said.

They only rode through the rain for another few minutes before arriving at a stone house. The man in black parked the motorcycle and welcomed Brett inside. Once they were out of the rain, Brett took off his wet jacket and looked for a place to set it.

"Here," said the man pointing to a peg near the door. "Hang it."

"Thank you," said Brett. He placed his jacket on the lower peg since the one above held a solitary glove. "I didn't get your name."

"Don," he said, offering nothing in the way of a handshake.

For the first time, Brett could get a sense of the man. He stood proud with broad shoulders and long, straight hair. The wrinkles in his face appeared as though they were earned and not forced into his skin by the magnitude of time. He moved throughout the tiny, one-room cabin with purpose and ease, as though he was gliding.

There were only two points of interest in the cabin—a cot that could never fit more than one person, and an oversized fireplace to which Don was tending. Once he built a fire and it grew to a comfortable roar, he sat down on the stone floor and motioned for Brett to do the same.

"Thanks for helping me out back there," Brett said. "You saved my life."

Don took a deep, slow breath as he reached for a kettle and canteen that sat next to the fireplace. "Mr. Builder is a damaged spirit."

"Mr. Builder. Franklin Builder, right? So is he the one that supposedly died in a mining accident in the early 1900s, or whatever?"

"July 25, 1902. Exactly two centuries, three months, and a day after I entered this world." Don emptied some water into the kettle, crumbled a substance into it, and placed it in the fire.

Brett wasn't sure if Don misspoke, if he heard him wrong, or if this man in black lacked an understanding of time and numbers. He didn't know how to respond.

Don continued, "Mr. Builder is without empathy." His pauses between sentences and certain words were long and patient. "His problems, his fate... they are the fault of the stars, he thinks."

Brett stared into the fire for what seemed like ages. He

didn't feel awkward or compelled to speak, but eventually his curiosity got the better of him. "So you've been dead for almost 300 years?"

Don guffawed. "Do I not sit before you?"

"You do, but you also said you were born in 1702." Don nodded once. "So you're over 300 years old?"

"No... I have not tallied my years. But I am only a visitor in your time." Don retrieved his kettle from the fire with a stick. He retrieved two clay cups from the side of the fireplace and filled them with the kettle's contents. "Here," he said, handing one to Brett.

"What is it?"

"Drink."

Brett blew into the cup to cool down the liquid. After a few moments, he drank what he discovered was some kind of poorly strained tea. When he finished, Don told him not to speak until spoken to. He heeded this advice as he sat in the fire's warm glow.

After a generous passing of what Brett formally considered the concept of time, he realized there was a powerful psychoactive substance in the libation. He brought his hand to his face, closed his eyes, and grinned. He was about to announce how hard he was tripping, but then he remembered Don, the 300 year old fellow to his left, had told him to keep his mouth shut.

"Mason," Don said finally.

Brett was surprised to be called Mason since he assumed they were still in character. With the effect of the tea intensifying every passing moment, he experienced a crisis of identity. Was he Brett or Mason? Who were Brett and Mason anyway? Who was identity more important to—the person who possessed it, or the person who used it to identify another?

"Mason," Don said again.

He looked down at himself. "I am Mason." Don nodded once. "How did you know that?"

"I know."

Mason nodded. "Alright, man." He wasn't feeling very curious or confrontational under the influence. He felt like he could just let the events unfold without trying to control them.

After another considerable pause, Don spoke again. "I am an immortal spirit."

"You do look good for a 300 year old." Don didn't even begin to crack a smile. Mason quickly attempted to recover from his failed moment of hilarity by once again respecting the somberness of the situation. "How have you managed to evade death?" he asked matter-of-factly.

"I appear in the minds of authors, and I live in the pages of books."

"How did you figure that one out?"

Don explained everything from the beginning of his life in what was then (according to Europeans) New Spain, to the moment his life almost ended at the hands of the Spanish soldiers who captured him. He escaped, but all other members of his warrior band were slayed. Despondent, he travelled to the burial grounds of his ancestors and surrendered his carbon back into the earth. As he lay unconscious, his soul began to seep from his being. Instead of letting the current take him to the afterlife—or where ever disembodied beings went—he fought it and forged his own path.

Soon he found himself in the thoughts and prayers of generations far removed from his own. But these thoughts and prayers were fleeting, and he only achieved consciousness the instant before they ended. Then one night he found himself in the collective hallucination of a group of scribes and healers. After a long conversation about life, death, and the afterlife, the group invited him into their prayers. After that, he began appearing in the thoughts of creators, and by extension, in their prayers.

"So at this moment, you're alive because you're in this story," said Mason.

"Yes," said Don. "I have appeared in many stories and spoken with many characters..."

"Do you ever get bored just waiting in the ether for someone to think about you?"

"No, conventional notions of time do not exist in my life."

"Is it fulfilling, this life?"

"Any life that has purpose is fulfilling."

"And what's the purpose of your life? I mean, um, you know, what gives your life purpose?"

"Saving people like you from damaged spirits like Franklin Builder. And talking to people like you who find life boring and without purpose."

Mason considered his words. "So… I'm bored and purposeless. Is that why I find life so unfulfilling?"

"You find no fulfillment because you think happiness lies in the past… You are too anxious to enjoy the present… And you fear the future."

Mason laughed. "You're right, I suck." Don didn't respond, so he continued. "Would you like to point out any of my other shortcomings? I have many."

"You lack confidence and poise…"

"This conversation," said Mason, "is not my favorite thing." Generally when Mason consumed a drug, he wanted to enjoy the showering of dopamine on his brain by confirming everything he liked about his life. He would dwell on his shortcomings the next time he was hungover.

"Calm down," said Don. "I am not criticizing you. I am extending an invitation to release your pride long enough to examine yourself."

Mason didn't utter a word. Obviously politeness and tact were not Don's strong suit, so Mason ceased wasting any energy taking offense to the brutal honesty. Once he put the sting of the insults behind him, he interpreted his words for what they were meant to be—unabashedly constructive criticism.

"What do you mean I lack confidence and poise?" He asked the question in an earnest, non accusatory tone.

"You have the spirit of a free man and the confidence of a man imprisoned by fear… Comfort is the enemy of contentment… You have sacrificed the former for the latter."

Mason dwelled on this assertion for a long time, the words reverberating in his mind until they became echoes of themselves. "Wait," he said. "In the past, I was constantly uncomfortable and it was the happiest time of my life. But if I seek happiness in the past, I will never be happy."

"This is what I speak."

"But what am I supposed to do with that? It's a mess of contradiction."

"That's life," he said. And that's all he said. Mason nodded and lost himself in the flames of the fireplace.

After he felt like he got through to Mason, Don lightened up a bit. At first he smiled, and then he leaned over to Mason and said, "Do you like to dance?"

"Sure," Mason said. "Why?"

"That is just something I really miss… Well that and sex, of course."

"Sure."

"We used to have huge gatherings where we would dance all night around a fire and then have sex until dawn…

It was great."

"Yeah," Mason said, nodding.

"That is the thing about these stories... I am always the wise soul, not the wild soul who gets to dance and make love... Having fun is just as important as sincerely analyzing life."

Mason shrugged. "My phone plays music. We could dance around this fire."

Don's face lit up and he nodded profusely.

"Alright, let's see what you'd like," he said, scrolling through his music library. "Not Shellac—too weird. Probably not Strike Anywhere—you can't slam dance with just two people. Here we go—Louis Armstrong. Let's get some 'Skokiaan' in here!"

The two danced to the entirety of Louis Armstrong songs that Mason had on his phone—even the ballads. He offered to skip the slower tunes, but Don wanted to sway to those as well. At one point during the two-man party, Mason took a break to catch his breath and get some water. As he watched Don dance for a few songs, he couldn't help but marvel at the ridiculousness of the situation. He had never tripped with a spirit—much less one that wanted to dance all night.

"You coming back?" shouted Don. "This one's a good one." He was convulsing to "Hello Dolly."

Mason put his cup of water on the floor and rejoined the party in progress. They danced until his phone battery nearly died. Then they rested by the fire.

When the effects of the mushrooms subsided, Don hugged Mason for a long time, thanking him. After they watched the sunrise, Don gave him a ride back to camp on the back of his motorcycle.

In the early morning light, Kelly began to stir in the tent.

She opened her eyes and glumness weighed heavy on her chest. It only took few moments to orient herself to the harsh aftermath of the events that unfolded the evening prior. Still paralyzed with fear, she was too traumatized to confront whatever lurked beyond the thin tent walls.

Before she could gather her thoughts, she heard a motorcycle pass by on the road nearby and then footsteps heading toward the campsite. She burrowed under the sleeping bags, nestled as close to the ground as she could get, and tried to breathe as quietly as she ever had. Just as they reached their loudest, the footsteps stopped. She held her breath as the tent zipper began to move. She closed her eyes tightly and she heard someone step into the tent. And she screamed when she felt a strong pair of hands clench tightly around her shoulders.

"Kelly! Kelly! It's me," said Brett, his hair disheveled, his face scraped, and his clothes tattered in places.

"Oh my god," she said, lunging to hug him in relief. "What happened? Are you alright?"

Once Brett calmed her down, he took a seat in the tent and began to explain the events of the evening prior.

"But Brett-" said Kelly after he finished recounting the story.

"You can call me Mason. That's my spirit name."

"Um, listen you! We need to find help before the killer returns." This line wasn't on her one-sheet, but she said it because she thought it might be a good way to conclude the scene. And she was right. Once she delivered the lines, the scene ended.

Chapter 20

Eileen stared at her phone with tremendous anxiety—as if it taunted her with its very presence. The small, handheld contraption possessed so much frightening possibility. With it she could reach out to an unknown world, and she feared the potential emotional landmines lurking therein.

And it wasn't as though she had a choice, either. Now that she discovered Karen's existence, she knew she had to call her. If she didn't she would lie awake at night concocting imaginary conversations and inventing wild scenarios in an attempt to fill in the blanks of the cursory information her ex-lover included in her email.

But she just couldn't bring herself to pick up the phone. In an attempt to procrastinate, Eileen ran two miles (something she hadn't done in years), showered, and went to the grocery store. When she returned, she made a large pot of quinoa, washed the dishes, cleaned the kitchen, and made all the beds in the house. She picked up the biggest book she could find on Mason's shelf—*Our Band Could Be Your Life*—and began to read.

When she was content with the sheer amount of time that had passed, she meandered over to her phone on the dining room table, where it lay during the entirety of her errands, and picked it up. Zero calls or texts. She hit the phone icon and quickly scrolled through her contacts until she found the only recently entered Karen Crowley-Gasovic. Then, without so much as a thought, she called her.

When Karen answered, Eileen immediately regretted the call and nearly hung up. But she had come this far, she reasoned, no use abandoning it now.

"Karen, it's Eileen."

"Shut the front door!" Karen said before screaming in delight. "Oh my god! I can't believe it. How did you get my number?"

"You sent me an email."

"Email? You mean the one I sent like a friggen year ago!"

"The very same."

"Dy-no-mite!" she said in the style of J.J. on the show *Good Times.* "So, how the heck are you?"

"Um," Eileen was taken aback by Karen's goofiness. When they dated she maintained a dour, uninviting armor that she allowed very few people to penetrate. "I'm doing alright, I suppose. I just started writing again."

"Oh sweet! Are you going to start *Grrrl Reaction* again?"

"I haven't ruled it out, but I think I might either start something new or pitch ideas to publications I read."

"Awesome, I think that's great. I mean it would be super cool if you started writing for, like, real publications instead of just doing a crummy zine. No one even reads zines anymore."

"I still do, but you're right. Most people don't."

"I haven't even heard anything about riot grrrls in years. I think everyone outgrew it."

"Really? You're not a feminist anymore? That's like saying Ian Mackaye isn't a punk rocker anymore."

"Eileen, that was, like, over a decade ago. Things change. I'm a mother now."

Eileen would have dropped the phone if she hadn't been gearing herself up for the admission. Back when they dated, Karen wrote long screeds about the irresponsibility of breeding and how any self-proclaimed feminist should get her tubes tied out of respect for the overpopulated planet and the beings that were already here.

But that's the troubling aspect of friends from the distant past—they remain the same in memories even though they took a different path on their way to the present.

"So are you married?" Eileen asked.

"Yes, to a wonderful man, my knight in shining armor. His name is Hank."

"And you have kids?"

"Two girls, Joan and little Tina. They're angels."

"Congratulations," Eileen said flatly. She knew she should be happy for her former lover, but she also realized that attempting genuine felicitations would be disingenuous enough to make her feel like phony of the year.

Karen's cheeriness and new cutesy swear words (like "friggen" and "heck") made Eileen pity her. Karen was a person she cared deeply about that helped shape her personality and outlook on the world. Sure they were both young, bisexual, and angry when they dated, and as Eileen aged, she realized their politics were at times naïve, unrealistic, and overly radical. But she retained a positive outlook on feminism and progressivism, and she wanted to make the better elements of these ideals a part of her life again. Had Karen known that, she would have pitied Eileen, and there was already enough pity in this conversation.

"So what about you?" Karen said. "How are things in your world?"

"Good, I suppose."

"You suppose? Well are you married? Do you have kids?"

"I… no."

"No? What are you still 'fighting the power?'" Karen asked, sounding slightly contemptuous. Eileen couldn't hear the air quotes over the phone, but the tone implied it all. "Come on Leeny, don't tell me you're still listening to Bikini Kill and blaming men for your problems."

Eileen couldn't imagine not being harshly judged and scorned for whatever came out of her mouth at that moment. She toyed with the idea of inventing a life teeming with status symbols, a nuclear family, and endless, non-punk amusement, but it would have been an exercise in futility made out of spite. And she had long since learned that actions made solely out of spite only felt good in the moment and eventually led to shame and remorse. So she simply hung up and turned off her phone. Not one of her more mature moments, she knew, but a necessary one nonetheless. When someone treated her with disrespect, she had a right to disengage from the situation.

Although the phone call wasn't a rousing success, she did get something out of it. There were three words that Karen said: "Everyone outgrew it." She said it as though the process of maturing was the natural result of aging. The sentiment intrigued Eileen. Maybe she didn't owe the past a damn thing. What if she had outgrown her angsty high school zine and wasn't beholden to it or anything like it anymore? When Uncle Ernest told her she needed to start writing again, he didn't specifically mean she should reestablish the zine. He probably meant if she were doing what made her happy, she'd be writing.

She attempted to call Mason from the landline because she wanted to bond with him over how he felt after his encounter with new Mark and Sheila. She could empathize!

Fucking Mason didn't answer of course.

· · · ·

He didn't answer his phone because the batteries had died and he was also engaged in a verbal tussle with Sophia. She remained equal parts angry and confused in the aftermath of the last scene.

"Brett… I mean Mason, the character of Brett was supposed to die back there. It says so on my one-sheet." Sophia held the sheet up for him to see, but he was the one driving back to Denver and couldn't take his eyes off the road. "The author had decided to kill you early."

"That wasn't on my one-sheet."

"That's because the author wanted to use the element of surprise to make it more authentic, or whatever."

"Well maybe he changed his mind and decided to let me live."

"It doesn't usually work like that. In all my years of doing this, I've never seen a recently revised one-sheet not followed to a 'T.'"

"But I'm sure things like that happen, right?" he said.

"I suppose. But that guy with the motorcycle you were talking about, he wasn't anywhere on my one-sheet."

"He wasn't on mine either. I've been thinking about that. I totally thought he was a character. I guess he isn't."

"No, he isn't."

"And what about the miner, Franklin Builder. Is he a character?"

"He's a local legend. There's a bit of historical fiction mixed in, so he is a character and whatever else, a zombie or something like that. That's the thing with works of fiction—it's the only time otherworldly beings like Franklin Builder get to live again."

"That's what Don, the guy with the motorcycle said. He was an otherworldly being too."

"So he snuck into the story."

"I guess that's what happened, I don't know."

"I wonder if the author is going to use it for the book."

"He's been given a gift, in my opinion. He'd be crazy not to use it."

She shrugged. She supposed maybe the author had been given a gift. Either way, it was out of her hands, so she decided not to dwell on it.

Chapter 21

As their car sped down the highway, the hum of the tires rolling over the pavement hypnotized Sophia. In her zen-like state, she didn't have much to say, which meant she felt comfortable enough in front of Mason not to fill silent moments with conversation in order to quell any awkwardness.

Meanwhile, he couldn't help but dwell on the bizarre world of character placement. No one had uttered a solitary word about coming into contact with the post-dead when he embarked upon this endeavor. If the Craigslist ad had specifically mentioned rubbing elbows with spirits, Mason thought, it would have received a lot more attention. Maybe they purposefully didn't mention it so they could avoid attracting hordes of weirdoes. Of course, he did encounter myriad strange and earthy-looking folks at Lachesis the morning he began this project. The unusual and free spirited always seemed to cultivate a connection— however tenuous or imaginary—to the supernatural.

He also marveled at how the events in the story unfolded in stark contrast to the one-sheet—and how apparently infrequently this occurred, according to Sophia. But it still happened, which led him to wonder just how much control the author had over the story. Sure, he could conceive a rough outline, but once all the characters were in place, anything could transpire.

And that's when it struck him. He slowed the car and pulled over to the shoulder of the highway.

"What's wrong?" said Sophia, who had been shocked out of her stupor by his erratic driving.

"Nothing," he said. "I just thought of something. You know how *Wrong Turn in Susurrant* has taken a wrong turn with the plot? How what we're doing is nowhere near what we're supposed to be doing?" Sophia nodded. "Well what if we hijack the plot completely? Take our fate into our own hands and have fun with the thing?"

Under normal circumstances Sophia would have been terrified of the idea and irate at Mason for even considering such a blatant lack of professionalism. But she felt a certain sense of freedom that had eluded her for years.

Since she had just returned from Lawrence where she broke up with her boyfriend Pete, she felt as though an incredible weight had been lifted from her shoulders. Before the separation, she was beholden to the aspirations her and Pete had created as a couple when the relationship was new and exciting. During their respective senior years in college, the couple met and rapidly fell in love. In the first year alone, they made plans to travel the world and elope in Copenhagen. But those plans never really panned out, and the only traveling they ever accomplished was a trip to his grandparents' two bedroom condo in Biloxi, Mississippi in the middle of July.

Eventually Sophia grew bored of Lawrence and repeatedly tried to get Pete to relocate to Denver with her—a move he never wanted to make due to his current proximity to his mother, who lived a few blocks from their apartment. After several heated negotiations—and repeated threats to end the relationship outright—Sophia finally convinced him to let her move to Denver alone, with the stipulation they keep the relationship open and communicate daily. This arrangement endured seven months of longing, anger, boredom, jealousy, and one passionate, sex-filled reunion the first time she returned to her hometown two months after she originally left.

Now that she'd severed the ties that bound her, she was beginning to enjoy the relief and liberation of a guilt-free existence. There was no shared past to stifle her present and now the future belonged to her. So caution was only good if it could be thrown to the wind, and she agreed with Mason about exploring the possibility of hijacking plots.

"Who's stopping us?" she asked with an alluring smile.

. . . .

Once he dropped Sophia off, and before he was scheduled to return to Susurrant, Mason stopped by his house to shower and change. Eileen was waiting for him with bated breath. She was sprawled across the couch in the living room when he walked in.

"Where the hell have you been?" she characteristically wondered.

"I was working," he said.

"I've been trying to get a hold of you."

"Last night I was out of the coverage zone or whatever. And my phone ran out of juice this morning. I used it as a sound system for an all-night dance party."

"You what?"

"It's a long story. Why were you trying to get a hold of me?"

"I talked to Karen."

"Karen Karen? What was her last name, Crowley?"

"Actually it's Karen Crowley-Gasovic these days."

"Really? She's married?" he said.

"Yes, to a man."

"To a man? Since when do radical queer feminists marry men?"

"Well to be fair, we're both bi and we both went on to date men. And we also became much less radical as we got older. Still, she's definitely not even close to the same Karen you knew from the '90s. She has kids and doesn't say swear words and, hell, she might even be republican for all I know."

"She sounds like new Mark."

"Yes, that's why I was trying to call you!" she said. "I wanted a shoulder to, well not to cry on, but, I guess a shoulder to talk shit on."

"You can always talk shit on my shoulder, Eileen."

"Thank you," she said. "So at one point in the conversation, Karen asked me if I still listened to Bikini Kill and blamed men for my problems, and I totally just hung up on her."

Mason nodded approvingly. "Good for you. Stickin' it to the… woman."

She laughed. At that moment she thought of a not so distant past when several months went by without someone like her brother to offer vehement support whenever she needed it. *How the hell did I do that?* she wondered. Or more importantly, *Why the hell did I do that?* She mused at how easy it was to neglect the things that mattered most, even when they were a mere text away.

"She was trying to stick it to me!" she said. "You know, it's like we've all made these choices and we're all living these lives and we're all so full of doubt about it. And I think that one symptom of this doubt is being really protective of the choices we've made. And anyone who lives different from us is threatening those choices, you know?"

"Yeah, I can see that. But do you think the reason a hard-core Christian like grandma won't talk to us is because she's full of doubt? Because there's no way that's the case. In her mind there is a god, and he hates you and me. So it's not just about doubt; it's about conformity too."

"It's about everything. Everyone thinks they're better than everyone else. Karen and grandma and new Mark—they all look down on us. But, you know, we look down on them."

"Yeah, we suck, too," he said. "But we do try to be better people. I mean, we accept others for who they are and they hate others for who they are, you know? Let me put it this way: Gay people don't choose to be gay. But homophobes choose to hate. We just hate the haters, and I feel like that's better, if that makes any sense."

"Of course it makes sense. But that's the thing; we're just as judgmental as anyone else."

"It's just our criteria are different," he said.

"Exactly," she said. "I suppose that's it—part of being human is being an asshole, like it just comes with the territory." She sat up from the couch and walked into the kitchen.

"Yeah, what are you gonna do?" he asked.

"Oh, I don't know... You want anything to eat?"

"Sure, I could eat, but I have to take a shower first."

"You got somewhere to be or something?"

"I'm still working for Lachesis. Sophia and I are headed back up to the mountains to finish the story we're working on."

"Can I ask you something?" she said. Mason nodded. "Why are you working there still? Shouldn't you be playing your guitar and trying to get a band going? That's what Uncle Ernest said you should do."

"I like Sophia," he said. "I'm doing it because, I don't know...
I get to hang out with her, I guess."

"Mason! Are you falling in love? I thought you were all
about the no strings attached relationships."

"There are strings attached to NSA relationships way
more often than you'd think. Besides, Sophia wants to be
monogamish, so I could still have my flings."

"Really? You think you're swinging enough to handle
that?"

"Oh, I don't know. We'll see, I guess. Right now, I'm just
enjoying her company—and the sex. I'm enjoying that too."

"I bet."

Mason excused himself to get prepared for the day ahead.
They had to be in Susurrant in the early afternoon and it was
already mid-morning. After he showered and shaved, he sat
down with Eileen on the couch to a bowlful of green chile
with black beans and quinoa.

"So tell me," Eileen said, "what's going to happen next in
the story?"

Mason stared into his bowl for awhile and then slowly
looked towards Eileen. "You know, I have no idea."

Chapter 22

Mason was still driving the bright yellow clunker from the early '80s that they borrowed from the Horror Camp Car Lot when he arrived at Sophia's house. He tried sounding the horn, but the only noise it produced was his fist hitting the middle of the steering wheel. So he double parked and ran up to the front door where he attempted to ring a doorbell that was also broken. He let himself in and walked into Sophia's room only to find her sleeping next to another woman.

"Sophia," he said, piercing the silence of the room.

"Mason," she said. "Oh shit, what time is it?"

"11:30. We really need to go."

"Damn it," she muttered, rubbing her eyes and surveying the room for signs of her clothing. When she sat up, she let the blankets fall to her waist, displaying her nudity without the slightest hint of shame. "Give me like five minutes."

Mason stormed back to the car, and by the time Sophia made it out—a full ten minutes later—he was incensed. "Who was that?" he demanded to know.

"It's this girl Coral. We dated briefly in college," she said.

"We've only been separated for a couple hours. When did you find the time to pick her up?"

"She spent the night with my roommate last night. I didn't

even know she was there. When I got up to pee, she was in the shower and she asked me to get in with her. So I did. And we gave each other mind blowing orgasms. That's why we both went back to sleep."

"Hmm."

"Oh, don't get jealous."

"I'm not jel..." He trailed off.

"Come on, Mason," she said. "Look, if we keep this relationship—or whatever you want to call it. If we keep it going, you'd be my primary lover and you'd get to have other sexual experiences on the side too. So please, try not to get jealous when I take another lover."

Mason thought about it for awhile. Then he sighed. "Fine, I'll do my best to try."

"Thank you. The more you think about it, the more you'll start to like the idea, I promise."

Mason agreed to think about it. And he remained a little too deep in thought when he almost ran a red light and came within inches of smashing into another car. Sophia screamed and he let out a string of expletives as he slammed the brakes just in time to watch the other automobile careen past in front of them. He quickly threw the gear in reverse and gave himself a comfortable buffer zone as she repeatedly questioned and belittled his driving abilities.

When the light turned green, he accelerated as though nothing out of the ordinary had happened. Once they both calmed down, Mason marveled at the sheer amount of times he narrowly avoided catastrophe and how nonchalant everyone acted afterwards. Had his car collided with the other, he would have spent his entire afternoon dealing with the aftermath, but since that didn't happen, he got to act like he didn't almost endanger his and Sophia's safety. He also wondered who would have been responsible for the wreckage, considering his lack of automotive insurance. But since he wasn't made to accept any responsibility for his shoddy driving skills, he took advantage of the fact he didn't have to worry about that either.

After they parked their car at the lot in Susurrant and procured a ride to the scene in the woods, very little had changed. The camp was just as they left it, so they took their places inside the tent. The one-sheet had been rewritten to accommodate Brett's non-dead status and his change of moniker. It also reflected Don's appearance and the aftermath of that episode. Kelly's name remained the same, but even that was about to change. In fact, everything was about to change.

Mason and Kelly spent the first part of the afternoon devising a plan. They had enough food to last another couple days, no car, and no clue when or if Franklin Builder would return. In order to maximize the daylight, they determined to begin a trek back to downtown Susurrant at daybreak tomorrow. Since Mason had stayed up all night tripping with Don, he was in no shape to begin at the moment. So they figured they would wait another night before seeking help.

As they lay in the tent—Mason sleeping and Kelly reading a book—she caught the sound of someone walking and whistling from the road.

"Mason," she said, shaking him. "Mason, wake up! There's someone walking down the road."

"But I'm just so tired," he groaned.

"Get up," she said. "Get out there and talk to him."

Mason groaned again, and whined, and whimpered, and threw a little fit in his sleeping bag. Kelly wasn't impressed with his efforts, so he reluctantly rolled out of bed, put on his shoes, and unzipped the tent. The whistling man was built like a bricklaying teamster, a very no-nonsense looking kind of guy who could mop the floor with Mason if he crossed him. He had stopped by the side of the road to urinate; otherwise Mason would have had to chase after him.

"Excuse me," said Mason as he approached him. "Excuse me, sir!"

The man did the post-pee shake, zipped up, and turned around. "Yeah?"

"Hey, my girlfriend and I broke down a few days ago on our way to the campgrounds up the road. Now we're just looking for someone with a car to get us back to Susurrant. Is there any way you can help us?"

"Well, I ain't got a car," he said. Mason looked crestfallen. "But I do have a truck."

"Oh," said Mason. He squinted at the character, unimpressed with his attempt at humor.

The man cleared his throat.

"Say, you don't happen to have a cute, naïve 19 year old daughter who would be charmed by a couple of fast talkin' city folk, do you?" Mason asked.

"Pardon?"

"If you did, maybe we could come over and spend the night at your house. Then when you slip off to bed we could drink your Old Crow and have some steamy sexy time. I know it's cliché and everything. But it'd be a lot of fun, nonetheless."

"What in the hell...?"

"I suppose it wouldn't be that much fun for you, since it is your daughter. And for all you know, she's never been deflowered."

"I ain't got a daughter."

"Okay, how about a 19 year old son? I mean it's not necessarily my thing, but my girlfriend might like it, and maybe I could watch. Of course, I'm not sure I'm into that either, but I did say I'd try..."

"Hey," said the man in hushed tones. "What the hell are you doing? Stick to the one-sheet."

"One-sheet, two sheet, black sheet, blue sheet." He chuckled. "Remember Dr. Seuss?"

His eyes narrowed. "I'm supposed to be playing an un-educated mountain man bearing an ominous warning. And you're supposed to be scared shitless flatlanders from Denver who are about to get killed. Get it right, asshole, or your union rep's going to tear you a new one."

"I'm not union and neither is my girlfriend, whose name is Sophia! Hear that author?" Mason yelled. "I'm not calling her Kelly anymore."

The man grabbed him by the shirt, and with clenched teeth he said, "Character placement 101, motherfucker. Never talk to the author."

Mason held his hands up. "Okay, okay," he said.

"See, this is what happens when they hire non-union characters—low wages and unprofessionalism. Now get back into character. Take some pride in your work."

"So you have a truck?" he said.

"Yeah, but I can't give you a ride."

"Oh no?"

"It's on the fritz."

"So what are you doing here?" asked Mason. Since the question didn't jibe with the structure of how the conversation was supposed to unfold, the man grinded his teeth and clenched his fist. Mason interpreted that as an invitation to adhere to the one-sheet as closely as possible. "I mean, we have enough supplies to make it another day at least. We figured we'd set out for Susurrant at day break."

"Just be careful out there. It's a full moon tonight and

that's when Old Man Builder has been known to prowl."

"Known to prowl? Is that a Hall & Oates album?"

"That's it," said the man. "I can't work under these conditions." He threw down his cowboy hat and walked away.

Mason picked up the hat and put it on. He walked back to the tent and popped his head inside. "Howdy partner," he said.

"Where'd you get that?"

"That guy in the road, he threw it down. What do you think?"

"It's very becoming."

"Thank you. Oh by the way, you shall now be known as Sophia for the remainder of this novel."

"How did you manage that?"

"I proclaimed it, for I am Lord Mason, king of the written word."

Sophia was so impressed by his grandstanding that she immediately tackled him and began stripping him of everything but the hat. Mason struggled to zip up the tent just in case any other characters happened to walk past. His concern was in vain, however, because as long as they had the tent a-rocking, no one came a-knocking.

After concluding their camping coitus—which is some of the best coitus around—they lay naked in the tent, their concern about the spirit of Franklin Builder subsiding to nil.

"Thank you kindly, cowpoke," Sophia said.

"All in a day's work, ma'am," Mason replied as he tipped his hat. Then he laughed.

"What's so funny?"

"Cowpoke is a funny name. It conjures up an image of a lonely rancher who knows no one's looking."

"Oh, Mason, that's some pretty low hanging fruit."

"I know. That's why I was drawn to it," he said. He tried to be ashamed of his own sense of humor, but he just couldn't make it happen.

She shook her head, which he understood to mean he couldn't make any seventh grade-friendly jokes in her presence. Accepting of his place, he removed the hat and made himself comfortable. He was so very tired.

Chapter 23

When Mason began nodding off to sleep, Sophia broke the long silence when she said, "So what are we going to do now?"

"Sleep," he said.

"Not like right at this moment," she said. "But we need to figure out some kind of plan."

"Yeah, you're right," he admitted as he contemplated the situation. "You know, there's this thing we used to do in our touring days called the Tortured Metaphor Action Plan. We would put it to use every time something shitty happened. So say we ran out of gas. None of us had Triple-A, so we would all sit cross-legged on the loft in the back of the van, close our eyes, and think nothing but positive thoughts. We would envision someone giving us a ride to the gas station. And every time, it took like 20 minutes tops for another motorist to show up with a gas can."

She laughed in derision. "You're telling me a van full of atheist punk rockers made a prayer circle whenever times got tough?"

"Yes! But that's the thing—it worked!" Mason described several accounts of the Action Plan's success—like the time in St. Louis when they didn't have enough money to eat. Literally while they were Action Planning in the back, someone put a flyer under the windshield wiper publicizing a Food Not Bombs event that afternoon. Then there was the situation in Durango where they couldn't find a hotel after a show because hunting season had just begun and it was too cold to sleep in the van. So they pulled into a neighborhood for an Action Plan session when they heard a knock on the side. They opened the door to a young woman in a Dead Kennedys shirt who had attended the show earlier. She had seen them loading up after the show and on her walk home, she recognized the van and offered them a place to stay. And in Seattle when their show was cancelled, they Action Planned until a guy on a skateboard ran into the van. They all got out of the vehicle to check on his well-being and offer him a ride if he needed it, and he turned out to be a promoter on his way to work at a venue across town. It just so happened he had a band cancel at the last minute, so he offered them an opening slot for a Dillinger Four/Avail show.

"That's all very impressive," she said. "But scientifically speaking, you can't change fate by willing it to happen."

"To tell you the truth, we had nothing else going for us at the moment, so it made more sense to be positive than to sit around feeling sorry for ourselves. Besides, that was real life. This is not. So I only have one question for you: What's our Action Plan?"

"What do you mean?"

"I mean what do you want to do? We've been handed this incredible opportunity and we need to take full advantage of it."

"Do you think we could bring people back from the dead and talk to them?"

"Maybe; I talked to a 300 year old, but he never properly died. I think we could probably rouse some disembodied souls as long as we also imagine a vessel for them to take shape in. But I don't think we could get Jim Morrison to come kick it with us."

"I was thinking about my dad," she said. "He died when I was young and I would love to bring him back long enough to have a conversation with him."

"I never even met my dad."

"Oh, that's so sad."

"Is it?" asked Mason. "Anyway, no one's dad is coming here today."

Sophia dropped the subject. Apparently, the discussion of parental units required a perfect balance of tone, sensitivity, and tact, lest they veer into the minefield of painful memories. Besides, she didn't want to ruin a jovial occasion such as this by dredging up unwanted particulars of the past.

"We could meet another hot couple for a crazy camping foursome," she said.

"Okay," said Mason a bit apprehensively. He tried to cover up his reluctance by saying, "They would need to bring a bigger tent, or maybe a tarp…"

"Wait a minute," she said, interrupting him. "Franklin Builder is still around, right? I mean, he's not a character; he's an actual disgruntled spirit. He could still come back and cause problems for us, right?"

"I guess so," Mason hadn't thought about it. "So what do you recommend?"

"You know what I was thinking?" she said. "That tree in the road that slashed the tires—it was put there for a reason, right? To stop us at that place because the setting was pre-determined." Mason nodded. "And when you were driving you turned off the main thoroughfare, and then we were on this god forsaken path for only a couple miles. I bet if we walk through the woods toward the main road we could find some civilization. I know there's a restaurant/bar kind of place north of Susurrant a few miles called The Boar Pour. My uncle's a biker and always talked about going there."

"The Boar Pour, like B-O-A-R?" asked Mason. She nodded. "Sounds like a redneck bar."

"Well, yeah. My uncle lives in Franktown and owns a Harley and a couple of trucks. He's as redneck as they come."

"So are we going to walk in the bar and hear the needle scratch across the record as everyone stops and looks at us?"

"Definitely be prepared for that—though surely they have CDs by now, or at least cassette tapes," she said. "But it's not like they won't serve us. I figured we'd get a drink and just kind of hang out in a public place where the spirit of Builder won't bother us."

Even though it hadn't occurred to him to fear the spirit of Builder, Mason didn't need any real justification to hang out at a bar in the late afternoon—especially since they were officially on the clock. Needless to say, he didn't offer much in the way of protest. So they got dressed and headed out.

The two began trudging through the woods in the general direction of the road. Aside from a few colossal boulders they were forced to traverse, the hike wasn't too strenuous. Once they arrived at the main thoroughfare, Sophia made an educated guess as to the direction of the Boar Pour.

An unsuccessful attempt to hitchhike necessitated a two mile walk, and soon they found themselves in the parking lot of the bar, which was overflowing with trucks and motorcycles. Mason didn't like the sight of the place. It looked like punker ass kickin' time happened in there.

"You okay?" said Sophia, sensing Mason's reticence.

"Yeah, I'm fine," he said. "Or at least I will be once I get a drink."

Since Susurrant and its surrounding areas lay in a heavily forested area, nearly all the structures were log houses, and the bar was no exception—though it appeared as though it was a double-wide log house. Above the door hung a rusted metal sign that once upon a time displayed the name of the tavern, but now, through squinted eyes, read, "Bo Po."

Sophia escorted Mason through the dimly lit room—filled with bikers, hunters, hippies, and other mountain folk—to the wooden stools in front of the bar. They took a seat and ordered drinks, but the bartender remained taciturn and unresponsive. When it became apparent that he had no intention of filling her request, she ordered again.

"Look, I ain't lookin' for trouble, okay?" the bartender said.

"We're not looking for trouble either," said Sophia. "We're just here for booze."

Mason couldn't help but feel his appearance was off-putting to the regulars of the bar. He wondered if he should roll down his sleeves to cover his tattoos, but he promptly decided against it. If this bartender found any fault with him, that was his problem.

"It's okay, Scotty," a man from the back of the bar yelled as he stood up to meet them. "They're with me."

Mason and Sophia turned around to a disheveled man with a five o'clock shadow, tinted glasses halfway down his nose, and haphazard dressing techniques to say the least. He had slicked back dark brown hair with gray strands mixed in and wore a short sleeve navy blue button down shirt and black corduroy pants.

"Are we?" Sophia asked.

"Of course. Scotty, put their round on my tab. They're my guests for the evening."

The bartender poured their drinks, and they followed the man into a room in the back of the tavern.

"Please, sit down," he said as he took a seat. Before him stood five glasses—three with melting ice and traces of whiskey, one half-filled with whiskey, and one entirely full of whiskey. There was also an ashtray full of cigarette butts and a laptop with an open document on its screen.

"Thanks for the drinks," said Sophia. "But I have to ask, who the hell are you?"

He smirked as he pulled a cigarette from behind his ear and tamped it on the table. "I'll give you a hint." He lit the cigarette. "I'm breaking a lot of rules right now."

"You mean by smoking?" Mason said. "Colorado clean in-door air act, or whatever it's called. It's why you can't smoke pot inside."

"I don't think that's what he means, Mason."

"You're breaking a lot of rules, too," the man said as he exhaled smoke above their heads.

"You're the author, aren't you?" said Sophia.

"Very good," he said nodding. "Lewis Wilcox. It's not a nom de plume. It's the name my mother bestowed upon me shortly after I was conceived. And don't bother introducing yourselves. I'm familiar with your handles—both real and fictional."

"Then we are breaking the rules, aren't we?" said Mason. "I was told in no uncertain terms not to talk to the author... Wait a minute, how the hell do you get to smoke in here anyway?"

"First of all, you're from Lachesis and you're a part-timer with Beforehand, so neither of you is union, which makes it easier for me," explained Lewis. "The last thing I need is for some overzealous union president breathing down my agent's neck. I'm already on thin ice with major players in the publishing industry as it is. Secondly, this is the fucking Boar Pour—Bo Po to the locals. There are no rules here. A six year old could walk in here with a cigarette in his mouth and the server would light it for him."

"Yeah well, if this place is so damn accommodating, why wouldn't they serve us?" Mason asked.

"Your reputation precedes you. A few of the characters come here to drink after their roles have concluded, and they're all talking about a couple of young provocateurs taking liberties with the one-sheets."

"How did you know that?" said Sophia. "I thought they weren't supposed to talk to you."

"They're not and they don't. This is the writer's room," Lewis said, pointing to a hand-written sign on the wall that spelled it out. "That's the great thing about Susurrant. If you make it clear what your boundaries are, everyone respects them. They know not to come in here and so everyone but the server leaves me alone. But I did overhear some tasty bits of gossip about you two."

"Are they threatening to run us out of town?" asked Mason.

"Pretty much." He stubbed out a cigarette and immediately lit another.

"How about you? What do you think about what we're doing?" she said.

He took a deep drag of his cigarette and exhaled it through his nose as he stared at the ceiling in contemplation. When he grasped one of the glasses of whiskey and focused on it intently without offering so much as a sigh, Mason and Sophia began to wonder if he had a response to offer, or if he was so intoxicated he forgot the question completely. Mason looked towards Sophia and shrugged, and they both reached for their drinks. Usually when the spirits flowed, the chatter of drunken souls echoed through corridors, but on this instance, silence dominated the room.

After a few minutes, Lewis took off his glasses to reveal deep bags under bloodshot eyes. "I never wanted to write horror novels," he said. "First my agent wanted a novella about a killer in the woods, so I made it happen. I even made the main characters unlikeable with no redeeming traits as people so it would be fun to kill them off. Then she decided that it would have more commercial appeal as a novel, so I had to expand it and gut huge portions of the conclusion. To say the least, I was disheartened at the sheer scope of the endeavor. But then in the middle of the story, you two shatter all the rules that characters are supposed to regard as gospel. I've never heard anything like it. It made me happy to be a writer again."

"What do you mean you had never heard anything like it?" said Mason.

"That's the other thing about this place—there are no secrets. A guy like me can sit back in a room like this where you can hear everything and soon enough, people start talking. And I listen and I write. Being an author requires two different skills: Writing, obviously, and the art of observation. If you're adept at both, you can tell a story. But you see, that's the thing. You can commission the best characters in the business, but it won't translate to the page if you don't record the story as it comes to you. You can't project your own demons and your own conclusions onto the characters. You have to let them choose their own path. There are no authors, just recorders of events."

"So you just sit here and listen to others retell what's happening out there?" Mason said.

"Pretty much. Some authors follow their characters around, acting as though they were extras in the story.

Sometimes I do that. I have a tent set up about a quarter mile from yours and I have rustled around in the bushes on a few occasions. But for the most part, I sit here and listen to the locals and the other characters."

"Now I know we're characters because that's what we were hired to do. But what about Franklin Builder and Don?" he asked. "Are they characters too?"

"No, I conducted a little research for the story by frequenting this bar a month before we even talked about procuring the characters. Franklin is a spirit of local lore that people around here can't get enough of. Don is infamous in writer's circles, and I knew I could summon him with a literary séance of sorts."

"So you did summon Don," said Mason. "We thought he invited himself to the story."

"No," said Lewis. "The trouble was, I thought the ending to the novella was solid, and I didn't know how to undo it. That's when I sought the help of Don, the notorious literary spirit."

"Can you control them?" Sophia wondered. "I mean, do they follow the one-sheet?"

"Not really, but that's the thing. When we pitched the arc of the story and the characters to the publisher, they were intrigued with the idea of uncontrollable elements. Any time you mix historical fact with otherworldly spirits, you have a recipe for attracting Hollywood interest. That's why I was so despondent about writing it. Once you reduce the creative process to the amount of money it might generate, it loses all appeal—for me anyway."

The server appeared from out of nowhere to remove the empty glasses and take another order. Sophia and Mason requested another round and Lewis asked for two whiskey and waters for himself.

"Why don't you just tell them to eat shit and write a sci-fi novel or something?" asked Mason.

"Eh, science fiction is the hardest to stage. Most often you have to rent out a theater and create myriad props. Plus you have to do all kinds of research so that your story is scientifically plausable. It's a lot of work, and I don't even enjoy reading sci-fi novels. I find them tedious."

"If you could write anything," Sophia said, "what would it be?"

"To tell you the truth, *Wrong Turn in Susurrant* is turning into one of my favorite stories."

Just then Lewis' cell phone rang and he excused himself to answer it. During the conversation, he spoke in hushed tones and made several fleeting glances at Mason and Sophia. When he ended the call and set his phone on the table, he took a deep breath.

"Have you ever heard of George Levin?" asked Lewis.

Mason was taken aback. "You mean the union representative?"

"Yes. Apparently he's had several of his union character workers 'mention' you—whatever the hell that means. He said he'd like to have a chat with you both."

"Well there's no chance in hell of that ever happening," Mason said.

"You might want to tell him that when he walks through the front door. He's on his way here now."

"Shit," Mason said. "I don't want to talk to that guy. Let's take off."

"How?" Sophia said. "Our car's in Susurrant. What, are we going to walk?"

"Relax," said Lewis. "I wouldn't worry about it. Besides, if you want to leave, we can all take my motorcycle and find a nice place to smoke some pot."

"They let you smoke cigarettes in the bar, but not pot? That seems odd," said Mason.

"Yeah, people up here are strange," Lewis said with a shrug. Then he motioned for the server and quickly settled his bill. Before they could leave through the front door, however, there was a terrible clamor in the other room. Mason leaned over so he could see what was happening and his face went white as a ghost.

"What?" Sophia said.

"Franklin Builder just walked in the bar," Mason said.

Chapter 24

At the very moment Mason should have been panicking, he sat stone-faced and motionless at the table, glaring into his drink. Bedlam had consumed the main room of the Boar Pour, as the clamorous spirit of Franklin Builder overturned tables and chairs, belligerently demanding the location of the "flatlanders from Sam Hill." Yet Mason seemed unfazed until Sophia screamed in his ear.

"What the hell are you doing?" she yelled. "Let's get out of here!" When Mason didn't bat an eyelash, she once again attempted to lovingly convince him to spring into action. "Mason you dumb fucker! Let's go!"

"Hold on, now," he said. "We don't need to go anywhere. This is his story." He pointed at Lewis. "He can write us out of this mess."

"Yeah, I can... I mean, probably," Lewis said, attempting to stand and falling over backward, kicking the table and bringing the chair down with him.

"Oh my god, are you okay?" Sophia asked.

"Ow," he said.

"I don't think he's in any condition to write right now," Sophia said.

Mr. Builder heard the commotion and quickly made his way to the back room. "Ah ha!" he said. "Them's here are the scamps I've been lookin' for."

Mason grabbed one of the glasses of whiskey that Lewis didn't spill and threw it in Franklin's face. The shattered glass and alcohol forced him to his knees as he let out a slew of rural working class swear words from the 19th century, which made Mason and Sophia laugh in spite of the situation. The remarks had lost much of their edge of the intervening decades.

Mason and Sophia helped Lewis off the ground as Mason closed his laptop and tucked it under his shoulder. Then they stumbled out of the bar and into the parking lot.

"Over here," Lewis motioned to a motorcycle complete with a sidecar. "This is me." He dug around his pockets for his keys, which he dropped in the dirt and gravel. His clumsy attempts to retrieve them would have been comical if he wasn't about to drive.

"He can't drive," Sophia said. "Mason, you drive."

"No way in hell," he said. "I don't know how to drive a motorcycle."

"It's cool," said Lewis. "Get in."

Lewis revved the engine as Mason and Sophia debated who would ride in the sidecar—he lost and she took a seat on the bike. When they made it onto the main road back to town, no one looked back. Lewis managed to get them all the way to beautiful downtown Susurrant, where he pulled into the gas station to assess the situation.

"What do you think we should do?" asked Lewis.

Before anyone had the chance to answer, Mason recognized a familiar voice from his vantage point in the confines of the sidecar. After awkwardly contorting his back and neck to catch a glimpse behind him, he confirmed the identity of the voice's owner. "Hey," he said in hushed tones. "Lewis, Sophia, come here." They leaned over him. "That's George

Levin over there." He pointed behind him to a gray-haired man in his 50s talking to two very large Teamster-looking folks.

"Hmm," said Lewis. "I've never met the guy, so I'll pump the gas. If you don't want to talk to him, just keep looking the opposite direction."

"Where are we going, anyway?" Sophia asked.

"We can go to my house," Mason said. "It's at Broadway and I-25 in Denver, if you know where that is."

Lewis nodded. As he pumped the gas, he played it cool and didn't give as much as a sideways glance toward the group at the other end of the parking lot. But when he put the nozzle back on the pump, he acquiesced to his curiosity and stole a look in spite of himself—and then he did a double-take. Franklin Builder was emerging from the woods and walking straight for George and his companions.

"Where the hell did he come from?" Lewis said.

"Who?" said Mason and Sophia together.

Before he could answer, Lewis leapt onto the bike and started the engine with a mighty roar. Almost everyone at the gas station stopped to look at them, including the very people they sought to avoid. As they sped away, Sophia watched George and his friends get into the cab of a truck as Franklin bounded into the vehicle's bed.

"They're coming after us!" she yelled.

Sure enough, about a mile outside of town, the truck caught up with them, ominously creeping closer and closer until its front bumper was inches from the tail lights of the bike. Lewis kept a watchful eye in his side view mirror as he navigated his vehicle under the influence of nearly a pint of whiskey. He hoped no one else noticed how close they were to peril, but he caught a glimpse of Mason contorting his body to improve his vantage point. Sophia saw him too and when she looked back, her independent motion had a detrimental effect on Lewis' driving and he nearly lost control of the handlebars.

Just as it seemed they were about to collide, the truck changed lanes and began to precariously pass the motorcycle on the tiny two-lane highway. One of the teamster guys started yelling, but no one could make out what he was saying. As the bed of the truck became parallel with Lewis, Franklin cackled and dove at him, but his dismount was flawed and he slipped. Consequently, he failed to lay a single finger on any part of the motorcycle as he landed with a thud behind them on the pavement. A minivan approaching them from the rear must not have seen Franklin on the road, since they ran over his body without slowing, decapitating him instantly. In all likelihood, the driver of the truck was concentrating more on watching the events unfold than on driving because he didn't even attempt to swerve out of the way of a white SUV that they met head on in a brutal wreck.

Lewis pulled to the side of the road just to make sure no one had died, but there were already another couple cars that had stopped and at least a few cell phone users around the wreckage talking to 911 dispatchers. Sophia and Mason were too dumbfounded to talk, and Lewis shook his head and said, "Some shit you just can't write."

They would have congregated longer had it not been for Sophia bringing to everyone's attention Franklin Builder, who was running towards them, holding his decapitated head by his side as if it was a pumpkin.

· · · ·

Night had fallen by the time Lewis pulled into the

parking space behind Mason's apartment. Eileen greeted them from the top of the stairs by audibly wondering where the hell Mason had been. After a brief introduction, they swiftly piled into the apartment and locked the deadbolt behind them.

"What's happening?" asked Eileen.

"We're being chased," said Mason. "Or at least, we were being chased. We lost them about an hour ago, but we don't need to take any chances."

"Was it an old guy and two big guys?"

Everyone looked over at Eileen. "Yes," Mason said. "How did you know that?"

"They came by the house right after you left this morning. I tried to get a hold of you, but you don't answer your phone."

"How do they know where you live?" asked Lewis.

"I had a meeting with him awhile back, and I gave him my contact info. What did he say when he was here?"

"He gave me his card and told me to have you contact him. He said it was of 'utmost urgency.'"

For the first time since the events unfolded, Mason had the mental acuity necessary to assess the whole situation. Other than the obvious explanation involving the complete lack of professionalism Mason possessed for the craft of character placement, he couldn't postulate a coherent reason why George Levin was looking for him with two hired strongmen, nor did he know what they intended to do once they met.

"What did George say to you when you talked to him on the phone?" Mason asked Lewis.

"He said he had spoken with both of your character placement firms—though I use the term 'firm' loosely in your case Mason. But basically he said he wanted to have a chat with you. He didn't sound mad or anything. I was a little surprised by your reaction at the bar when I told you he was looking for you."

"But why would he team up with Franklin Builder?" Sophia said.

"Now that I can't answer," Lewis said.

"Well who knows if Franklin knows where we live?" Mason said. "And who knows if he'll even come after us. The only reason he's even around is because of *Wrong Turn in Susurrant*, which makes—I don't know… It confuses the hell out of me. I mean, is the story still happening? Are we in the story right now?"

"That's for me to decide. It's my story," said Lewis.

"So you are writing yourself into your own book?" Sophia said.

"Why not? I've always had too much respect for the fourth wall as a writer—until now anyway."

"Hell yeah," said Eileen, holding up her fist. "Burn that wall to the ground."

Lewis looked at Eileen with a newfound respect—almost as if he noticed her for the first time, which was the intention of her comment. "Hell yeah," he agreed.

"So what's going to happen next?" said Sophia.

"Oh, I don't know. I can conjure up spirits like Builder, but I can't control them."

"So you didn't know what Franklin was going to do to us?" asked Mason. "What if he hurt us? Like actually caused us physical harm?"

"You would have been fine. Everyone in this business has insurance."

"That's not the point," Mason said. "It's fucked up that you put people in situations where they can be harmed."

"I'm a writer. That's what we do. We put our characters

in states of peril and do terrible things to them for entertainment."

"Is that why characters unionize?" Mason asked.

"More or less," Lewis confessed. "That's why we tend to go non-union when we write slasher books with supernatural beings."

"That's kind of a dick thing to do, isn't it?" said Mason.

"Relax, it's my job. Even if Don didn't appear and save you in the night, you all would have been fine. No one's ever been seriously hurt. Besides Builder came after me when we were on the motorcycle, and nothing happened, did it?"

"I guess not."

"And honestly, guys, you took the hazard pay, so what did you think would happen?"

A perplexing look fell over Mason's face. "Hazard pay?" he said. "What the fuck is hazard pay?"

"You're not getting any shift differential?" asked Lewis.

"Mason works for Lachesis," said Sophia. "He's working for weed."

"No, I'm not. I only get a 10% discount. Well that, and $450."

"$450 for the whole week?" Lewis said. "Do you even respect your own time?"

"Sure I do... Wait a minute Sophia. Are you getting hazard pay?"

"Uh," she blushed.

"God damn it," Mason said. "So I guess I'm a sucker... But you know what? I'm not even doing it for the money. I don't even need the money, so there."

"Thank god for that," said Lewis.

"Why are you doing it then?" Sophia said.

"For the adventure," said Mason. "And for you."

"Aww," Eileen said.

Sophia would have melted and collected in puddles on the floor if she was that kind of girl. Instead she smiled and immediately thought of sex, which was a nice change of pace from thinking about how she could avoid becoming a character victim to the scary ghost who held his own head in his arm as though it was a pumpkin.

"Alright you two," said Lewis. "What are we going to do now?"

"What are we gonna do now," sang Mason. A look of exasperation and annoyance came over everyone but Mason's face. "What? It's a Clash song. 'The Clampdown.' On *London Calling*? What are you all, uncultured swine?"

"You're such a punk rocker," Lewis said. "Does anyone else want to answer my question?"

"Just stay here tonight," Eileen said. "Lewis, I'll make you a bed on the couch."

"Yes," said Mason. "And Sophia, I'll make you a bed in my bed."

"That's fine and all," said Sophia, "but it is only nine o'clock. And that's drinking time where I'm from."

Everyone seconded her notion and soon the quartet was drinking and arguing about which record to put on the turntable. Mason wanted to hear Future of the Left, Eileen: 7 Year Bitch, Sophia: Modest Mouse, but only the early material, and Lewis: They Might Be Giants—a request Mason flat out denied.

"So why do you have the record if you have no intention of listening to it?" asked Lewis.

"Because," said Mason.

"Because you like it," said Lewis. "You wouldn't go through the motions of procuring a record if you had zero intent of putting it on your turntable."

"We're not listening to They Might Be Giants."

"Fine, we won't listen to the record you purchased, brought home, and filed in your record collection with all the other records you like."

"I know you're trying to make a point sarcastically, but I still think we shouldn't listen to it."

Defeated, Lewis didn't pick another record as Sophia and Eileen argued to hear their choices first. When Mason pulled the old, "It's my fucking record player," he whined himself into first rotation and the others acquiesced.

Of course, the music didn't make much of an impact on the evening as the four of them drank and laughed into the early hours of the morning—the output of the record grooves relegated to background noise.

By the time everyone was ready to stumble off to sleep, Eileen's sheer exhaustion precluded her from making Lewis a proper bed, so she invited him to room with her. And even though the occupants of the apartment went to bed in pairs, no one engaged in sexual congress, for the alcohol coursing through their veins completely overwhelmed the 30 year old-plus penises in attendance. Sure there was a bit of making out, maybe even some groping. But when it came down to sweet, hot coitus, the booze did not cooperate.

The last thing Mason said to a sexually frustrated Sophia before he passed out was a slurred comment recognizing the irony of an inebriated state that brought unlikely sexual partners together and only allowed some of them to physically perform.

"Do you think that alcohol has prevented as many pregnancies as it's caused?" he asked.

Before Sophia could answer, he was asleep.

Chapter 25

At dawn, all was quiet in the apartment when Mason groggily staggered to the kitchen to get his parched throat some water. He spilled nearly half the glass by the time he sat down on the couch to drink it. He probably would have fallen asleep after he put the empty cup on the coffee table, but he was jolted awake when he heard scampering on the roof. Normally the high jinks of neighborhood squirrels wouldn't have bothered him, but his mind was on edge from recent events. After fifteen or so minutes of Mason intently listening to the small mammals run back and forth above him, checking the front door for intruders, and pulling back a few curtains from the windows, he felt satisfied he was under no direct threat.

When he turned to walk back to the couch, he saw Eileen standing next to the stereo and nearly fell backward.

"Jesus!" he yelled.

"Relax, it's just me," she said.

"What are you doing up?"

"I heard the squirrels on the roof and then I heard someone milling around."

"How's Lewis doing?" Mason asked before taking a seat on the couch.

"He's still breathing," she said, sitting down next to him.

"Before he passed out cold, he told me he'd been drinking all day."

"Yeah, that's true."

"Did he drive you home all the way from the mountains?" she asked. Mason nodded. "Well that was stupid."

"We were being chased..."

"By the spirit of Franklin Builder, so I've heard. Listen, did you ever stop to think why he's chasing you? Or what would happen if he caught you?"

"He's chasing us because he's the villain in this story and this story isn't over. And I'm not sure what he would do if he caught us. I did have a wrestling match with him, and when I was on the ground, he lifted a shovel above his head like he was going to hit me with it. But I don't know what he'd do. Lewis seemed pretty convinced that characters in stories aren't in any serious danger."

"So are we in the story now?"

"Yes, but I think this conversation might go undetected."

"That's interest..."

She didn't even finish the word when a violent crash interrupted their conversation. They both leapt off the couch and assumed protective poses as they watched Franklin Builder's head slide towards them across the floor with shards of glass on all sides. He was cackling and howling. They screamed in fright at the cranium, which was close enough for Mason to reach over and slap if the thought would have crossed his mind. Then they looked at each other and screamed again—both so paralyzed with fear they couldn't think straight enough to offer any solutions to a situation with which they've had so very little experience.

Even before they caught their breaths, the clamor at the front door commanded their attention as the body of Franklin reached through the broken window and attempted to unlock the deadbolt. His head faced towards his body, as if he was watching himself. All they could see was the back of his skull, which still clung to generous clumps of hair and skin.

"I hope yer fixin' to face yer doom, ya danged sapheads!" said the mouth of Franklin.

"No... We're not," said Eileen.

"No, we're not?" said Mason. "That's your comeback? Come on, Eileen."

"Seriously? You of all people are going to say that to me right now?"

"Sorry," he said. Then he turned toward her. "What are we going to do?"

"I don't know. I don't know."

As they engaged in debate, Franklin's body managed to throw the deadbolt and charge into the apartment with a shovel in his left hand. He ran over to his head and situated it on the floor so he could see Mason and Eileen. Then the body stopped abruptly a few feet before Mason, pointed at the window behind him like Babe Ruth calling his shot, and grasped the shovel like he was holding a baseball bat. Just as he was about to take a swing, Sophia appeared out of nowhere and kicked Franklin's head out the front door and down the steps.

Eileen's jaw dropped in amazement, and after a few moments of stunned silence, Mason held up both hands and yelled, "She was on the soccer team in high school!"

"Ow, his fucking 200 year old skull hurt my foot," Sophia said.

"That was amazing," said Eileen.

Franklin's body ran after its head with the shovel in hand, which he dropped at the top of the stairs, causing his body to trip and fall neck-first in a mean trajectory.

"What the hell happened?" Sophia said.

"Franklin's body threw his head through the window," said Mason manically. "And then his body reached over and opened the front door. He was getting ready to hit me with a shovel."

While Mason offered his explanation, Eileen ran to the front door and locked it. "That bought us a few seconds," she said. "He's going to unlock it again. What are we going to do?"

"How do you even kill the undead?" Sophia asked. "His head's off. If that didn't do it, I don't know what will."

"I don't know either," said Mason, who ran into the kitchen looking for anything to fend off his attacker.

"You think we could slow him down with food?" asked Eileen.

"I don't think the undead need to eat," said Sophia.

Mason rummaged through every drawer in the kitchen. He turned around and said, "Okay, I got a knife, a fire extinguisher, a cigarette lighter, and an empty vodka bottle."

"Wait," said Eileen, "I have an idea." And then she ran out of the room.

"And then there were two," said Mason.

"What are you planning on doing with all that?" Sophia asked about his handfuls of random kitchen items.

"I'm not quite sure. I just started grabbing shit that looked destructive."

She laughed, but only for a moment. Franklin was at the broken window again, reaching for the lock. He must have learned a valuable lesson from the whole getting-kicked in-the-face-by-a-former-soccer-player-and-flying-down-the-stairs experience, and so he held his head closely by his side. It didn't take long for him to have the door opened, nor did he squander any effort on the scare tactics of cackling and howling. But before he began charging them, Mason lit a paper towel he had retrieved and jammed into the neck of the bottle.

"It's a Molotov," he said. "I've always wanted to throw one of these."

"It's not really a Molotov," said Sophia as Mason threw bottle, which hit Franklin square in the jaw, fell to the ground, and shattered, joining the other glass shards on the floor. "See?" she continued. "A Molotov has gas inside so it explodes on contact."

"Hmm," said Mason.

The bottle temporarily stunned Franklin, but he quickly regained his composure as he stomped angrily towards them.

Meanwhile in the other room, Eileen had awoken Lewis and was trying to get him to write the demise of Franklin. But due to his heroic whiskey consumption the evening prior, he lacked the necessary motor skills to sit up properly, much compose any words of coherence. So Eileen jostled, yelled, clapped her hands, stomped around the room—even gave him a wet willy. None of these techniques had any effect on his ability to sit up and write.

That was when Eileen bolted out of her room and into the living room. She was going to run blindly into the kitchen to get a glass of cold water to throw in Lewis' face, but when she realized she was facing the back of Franklin and he didn't seem to notice her, she stopped. His dramatic stomping gave her an idea. Just as he was closing in on Mason and Sophia, Eileen snuck up behind him, and when he lifted his right leg high into the air, she grabbed his foot and pulled as hard as she could. Immediately, he did a neck- and face-plant on the hardwood floor. Wasting no time, Sophia jumped on his back and emphatically attempted to wrestle away his own head from him.

In the meantime, Eileen filled up a glass of cold water and ran back to her room, splashing it with brute force into Lewis' face. He awoke with eyes wide open.

"Why?" he yelled.

"You need to take care of Franklin," demanded Eileen. "This is your story and if you don't find a way to kill him off, he's never going to leave us alone."

"Okay, fine. Hand me my laptop."

Eileen already had his laptop open and ready to go. She presented it to him after offering him a towel.

"Before I type anything, I need you to do me a favor," he said.

"What?"

"Come here. Since doing what I'm about to do is highly uncouth, I need to whisper it to you."

She leaned over and he spoke softly in her ear. Then she left the room as he typed on his computer.

When Eileen returned to the living room, Mason was sitting on Franklin's body as Sophia had his head on the coffee table. She was playing "I got your nose" and pointing to a fictional stain on an imaginary shirt and asking, "What's that?" When he looked downward, she lightly slapped his chin and said, "Gotcha! Ha ha."

Eileen went over to the turntable and put on a They Might Be Giants record at full volume. "Everyone dance as freaky as you can!" she yelled.

She expected Mason to make a face, but instead he smiled as Sophia stopped paying attention to Franklin's head and began dancing lasciviously. Eileen joined her and soon the body of Franklin started writhing violently. Mason tried to keep him pinned to the ground, but before long he was overpowered and cast aside. Sophia and Eileen didn't stop dancing as the body lunged towards the coffee table, quickly cupping Franklin's ears with his hands. To his chest, he held his head, which had a pained expression on its face. Just as the chorus of "Ana Ang" blared through the speakers Franklin turned and ran as fast as he could out the door and down the stairs.

The three of them cheered and Eileen reached over to turn down the stereo. Shortly after, Lewis came sauntering in as though nothing had happened.

"He didn't seem to like the tunes," Sophia said.

Lewis laughed. "No," he said. "I created a back story for him, which is probably not too far from the truth, I assume. He was a simple man who only enjoyed songs played with a banjo and jug. Plus he was confused and offended by the newfangled way you were dancing."

When Mason went to close the front door, shards of glass crunched under his feet. "What are we going to do about this window?"

"Don't worry," said Lewis. We have a licensed repair man on-call at the prop depot. I can page him and he'll be here later today."

"Well alright," said Mason.

"What about your neighbors?" asked Lewis. "Are they going to call the cops or anything?"

"Nah," said Mason. "My downstairs neighbors are gone and the highway drowns out almost everything we do up here."

Lewis sighed in relief. "Well, thank god for that."

Everyone settled around the coffee table, weary and anxious. They were too agitated for sleep and too hungover to feel resilient.

Eileen surveyed the expressions of exhaustion and

decided to take action. "I'm making coffee," she said. "Who wants some?" Three hands shot into the air.

Chapter 26

After a couple of days of recovery, the Jarmans resumed their respective conventional lifestyles with a few exceptions. First, Sophia went home once to shower, change, brush her teeth, and pick up her car. She and Mason were in the throes of an intense honeymoon period and they relished the amount of sexual exploration the novelty afforded. Second, Lewis had been sleeping in Eileen's bed, despite the fact that they hadn't consummated the relationship, nor did they have any burning desire to do so.

Lewis was on the verge of sending his agent the first draft of the second part of *Wrong Turn in Susurrant* after several grueling binge writing sessions. He worked in the house, typing away on his laptop in the kitchen, only taking breaks for smoking, refilling his coffee, emptying his coffee, and eating very brief meals. For the most part, he remained unnoticed once the clicking of the keys blended in with the usual ambient noises of the apartment.

On the afternoon of Uncle Ernest's big party, they finally heard from George. He appeared at their front door leaning on crutches with his foot in a cast. He was alone this time.

"Well, look who it is," said Mason when he answered the doorbell. Sophia joined in greeting their guest.

"Hello Mason, Sophia," George said.

"You don't look so tough without your muscle men by your side," Sophia said.

"Muscle men?" he said. "What are you talking about?"

"Those guys that you were chasing us with," said Mason.

"They aren't muscle men. They're just good union men. But anyway, I have matters of business to discuss with you. Can I come in?"

Mason didn't trust him, but he appeared so feeble and indisposed that he didn't fear him either. "Hold on," he said. "Just tell us what you want."

"It hurts to stand, Mason," said George.

"Sorry if I'm not taking pity on you, but you and Franklin Builder were chasing us down in a truck earlier this week."

"I can explain that. We didn't know his motives. We didn't know he meant to hurt you. Hell, we didn't even realize he jumped on the back of the truck until we were right next to you on the road. All I know is that we were both desperately trying to reach you. Besides, you all didn't get hurt. I got hurt." He held up his injured foot and started to laugh, but he quickly clutched his sides in pain.

"So you weren't trying to hurt us?" Mason asked.

"No, far from it."

"Then why did you have the huge manly men by your side?" said Sophia.

"They were… Look, can I just come inside?"

"Alright," said Mason.

George awkwardly maneuvered his way through the living room and threw himself on the couch. He was winded and sweaty. Even Lewis' curiosity got the better of him, as he stopped typing to watch the events unfold.

"Okay, here's the skinny," said George. "Several of our union members complained about how you and Sophia were straying from the one-sheet. So I spoke with Mr.

Wilcox's agent about how the story was progressing, and when she told me a few of the plot twists, I was intrigued. So I called up a few of our story closers, and we set out for Susurrant."

"What the hell's a story closer?" asked Mason.

"They come and help an author with writer's block," said Lewis. "For example, if I had a one-sheet that didn't allow for character development, or if the plot didn't thicken, as it were, the story closers would come in and stir up the pot, so to speak."

"They provide writers with the tools to effectively finish their stories," said George.

"Great," said Mason. "So why were they with you?"

"Because I wanted them to help me persuade you to join the union before *Wrong Turn in Susurrant* ended," said George. "They've been closers for 15 years and I was going to have them explain the ins and outs of the job."

"Why was it so urgent?" asked Sophia. "You put us all in a lot of danger."

"Let me explain something about what I face at my job. Unions are getting weaker by the day and freelancers like you are taking over the field. This story you're working on, it has all the makings of a best-seller. It's meta-fiction with mass-appeal from a rising star in the fiction market, and I wanted Union Local 2557 to be involved with it. I need to reinvigorate union involvement with a high-profile project. The union is dying and I can't let it. I won't let it!"

"The character placement of the story is over," said Lewis.

"I know," said George.

"But thank you for calling me a rising star."

"Thank yourself. I've read your stories in the *New Yorker*. Everyone in the industry wants a piece of you. Of course, before this, I would've never sent a union man into a slasher story..."

Mason scoffed and glared at Lewis, who completely ignored him.

"...but you're going to take a trite premise and make it into a masterpiece. That's going to get publishers interested in everything you do from this point on. And if the union was a part of it, they wouldn't change the formula that made it a success. They'd come to me for characters every time."

"But I had a guarantee with the story," said Mason. "And so did Sophia."

"Guarantees aren't contracts," George said. "I would have bought you out."

"Bought us out? Does that mean we're going to be in demand?" Mason asked.

"Most definitely," said George. "That's why I want you to join the union now and we'll make you story closers immediately. This whole meta thing could be a trend."

"I'm going to need to think about that," said Sophia. Mason agreed.

"Fine," he said. "Think about it all you want. I'll be right here."

"We're going to need at least a few days," said Mason. "We have a party to go to in a couple hours and we don't want to think about it right now."

George reluctantly granted them 48 hours, but he refused to leave the couch until they agreed to negotiate with him at least once before Lewis turned in the manuscript. No one felt totally satisfied at the conclusion of the meeting, but that was how these negotiations worked sometimes.

George finally hobbled to his rental car and left the premises, and the Jarmans and their company embarked upon the journey to Pueblo shortly after. Mason drove Sophia's car, and with traffic and three unplanned stops—two for

Lewis' smoke breaks and one for Mason's bladder (during which Lewis smoked another cigarette)—the trip ended up taking well over two hours. When they pulled into Uncle Ernest's driveway, they were greeted by the loud bellowing of his Australian cattle dog, Toby. As they walked up to the house, Ernest appeared in the doorway.

"Now we can get this party started," he said before bestowing upon everyone giant bear hugs, including Sophia and Lewis, the latter of whom chuckled as he hugged him back.

"We didn't bring any booze or anything," said Eileen. "But we assumed you had that covered."

Ernest looked offended. "Of course I have booze and food covered. I even got vegan hot dogs for you two." He nodded towards Mason and Eileen. "Chips and salsa, fruit, all you can handle. Plus I got plenty of whiskey and vodka."

"Hell yeah," said Lewis who made a bee-line towards the whiskey.

"Someone's champing at the bit," said Ernest.

"He's a writer," Eileen said.

"Say no more," said Ernest. "We used to say, 'What's the difference between a writer and an alcoholic? The writer has an ego and a pen.'"

"He's been working hard on his novel," she said.

"Yeah, it looks like it," said Ernest as he watched Lewis fill up an entire cocktail glass with whiskey and ice.

Eileen didn't really feel like defending him any more than she already had, so she went and made herself a drink as well. Sophia and Mason followed, and soon the dopamine was flowing and laughter and mirth filled the house.

As the celebration progressed, the party-goers became increasingly intoxicated and aggressively social—all the necessary elements that sometimes led to uncomfortable and annoying situations, such as the conversation in which Mason and Sophia found themselves. The perpetrator of chatter was named Nick Plouff, a retired security guard who assumed his former job was the most interesting topic of conversation on earth. He took advantage of Sophia's politeness by using it as a tool to keep her from leaving or finding an appropriate way to exit the discussion. "Hello" was all she said to cement a firm social contract obliging her to the most inane dialogue at the party.

Plouff said, "I used to work the night shift at the museum, and a lot of folks, they said, 'How'd you do it?' And I'd tell them, 'I clock in at seven at night, after most all the day workers went home. Then I'd clock out at eight in the morning when the day workers were coming in.' Yep, it was four tens, an hour for lunch each day, and then I'd get three days off every week. I was happy as a jaybird."

"Um, I think it's, 'As naked as a jaybird,'" said Mason.

"Oh no," said Nick. "I had to wear the same uniform every night. A security officer has to wear his uniform."

"My mistake," said Mason. "I'm going to use the restroom."

"Okay," Sophia said. "Well it was nice talking to you."

"It's nice talking to you too," said Nick. "Then they got me back working the day shift with the public. A lot of times I had to tell the kids not to be naughty because the parents just let them run like wild beasts through the halls. And you know kids, how they scream and play."

As Sophia politely nodded, Mason went to find his uncle. He inquired about his whereabouts to several shorter winded guests, and finally found him smoking weed upstairs in his room with his girlfriend, Jenny.

"Hey Mason," he said, patting the floor. "Sit down and smoke some grass with us."

Mason couldn't think of a reason in the world why he would refuse the offer, so he sat cross legged next to his great uncle and pulled a thunder hit from the bong. And then he coughed like crazy.

"Whoa there, cowboy," said Ernest. "Take it easy. This stuff is potent. It's powerful. It's p- p-... Someone help me out with another p-word."

"Posse-gathering," said Mason, who immediately realized how horrible it sounded the second it left his tongue.

"No," said Ernest shaking his head. "That just won't do. Think harder."

"Puissant," said Jenny.

"What does that mean?" asked Mason.

"Strong, powerful," she explained. "It's a synonym of potent as well."

"I'll have to take your word on that," said Ernest, then he looked over to Mason. "Most of the time it's too risky to doubt people who have constantly proven they're smarter than you. Looking dumb is one of the more embarrassing social blunders out there. That's especially true if you consider yourself a smart man."

"Yeah, I know," said Mason. "Speaking of social blunders, who's that Nick guy?"

"Nick Plouff? He's a retired security guard," said Ernest.

"No shit. That's all he could talk about."

"Did he tell you about the difference between the night and day shift?" asked Jenny.

"Yeah, he bored the living shit out of me. In fact, I had to sacrifice Sophia just to save myself."

"You just deserted her?" she asked.

"Yes, indeed. Boy is she going to be pissed."

They all laughed.

"You know, all kidding aside," said Ernest, "you should take it easy on the guy. His wife died and he lives by himself. And people who live alone tend to talk a lot in social situations because they don't have anyone else to talk to."

"I wasn't a jerk to him by any means," said Mason. "I excused myself to use the restroom. And I can guarantee that Sophia's being nice. That's just how she is."

"At least it was nice of you to leave Sophia for him to talk to," said Ernest.

Mason laughed. "It's weird how being nice to one person can often involve being mean to someone else."

Everyone in the circle agreed with the sentiment and dwelled on the subject matter for as long as their marijuana-addled brains allowed—which seemed like forever but was really only around 18 seconds. Once Jenny started laughing at how quiet the room had become, everyone else joined her. It was a curious sight: Two grey haired proto-hippies laughing and smoking weed with a 36 year old punk rocker in a cross generational, counter cultural gathering.

The bong made a few more rotations before it dawned on Ernest that his hunger was getting the best of him. He relied on marijuana to stimulate his appetite, and these days he only ate when he was stoned.

"Hey Mason, I got you your own grill for the party so your vegan dogs don't have to get contaminated with meat juice," Ernest said. "When the party's over, you can take it back to your place."

Mason thanked him profusely, but Ernest was glad to do it. He wasn't going to need a grill after the grand inevitable.

All that thinking and talking about grilling made him realize there was a fridge full of food just waiting for consumption, and he invited his fellow potheads to join him for a cookout.

As they sauntered through the kitchen, Mason caught a

glimpse of Sophia still talking with Nick. When she made eye contact with him, she attempted a facial expression that conveyed the totality of righteous retribution that would rain down upon his blackened soul if she ever managed to find a way out of the conversation. It was menacing, exasperated, and longing for sweet revenge at the same time. Sophia was a very talented woman in this regard.

After procuring all the sustenance suitable for his diet, Mason took pity on her. "Hey Sophia, can you come and help me out with the grill?"

She politely excused herself from the conversation, which at that point had deteriorated to a meandering, unnecessarily detailed account of his television-viewing schedule.

"Sorry, Mr. Plouff," she said, "but I need to have a word with someone."

Chapter 27

"You are a terrible fucking person," Sophia told Mason once they were out of earshot from Mr. Plouff. "What were you doing? You were gone for like fifteen minutes."

His bungled attempt to explain his recent dalliance with cannabis was all the confirmation she needed that he was stoned out of his mind. And it was all the more reason to remain upset with him, since she missed out on a pot smoking session in order to converse with the dullest man she had ever met.

"It's not my fault you're too nice to excuse yourself from a boring conversation," he said.

"No, but it is your fault that I got stuck with him," she said, following him outside to the grill. "You see, that's why I need you—to like, use your assholism for the betterment of me."

"Aww, you just said you needed me."

"Yeah, but it wasn't meant to be a compliment, so don't let it go to your head."

Just then an object did go to his head—or at least, near his head. It was an ice cube, a big one too. One of the ones that froze to all the others and created a magnum clump. Eileen threw it at him from the roof, where she and Lewis had been sitting.

"Damn it, Eileen," said Mason. "That would've fucking hurt

if it hit me."

"I was just trying to get your attention," she said.

"Hey, I want to get... wait for it, 'Up on the roof,'" Sophia sang the last part from The Drifters' song she loved so much.

Eileen encouraged her to join them and Lewis held the ladder as she climbed atop the lowest part of the roof over the garage. Mason was invited, but he declined, opting instead to put his outdoor culinary talents to good use. Besides, at the moment he was stoned and afraid of ladders and heights.

"Who wants a veggie dog?" Mason called out. Eileen was the only one who raised her hand. "Are you not eating, Sophia?"

"I am," she said. "But I want a burger."

Mason's heart sank. Since she had tattoos and seemed to nestle so comfortably into the counterculture, he just assumed she didn't eat meat, much less red meat. All the occasions Mason observed her relationship to food had hitherto been vegetarian. During work, she had mainly subsisted on energy bars and bottled smoothies. Her character just ate grilled pickles. And when she stayed at his house, she ate whatever was being served.

Her request for meat brought about two uncomfortable realizations for Mason. One, he unfairly stereotyped people. Even though he ascribed to her a dietary choice he valued, it was still an unrealistic categorization. And two, Sophia wasn't perfect—or at least, not his perfect match (as if there was such a thing).

"Uncle Ernest's going to have to make it for you," said Mason glumly.

Ernest walked through the back door just as Mason finished talking. "I'll make it!" he said. "What am I making?"

"A burger for Sophia," he said sullenly.

"Uh oh," said Ernest under his breath. He quickly extrapolated from Mason's tone that he just discovered his new lady friend's dietary habits, and he knew right away his grand nephew was not going to be particularly thrilled by this bit of news. All of Mason's previous girlfriends espoused the tenets of veganism, so he wasn't used to dealing with the issue. And any time loved ones don't share tightly held convictions, there is bound to be hurt feelings and friction.

Mason tucked away his resentment towards Sophia, while his subconscious mind made a mental note to return to the topic at a more opportune time when the occasion was less jovial. With his irritation out of the way for the time being, he made two veggie dogs with the works for him and his sister. Ernest grilled a burger for Sophia and a hotdog with half a bun and one line of mustard for Lewis, as per his request. Lewis retrieved the food and brought it up on the roof to the others, as Mason ate in a lawn chair next to his uncle, refusing to even so much as glance in the direction of his lover while she devoured a slab of beef between two buns. He also made a very conscious mental note not to kiss her later.

Ernest had a difficult time eating because his friends kept coming up to him with somber reflections of life. He didn't want the party's attention to center around his impending demise, however. So whenever guests offered bromides about life or became overly emotional, he quickly changed the subject. This was his last celebration with friends and family and he wanted to avoid feeling like everyone was offering him encouragement on some sort of march towards death.

There were around fifty people at the party, most of whom Mason and Eileen knew—including Ernest's son Darren, who arrived as most guests finished their meals and refilled their cups with booze. After he filled a glass with soda water and ice, he proposed a toast to his father. All in attendance raised their glasses and cheered, and a few began crying.

"Well, since we're all gathered here tonight to honor the amazing life of my father, Ernest Learner, why don't we get him to say a few words?" said Darren to a round of applause.

Ernest knew this moment was coming and had been bracing for it all night. He thought about what he could say to make everyone feel better about his passing, but he came to the conclusion that the process of grief was too personal and individualized for blanket statements about his perspective on life to have any grand effect. He also didn't want to sound as though he was eulogizing himself at his own funeral. Still, they expected him to say something profound and meaningful.

"Of course you know that in a few days, I will no longer be here. And for this I am not sad or afraid. Some of you may remember me as a younger man full of piss and vinegar with a head full of hair and an ego the size of Montana. And some of you probably didn't meet me until a few wives later when my proudest parts began to sag and I had done too many drugs to pretend I gave a shit about what you thought of me. Well now I stand before you, a shadow of myself, robbed of my healthy physique and the last few years of my life by this wretched disease, for which there is no cure. But I don't curse fate. I outlived an equal share of bastards and saints. And through all the ups and downs of this—whatever the hell this is—life, for lack of a better term, I did the best I could in most situations. Do I have regrets? Sure, I do. But who the hell doesn't? This right here is what I wanted it all to come down to. Looking out at all of you, only one thing comes to mind. I'm damn lucky that I didn't get stuck with a bunch of assholes for friends and family. And before I say I love you all, let me say this: If you give me an open casket at my funeral, I'll haunt the holy hell out of every last one of you. Thanks, everyone for coming. I love you all."

Ernest brought the house down as everybody held their glasses in the air and cheered uproariously. There wasn't a dry eye in sight.

His speech was equal parts gratitude and self-deprecation, which fit perfectly with his outlook of life. He referred to himself as a realist, which a peer of his once described as "off-putting," though it wasn't as if he didn't enjoy finer moments of existence. But he always had a sense that pure happiness was as fleeting as depression and tears, and he would often elucidate the simple truth that humans spend most of the time somewhere between intense feelings of elation and melancholy. He also didn't mince words when discussing the darker side of life—the doubt, the ominous sense that everything was wrong with everyone most of the time. And since he spoke about the genuine core of life, rather than its feigned exterior, he carried the designation of pessimist in certain circles.

After his oration, Ernest slyly handed Mason a breath mint on his way back in the house. For an instant, Mason wondered if his breath was really that atrocious, but then he realized it most likely contained a mind-altering substance. He popped it in his mouth without a second thought.

In order to receive the sheer amount of guests who wanted to converse with him, Ernest situated himself in his living room, which contained ornate couches and chairs surrounding a coffee table with a tea set at its center. Guests crammed into the room to laugh, carouse, and reminisce.

Mason was notably absent from the gathering. First because he had to explain to Sophia that he wasn't mad at her for anything, even though she could tell he was upset. And then because the substance on the breath mint was most definitely acid, and he needed at least 45 minutes of alone time to quell the anxiety and come to peace with the drug.

Eileen, Lewis, and Sophia joined the gathering inside as the sun was setting so Mason could pace in the backyard by himself. He could have powered half of Pueblo with the sheer amount of nervous energy emanating from his being. Eventually though, he accepted the drug and became comfortable in his own skin. And once he did, his confidence came cascading back. It was then that he climbed to the top of the roof and stared at the stars for what seemed hours.

With an intense appreciation for the sheer scope of his own insignificance, he did a lot of ruminating up there. He imagined himself in a parallel universe with a wife and kids, living in the suburbs, wearing a suit and tie to the office every day. And he tried to strip down his identity, the personal narrative of his life, to determine if any part of that lifestyle actually appealed to him. He knew the story he told himself and others—the traditional prizes of western society guaranteed a vapid existence. A wife limited options. Children threatened both personal freedom and a beleaguered environment. Suburbs killed creativity and diversity. And desk jobs obliterated the soul.

Mason, as he knew himself, as the protagonist in the story of his life, believed these things. But he wasn't sure he had to keep playing this character—or even if he wanted to. If his work in character placement taught him anything, it was the fluidity of identity. People could flip the script—or disobey the one-sheet—and suddenly they'd be worlds apart from their former selves. New Mark, Karen, grandma—they shed their old identities like a snake molting skin. And while he found the prospect freeing in a way, it also seemed disingenuous to him.

His thoughts were happening at such a rapid-fire pace, he couldn't process them properly, and soon he lost any semblance of himself and his surroundings. So when Eileen came to the top of the ladder and shouted his name, he didn't answer right away.

"Mason? Mason, I know you're up here," she said.

He moved his head toward the sound of her voice, but he still couldn't properly process what was being said.

Using her phone as a flashlight, Eileen located her brother and sat down next to him. "Are you dead?" she asked.

"Hey Eileen," he said finally. "Uncle Ernest made me trip."

"I know, he told me. He said you were probably going to be up here for awhile."

"I think I'm ready to come down now."

"Good. Everyone else either left or crashed out. I've been talking to Uncle Ernest for the last couple hours. But I'm tired and he wants to talk to you now."

"What time is it?"

"It's after midnight," she said.

"Really? It doesn't feel like I've been up here that long."

"That's because you're on acid and you have no sense of time."

He nodded. As they were readying themselves to climb down the ladder, Mason held her shoulder and said, "Eileen, do you like who I am?"

"Seriously?" she asked. But then she looked into Mason's eyes and understood his statement was sincere. "Mason, don't be a dumbfuck."

He chuckled. Then he nodded. "Okay," he said.

Chapter 28

When Mason walked through the back door to his uncle's house, his perspective on life completely changed. No longer was he an insignificant trace of life floating aimlessly through the vast universe. The bright lights, walls, and ceiling subdued his sensation of infinitude, and he felt much more grounded.

As he walked through the kitchen, he saw the sink and realized he hadn't consumed any water in hours. He immediately drank two pints of water in succession and then mixed himself a proper drink. When he made his way into the living room, his uncle was sitting on the couch, drinking tea.

"How're you feeling?" he asked.

"I just went to the moon," said Mason.

His uncle laughed. "I thought you'd enjoy that."

"How are you still up?" Mason wondered.

"My doctor prescribed a pharmaceutical amphetamine. I have pills for everything these days."

"How did the night go?"

"It was unreal. Everyone said good things about me. There were more smiles than tears. And I got to say goodbye to all the people I wanted to say goodbye to."

"I'm sorry I missed it."

"You're still here," he said. "I wanted to talk to you and Eileen separately."

Mason took off his shoes and slouched in his chair. It was integral for him at that moment to get as comfortable as humanly possible. He took a deep breath. "Thanks for the acid," he said.

"You're welcome. I had a buddy come and stay with me awhile back and he brought it with him. He gave me three and I only took one that night."

"Did you take the other one?"

"Yes, I dropped it shortly after I was diagnosed with cancer," Ernest said. "The first few weeks after the diagnosis, I was distraught—full of depression, self-pity, anxiety. I couldn't sleep because every night I imagined it to be the last time I closed my eyes. I resented Jenny because I didn't want her to watch me become weak and feeble and helpless. And most of all, I resented my own body because I just couldn't accept my limitations. I felt trapped in a decaying vessel.

"Then one morning I was smoking some grass to work up an appetite for breakfast, and I was just so sick of being stoned. I didn't want to spend another day high and I remember wishing I had another drug to do. Then I remembered the acid in my drug drawer, and without thinking, I walked over and swallowed it. The whole experience really grounded me. I realized I had been obsessed with myself and my fate. But I'm 82 years old. I got to live a long, fulfilling life. And because I was lucky in so many ways, I had no right to my own feelings of bitterness and resentment. I had no business pretending I had any reason to feel remorse."

Mason had finished his cocktail and he momentarily excused himself to make another. When he returned, his uncle was standing by the window, looking out into the darkness.

"What are you drinking?" asked Ernest once he turned around to acknowledge Mason's presence.

"Vodka soda," he said. "I like to drink at this point in the trip because coming down always depresses me."

"That's why I smoke grass when I trip."

"I do that sometimes too, but every now and again the pot just makes you trip harder," said Mason. Ernest nodded. "It feels like my face is melting off. This is some powerful acid."

Ernest laughed. "Yes. Yes, it is." He returned to his seat on the couch.

"When I was up on the roof, I went into this thought spiral where I lost my identity—or at least I lost the concept of identity," he said. His thoughts were happening too fast for him to physically convey by means of speaking. His "reducing valve of the brain"—as Aldous Huxley once put it—had opened, and with it a torrent of consciousness came pouring out. Consequently, by the time he came to the end of speaking a sentence, his brain was already three sentences ahead.

"You know how you thought you had no right to your own feelings?" Mason continued. "I thought the same thing, but I felt I had no right to me, to who I think I am."

"It's liberating when you realize you're not that big of a deal," said Ernest. "It lowers the stakes of life."

Mason nodded. Since his mind was travelling at warp speed, he had forgotten where they were in the conversation. He was busy imagining his uncle's death and reconciling that vision with what he knew about Franklin Builder and Don. He wondered if his uncle had ever entertained the idea of immortality, or if he was the sort of person who would want life to take its natural course.

Mason attempted to explain his experience with character placement, his rendezvous with Don, the quarrel with Franklin. But the words came out so fast Ernest had difficulty comprehending him.

"Hold on," said Ernest. "Eileen already tried to explain this to me. Immortality through literature? Is that right?" he asked. Mason nodded. "Seems a little hokey," said Ernest.

"Hokey? What do you mean?"

"Fanciful. Fake. It sounds like something certain people would want to believe because they're overly sentimental about life and they fear death."

"I can see where you're coming from," Mason said. His thoughts had moved to a different topic and he abruptly changed the subject. "Give me some life-affirming advice."

"No."

"Why not?"

"What is it with you? Why do you need to be reassured every step of the way? You're a smart man. You were a smart kid too. You're just too god damn gloomy and self-absorbed to let your brain enjoy yourself. You think I'm going to say some platitude and it's going to change your outlook on life? Well I'm not and it's not. Here, how about this? There are no easy answers. Stop looking for them. How's that for life-affirming advice?"

"It's good," said Mason. "I can live by that."

"Don't live by that. God damn it, Mason. Now you're just trying to piss me off."

"No, I'm not. I'm just sick of being full of doubt all the time. The reason I'm asking you about it is because I'm hoping one day I'll get to the other side where doubt doesn't exist."

"Where doubt doesn't exist?" Ernest contemplated the sentiment for what seemed, to Mason's drug-addled mind, like several lifetimes. Then very deliberately, Ernest leaned forward and said, "Let me save you the suspense: Doubt never ends. I'm still steeped in doubt and I'm days to death. You're missing the point when you think about it. Don't use doubt as a crutch; use it as a tool. Use it for the betterment of yourself and those around you. When you stop doubting yourself, then maybe you're really fucking up... Or, I don't know… Advice is always easier said than done. There are no easy answers."

During the course of Ernest's answer, Mason understood how intellectually needy he had been. In the face of his inquiries about death, his uncle felt stereotyped as the wise old man with all the answers. And since he didn't have the answers his grand nephew sought, he felt inadequate and defensive. It was the same way Don felt typecast as the wise old spirit when he really just wanted to dance. Maybe Ernest just wanted to dance.

"Should we listen to some records?" said Mason.

Ernest smiled. "Yes. I thought you'd never ask."

They spent the rest of the early morning alternating as DJ, per Ernest's rules: Whenever someone put a new record on the turntable, he had to defend his choice with an explanation of how it personally affected him. For example, when he played *Electric Ladyland* by Jimi Hendrix, Mason said he wanted to hear the track, "Burning of the Midnight Lamp," since he once had the best sex of his life to that song. Ernest spun Herbie Hancock's *Takin' Off*, because his fourth wife, Sharon, played it on the jukebox on their second date—and it was the precise moment he realized he would marry her.

They continued playing records as the morning light started illuminating the room. At one point, when it was Mason's turn, he came across his band's records and smiled. He didn't play them, since neither he nor his uncle would have appreciated the self-indulgence, but it still made him smile to see them there.

When the sun rose, they climbed to the top of the roof to watch it. Mason never understood why watching the sunrise was anything special. Ernest, on the other hand, had learned to savor the smallest bits of dignity in life. When he had the opportunity to appreciate the sun peaking over the horizon—instead of hiding from it in a hurry to get ready for work—he felt grateful and untroubled.

Soon the temperature began to rise, and Mason could once again sense his dehydration and climbed down to get himself some water. Ernest followed him, and they returned to the stereo to play alternating DJ until the overnight guests started stirring.

Eileen made breakfast for everyone and they ate together as they relived the best moments of the evening prior.

The Jarmans took their time as they gathered their belongings to leave, since it dawned on them that this would be the last occasion in their uncle's presence. Eileen dragged her feet more dramatically than Mason did. A sense of panic was beginning to well inside her.

Ernest had fallen asleep on the couch by the time Mason convinced Eileen they needed to leave. It was one o'clock in the afternoon.

"He has things to take care of, Eileen," said Mason.

"Just a little more time," she said.

"Eileen, there's not enough time in the world. It's never going to be enough. We have to go."

She was crying. "I can't do it. I can't leave. I have to stay. I'm staying."

Mason and Eileen both looked over to Jenny who was also standing in the kitchen with them. "It's fine with me if you want to stay," she said. "But it's about to get pretty dramatic around here."

"That's okay," said Eileen sniveling.

"I don't have enough tears for what's about to happen here," said Mason.

"That's alright," said Jenny. "I think Ernest would have a hard time dying around you, Mason. He always talked about how competitive you two were. How you'd send him your new record and it would inspire him to play his guitar for hours. He would write songs too. He said he didn't realize it at the time, but he would try to write enough new songs for an entire album just to keep up with you."

"Seriously?" he said. "I guess that's why he's so adamant about me playing music again."

"It is," she said. "And Eileen, he was tickled to death about the pamphlets you used to write."

"Zines," said Eileen.

"What?" said Jenny.

"Sorry, that's just what we called them—zines, not pamphlets... Never mind, it's not important."

"Well, whatever they were called, he loved them. He still has them. In fact, whenever he needs inspiration to write lyrics for his songs, he takes them out and reads them for the thousandth time."

"Ooh," Eileen said with a loving voice inflection as she began to cry. "That's so sweet."

"He has something to give you," she said. "Let me go wake him up." She walked over to Ernest and jostled him. "Mason's leaving, dear. Get up and say goodbye."

It took him awhile, but Ernest got off the couch and shambled upstairs to his room. When he returned, he was clutching a small stack of records. "Here you go," he said, handing a copy to Eileen, Mason, Lewis, and Sophia. The sleeve was white with a sticker on the corner with Ernest's band name on it.

"What is this?" Mason asked.

"It's the essential Rock Lingo," he said. "I finally got it a few days ago. I curated the whole thing myself and had 100 pressed. It's our first time on vinyl."

"No shit!" said Mason.

"Are you sure you want to give me one?" Sophia asked.

"Yes, I am. I've already given away about 70 to friends and family, and to friends and family of the other band members. I figure I'll still have at least 20 or so to give away at the funeral. So please, take one. Otherwise they'll just sit in storage."

"Let me have another one," said Mason. When Eileen demanded to know why he needed two, he said, "I have two copies of all my favorite records. That way, if I ruin one by listening to it too much, I'll have another one."

"It's fine," said Ernest as he handed him another one.

"I can't wait to play it," said Mason.

They thanked and congratulated him profusely as he beamed with pride.

"Oh, and Mason, one more thing," said Ernest. "I got you this." He handed him a CD. "It's some of my singer-songwriter stuff that a buddy of mine recorded mostly on his laptop."

"Thank you, Uncle Ernest."

"I think you'll like it."

"I'm sure I will."

As the conversation reached its natural conclusion, they began offering words of parting. Lewis and Sophia were the first to excuse themselves and wait outside. Then Mason hugged his uncle as tears streamed down his face.

"I love you, Mason," said Ernest. "You've always made me so proud."

"I love you too. You're the best uncle a guy like me could

have."

"You've got to keep playing. You know that, right? Don't give up on the things that make you who you are. You can't float through life without an identity."

"I know. I know…" he sighed. "I'm really going to miss you. I mean, who else is going to be a huge pain in the ass about me playing my guitar?"

"If you don't pick up a guitar, I'm going to haunt you."

Mason laughed. He didn't want the moment to end. "Bye, Uncle Ernest," he said. "I love you."

"Bye, Mason. I love you too."

Mason made it out the door and all the way to the passenger seat of the car before he broke down into uncontrollable sobs.

"Don't go yet," he said to Lewis and Sophia. "I need… I need a minute."

Just when he seemed to compose himself, he looked towards the house and lost it again. But with affection from Sophia and reassurances from Lewis, he eventually gained enough self-possession for Sophia to slowly drive away.

It wasn't until they passed the Air Force Academy outside of Colorado Springs that he finally calmed down. They had put Ernest's CD in the car stereo when they were north of Pueblo, and it had played past a dozen songs when a live recording of the time Mason sat in with Rock Lingo blared through the speakers. It was recorded when he had driven to Pueblo to see the band and Ernest surprised him by asking him to play a guitar and sing backup vocals for the songs, "Twist & Shout" and "That'll Be the Day." Ernest had placed those songs as tracks 13 and 14 on the CD. And while the recording wasn't high quality, Mason turned the songs up almost as loud as the stereo would allow. Tears streamed down his face and over his lips. And even in profound grief, he still managed a half smile.

The last track on the CD was a Johnny Thunders' cover, "You Can't Put Your Arms Around a Memory"—a song that Mason had introduced to Ernest several years before. When it ended, he ejected the disc and pondered the reasoning behind including that song, since death always sends the soul searching. When he couldn't formulate a satisfactory rationale he asked the other passengers. "Do you think my uncle put that song at the end of the CD for a reason?"

No one in the car knew his uncle well enough to know if it was something characteristic of him or not, so after offering a couple I-don't-nos, they listened to Mason attempt to suss it out on his own. "You think he's talking about my past or about him as a person? Because if it's him as a person, that's kind of messed up—like he's deliberately trying to make me sad. But he wouldn't do that. At least I don't think he would..." He thought some more.

After a moment or two in silence, Lewis said, "Or maybe it's just a good tune and he has no ulterior motive."

Mason considered it and slowly began to nod. "Yeah," he said. "That could be true." He turned around and met Lewis' eyes. "You know, maybe I shouldn't be trying to analyze everything to death all the time."

"Maybe not," he said flatly. "But it makes sense. You're looking for deep and meaningful answers in the face of death. We all do that."

By the time they passed Castle Rock, Sophia had managed to brighten the mood in the car by broaching a few other subjects—the Renaissance Festival (as they passed Larkspur), Star Wars (since they were on the subject of nerdy pursuits), and how they could all use some caffeine.

Chapter 29

Back at the apartment, Mason made coffee and everyone took a cup and sat around the record player. He filed his uncle's records into his collection for another time, since they all just listened to his CD.

Mason put Alice Donut's *Donut Comes Alive* on the turntable because he used to listen to it when he took mushrooms in high school. Even back then, the album always made him feel so appreciative that he was different.

By that time he had his first taste of coffee, and Mason was too emotionally exhausted to dwell on his uncle's fate. And since he was still wired from the acid, he joined Sophia and Lewis in conversations far removed from matters of life and death.

"So," Sophia said nodding, "you and Eileen, huh?" She made a lewd gesture of her right index finger entering and exiting a circle created by her left index finger and thumb.

Lewis smiled. "No, it's not like that at all. I have a wife and house and dog up in Fort Collins. Eileen and I have just been sleeping in the same bed. Maybe a little bit of foreplay, but nothing spectacular."

"You mean, nothing spectacular like sex?" She asked. He shook his head. "Because you're married?"

"No… Well we're married, but we're in an open relationship, so sex isn't off limits. But sometimes it's better just to talk to another person, you know? Someone new who isn't your wife and doesn't already know everything about you. They say sex can get stale in long-term relationships; well, so can conversations."

"What do you talk about that's so special?" she said.

"See that's the thing. That's just it. We talk about writing! And I love it. My wife is not a writer; she's a veterinarian. And she can't talk to me about putting words on the page the same way I can't talk to her about mending animals. I mean, sure we have plenty of topics we can speak passionately about to each other, but writing isn't one of them."

"And it's not like you can go into the office and talk to your coworkers about writing," said Mason. "But I bet that's what your wife does every day. She goes and talks about being a veterinarian with all of her veterinarian coworkers."

"Exactly," he said.

"Man, being a writer like that must suck sometimes," said Sophia. "I mean, it must be lonely sometimes."

"It has its drawbacks for sure. But that's just a part of it. And it's not like I can imagine doing anything else. It's like you and your guitar, Mason. Or your uncle and his guitar. Or Sophia and her character placement."

Sophia was surprised to be included at that particular point in the conversation. "Um, I'm not sure I would call that a passion. It's more like a job than anything."

"Yeah, but it's a job you take pride in," said Lewis. "Not a lot of people can say that about what they do for a living. Most people's jobs are the worst part of their lives. That's not true for you."

"Yeah, I guess."

"What do you mean, 'Yeah I guess?' I've seen you work,

and it's incredible. I've read a few of the stories based off your performances. They're all great too."

"Yeah, but it's not my passion. It's just what I do for money."

"But it doesn't have to be; that's all I'm saying," said Lewis. "You know how many former characters I know who became writers later in their careers? At least half a dozen. And their character work wasn't half as good as yours."

"Seriously?" She blushed. "I always thought about writing fiction—how I could at least write a better story than half the stories they place me on."

"That's how you start," said Lewis. "You take a look at some of the shittier books out there that still get published and you say, 'Well, I can at least do better than that.' Then you write your first novel and it is better than a lot of tripe out there, but it still needs work. And after you get one or two under your belt—that's when you say, 'I've done it, so I know I can do it. Now I want to make it good.' And that's when you hit your stride."

"Yes!" said Mason. "That's the exact same process of starting a band. You see someone with less talent and more nerve on the stage and you're like, 'Why aren't I up there?' Then you make a record, practice a lot, play some shows. Then you make a good record and realize how much your first record sucked."

"You know what I really want to do?" she said. "Write a sex and relationship advice column. It's not fiction or anything, but I think I'd be ready good at it."

"Well," said Lewis, "what's stopping you?"

"Yeah, Sophia," said Mason. "What is stopping you?"

"Nothing, I guess. I could just make it a blog at first. Get my name out there..."

"So?" said Lewis.

"So…" she said. "I suppose I could just do it, right? Because nothing is stopping me." She whispered that last part, but everyone heard her.

"Nothing is stopping you," repeated Lewis.

Sophia smirked. "I feel like I'm having a… What's that word again? The one where you realize something big? Like there should be real dramatic music playing in the background?"

"An epiphany," said Lewis. "You're going to have to learn that word if you're going to be a writer."

"I know it, I just forgot it," Sophia scoffed.

"So that's it," said Mason. "You're just going to do it?"

"Yeah," she said. "I could easily do it. I can have people send me questions from Facebook."

Sophia hadn't imagined her own future with such unbridled enthusiasm in years. And for the first time since college, she didn't have any ties to her past. It was as if she were witnessing her fate aligning itself perfectly in front of her own eyes.

"Maybe your sister and I could start a writer's group," Sophia continued. Her excitement was growing by the second. "We could meet right here on the couch."

Lewis smiled and Mason laughed. "I'm sure Eileen could use the support," said Mason.

"And you could be there too and work on your songs," she said.

"Nah, you wouldn't want that," said Mason. "I'd be singing and playing my guitar and you'd keep telling me to shut the fuck up."

"You could come," she said to Lewis. "And we could all talk about writing and not about veterinarian shit."

Lewis laughed. "Sure, I'd like that," he said. Then he finished his coffee and put his mug down on the table. "I need to get going. My wife's coming home from her folk's house today and it would be nice for me to be there."

After a round of goodbyes, Lewis fired up his motorcycle and sped off into the distance, leaving Mason and Sophia alone. Almost immediately she broached the subject of his obvious disapproval of her dietary choices the evening prior—a conversation she had been dying to initiate the second she found an appropriate moment.

"So what? Do you like totally hate me now?" she said.

"No," he said. "Wait, what do you mean? Of course I don't hate you."

"You know what I mean. Last night, after I ate a hamburger, you got all fucking wienery on me."

"Wienery? Is that a word?"

"Mason, come on. Let's have a real conversation here. Why did you get so butt hurt?"

He couldn't imagine the apposite response. He didn't want to tell her eating the wrong type of food for dinner really diminished his opinion of her. He prided himself on being an open-minded vegan that didn't endlessly persecute and criticize meat eaters. But it's always difficult to consistently explain and defend firmly held beliefs to friends and family who don't agree for whatever reason.

"I don't know," he said. He contemplated the situation in silence for a few moments. "Here's the deal: Yeah, I was a little butt hurt about it because I've been vegan for so long and it's something that's really important to me, you know? I mean, you always want people close to you to share your beliefs. You don't want to be alone out there. And besides, I've been the vegetarian in a few of my shorter lasting relationships and it's really emasculating if the girl eats meat."

"Ha! You're concerned about gender norms? You're worried you're not going to get to be the manly man in the relationship because I eat meat?"

"Well, when you put it that way it makes me sound pretty damn petty and bigoted..."

"Well?"

"There's more to it than that," he said. "This might sound shitty, but kissing someone who just ate a hamburger is like making out with someone who just smoked a cigarette. It's, I don't know...kind of gross."

Sophia grew silent. Criticizing anything related to sexual performance in such a sexually critical culture invoked a strong sense of shame—even if it was related to something as simple as kissing. "I guess I'm sorry," she said.

"No, goddamn it. Don't feel bad."

"How can I not feel bad? I'm a smoker and a meat eater. And you just called me a smoky rotting meat mouth."

"I don't think I used those words..."

"This is why everyone hates vegans—and to a lesser extent, non-smokers."

Mason realized he had painted himself into a corner. As far as he could tell, he had a few options of how he could be perceived from this moment on—a martyr, an authoritarian, a plain old fashioned dick—none of which were very appealing. "Look," he said. "Let's just drop it."

"How can we just drop it?"

Mason sighed internally, since he knew if he performed such an action externally at the moment, he would have cast even more shovels full of dirt out of the hole he was digging. He may not have been the best at relationships, but he knew when to stop digging.

As the conversation progressed, he spent any and all of his allocated speaking opportunities convincing Sophia nothing was wrong with her. She would describe her newly realized insecurities and he would backtrack his previous logical arguments and understate the importance of his convictions. Then when he could sense that she was mentally preparing to leave, he pulled the ace out of his sleeve.

"I'm sorry," he said. "I'm just a little upset about my uncle, you know? I'm sad. I'm grief-stricken."

While it was a cheap, desperate way to win the argument, Sophia had to respect the power of the ace up his sleeve. His cool great uncle—who meant so much to him—was perilously close to the end. She had to acquiesce. "Fine," she said. "Let's just drop it."

Mason successfully fought the urge to smile, which was wise. He may not have been the best at relationships, but he knew when to quell a smile.

"Come with me to the B-Street," he said. "I need a drink."

"But you just spent the entire night drinking..."

"Yeah, and it wasn't enough. Look, I just need to drown out the sadness for one more day. I don't even want to try to process anything right now. I just need a drink. Are you in or not?"

"I'm in," she said.

Mason and Sophia drank until the sun went down and then they went to her house where they joined her roommates in a party already in progress. When he finally fell asleep next to the bodies of Sophia and her ex-girlfriend Coral, he had been awake for nearly 40 hours. And while they technically enjoyed a threesome, it was really more of a Coral-Sophia two-way with a Mason spectator. Still, no one complained, and he took a small but important step of becoming more comfortable with the entire monogamish situation—especially when right before he fell asleep Sophia whispered into his ear, "I love you." He didn't think twice before he said, "I love you, too." He smiled as he spooned Sophia who spooned Coral. The night would be granted prime real estate in his catalogue of mental images upon which he relied to get him through his lonelier moments.

After a solid eight hours, both women awoke and left Mason to sleep alone. He slumbered uninterrupted for 15 hours before his phone disrupted his peace. It was Eileen and she didn't have good news.

. . . .

The afternoon Eileen called, Ernest had taken a turn for the worse. His body was worn out from the cancer and weary from the amount of pharmaceutical amphetamine he had taken to stay alert in the days leading up to his party. After the festivities, he napped all day and slept the rest of the night. When he awoke in the morning, he felt weak and short of breath. Instead of heading to a hospital, he remained in his bed where he ingested a large portion of the drugs he procured for the situation.

By that afternoon, he had fallen into a deep sleep, and by the evening he had passed. In his final moments, he was surrounded by Jenny, Darren, and Eileen, and he seemed free of pain and torment. His last words weren't exactly audible. Eileen liked to think he was trying to say, "This was so unreal."

Chapter 30

"I appreciate your help over the past couple of weeks," said Jenny on the way to Denver.

"My pleasure," said Eileen.

After Ernest's passing, Darren and Jenny were busy planning the funeral and tying up loose ends while Eileen ran the day-to-day errands—procuring groceries, picking up holds from the library, cooking and cleaning. Mason, Sophia, and Lewis all attended the funeral, and at the wake, they drank enough booze to kill most of the fish in Pueblo Reservoir. While they all returned to Denver the next day, Eileen remained at Jenny's house, basking in the emotional support of the rapport the two had developed.

"It means a lot to me to have a connection with Ernest's remaining family," Jenny said.

"It means a lot to me to have a connection to you," Eileen said.

While it was integral to her well-being to remain in southern Colorado for her uncle's death and the aftermath, Eileen was excited to go home. During the wake, Sophia explained her vision to create a sex and relationship advice column and her enthusiasm was contagious. A grand aspiration of Eileen's own had been percolating in her head and she realized she finally had the tools to put it into motion.

"You seem better than you did when you first got here," Jenny said as they passed the eyesore that was Denver's southernmost suburbs.

"I feel better," said Eileen. "I'm seeing things more clearly."

"How do you mean?"

"Things just don't seem so serious anymore."

"Yeah? How so?"

"It's like, hold on, let me think about it..." She stared out the window for a while. "Having kids, for example. I know I don't want kids, but I was constantly second-guessing my decision. Now I don't care."

"I knew I didn't want kids from a very young age and I never really thought about it much. They say you really start to think about it when you get older and need someone to take care of you. But I'm 77 and perfectly healthy. And if my health does take a turn for the worse, there's always Medicare and hospice. I'm not worried."

"There was a very specific incident that completely confirmed my impression of being a parent. It was when I was picking your books and CDs up from the library. This mom or nanny or whatever was in there with three kids and they were just awful. There was this two-year-old who went into a jealous rage, just crying and screaming every time another kid tried to play with one of the toys in the children's section. One of the kids was eating Cheetos and smearing her orange hands all over books. And the other one was taking entire racks of books and dumping them on the floor—all while the grownup sat there on her phone. Then when I got up to the counter, some other little sixth or seventh grader was trying to get the librarian to check out a stack of DVDs without his library card and he was being so disrespectful. He called her an idiot. It was horrifying."

Jenny laughed. "Kids aren't all like that. But I understand the point you're trying to make."

"I guess that's not even the point. The point is that I think a lot of people have kids for the wrong reasons. Like they think they should. Or they want someone to look after them in old age. Or, I don't know, they want smaller versions of themselves running around. I'm not entirely sure what the right reasons are, but I know if you're having kids to enhance your own ego, then you're missing the point. And if you don't care enough about them to raise them properly—with respect for others and themselves—then you're *definitely* missing the point."

"You know, just to play devil's advocate here, there are a lot of good reasons to have kids," said Jenny. "A strong biological drive to procreate is probably the first."

"Yeah, but that's the thing, I don't know if I care anymore. I just feel better about it now. We've been through some powerful, life-changing events. And now that everything's over, it's all different. Nothing can be as serious as that."

"Nor should it be," she said. They grinned.

Not even the conversation they were having maintained its graveness, as it veered into topics like finding meaningful work, the ridiculousness of road rage, and Eileen's idea for a novel, which Jenny met with extreme enthusiasm.

When Eileen arrived at the apartment, Sophia was the only one home. Her brother's lover had already begun work on her sex and relationship advice blog, which she called *Begging the Question*. She was answering her very first letter about a woman's religious boyfriend who was struggling with issues of guilt about engaging in premarital sex. Immediately after he reached orgasm, he became extremely jealous and judgmental. He would come and then grab her phone and go through her Instagram, yelling at her for pictures where she appeared with other men, including relatives. He called her names and issued ultimatums.

In Sophia's response, she was trying to provide and expound upon as many courses of action as she could imagine, while gently nudging her towards finding a partner who didn't project feelings of guilt and shame for having premarital sex onto her—or the "only real way to make the problem go away," as she put it. But she was having difficulty crafting coherent guidance. Every time she settled on any one piece of advice, she thought of why it wouldn't work in this situation.

"How's the column coming?" asked Eileen as she threw her purse on the couch.

"Not great," said Sophia. "This one is about a guy who gets angry and jealous after he has sex with his girlfriend. Once he comes, he yells at his girlfriend for showing any kind of affection towards other males, including her brother."

"People like that still exist?" Eileen said. Sophia nodded. "Where do people like that still exist?"

"I have no idea. The suburbs, maybe."

"Yeah, that makes sense," said Eileen. "I lived in suburban hell for a few years. I never understood why anyone would want to live in a suburb. It's like, 'Let's go where there's no culture and everything looks the same, where all my neighbors are judgmental assholes...'"

"'...And everything closes at nine.' That's some scary shit. I shudder to think... I just want to tell this woman, 'Move to the city and find an artist,' but I could see myself telling that to everyone who writes in, and I don't want to pigeonhole myself on the first column, you know?"

"I've met some shitty artists, too."

"That's true," Sophia said. She stared away from her computer screen in contemplation. "I guess everyone has the capacity to be a jerk."

"Yeah, that's tricky."

"Mm-hmm." She looked back at the screen, hoping the answer would come to her—some kind of eureka moment—but she kept settling on the ditch-your-boyfriend response.

"Hey, where's Mason?" asked Eileen.

"He went to pick up some lunch. I can text him if you want something."

"Sure," she said. "There's also something important I need to talk to you all about."

"Alright, is everything okay?" Sophia wondered.

"Yeah, everything's peachy. It's just this idea I had. I want to tell you about it."

Sophia forwarded her lunch order to Mason, hoping he would see it in time. Eileen retired to the shower and Sophia kept typing away as she carefully crafted each sentence, writing and rewriting until it sounded somewhere near articulate.

When Eileen reemerged, Mason was walking through the front door. He unloaded the food, doled it out, and put Big Boys' *No Matter How Long the Line at the Cafeteria, There's Always a Seat* on the turntable as they gathered around the living room to eat.

"I got your text after I paid for our order," said Mason. "I had to get back in line to get yours Eileen."

"Well thank you," she said.

"They didn't have the quinoa salad, though," he said. "So I got you the steamed kale."

She shrugged. "Whatevs, I just wanted some kind of vegetable."

"*Some Kind of Vegetable*, wasn't that a vegan propaganda film from the '80s?" Mason said.

Sophia sneered.

Eileen laughed. "You're thinking of *Who Liberated Roger Rabbit?*" she said.

"Okay, that's enough, you fucking salad shooters," Sophia said. "Vegan self righteousness on its own is real shitty. When you add fake humor to it, it's like the shittiest thing in the world…" She turned to Eileen. "You wanted to talk to us about a project or idea or something."

"Yes," she said. "I have an idea for a story…"

Since the past few weeks gave her ample time to think, Eileen described her idea meticulously—even referencing notes she had created. It was a rough outline, sure, but it was all she needed to initialize character placement and begin production.

"The story begins with Chloe, an emerging sex and relationship advice columnist who struggles to field questions since she lacks experience," said Eileen. "So she has to go out and research them, but her boyfriend gets jealous since he's not invited to partake in a lot of the research. He's a has-been rocker who plays guitar but has a wishy washy future at best. On her journey, she encounters discarnate spirits, crazy sexual experiences, and life-affirming events."

"That's enough for the first one-sheet right there," Mason said.

"It is," she continued. "Lewis got me into contact with his agent, who said she wouldn't represent me because I didn't have any name recognition or contacts within the industry. And that's when I thought about you all and George, and how he's desperate to get you working for him."

Mason smiled. "Holy shit," he said with an enormous grin on his face. "That's a fucking plan!"

Hitherto this moment, Sophia and Mason had very little motivation to get in touch with George—a man who seemed to keep people in his life long enough to use them for the benefit of his ends. But now that they had the chance to use him, they wasted no time establishing contact. Before she even finished eating, Sophia called him and set up a meeting for that afternoon.

"He says he can't wait to see us," she said when she hung up the phone.

. . . .

George's relief was palpable as they walked through the door of his office. He took a deep breath and relaxed his shoulders as he told them about the sheer amount of unfinished stories coming across his desk that could use a pair of good closers. Needless to say, he said, he was eager to enlist them. Sophia and Mason could hear a slight twinge of desperation in his voice, which they would use to leverage their situation. They had brought the one-sheet and a list of their own demands.

"We look forward to helping you with the projects you mentioned," said Sophia. "But we have a project of our own that we want to work on first."

"Oh?" George raised his eyebrow.

"It's a work in progress," said Mason.

"What's it called?" he said.

The project had yet to be named. That was the one thing all industry lifers like George needed before they could grant any kind of legitimacy to the venture.

"Um," said Mason.

"It's called *Begging the Question*," said Sophia.

"Isn't that the name of your…"

"Shh."

"*Begging the Question*..." George thought about it. "What's it about?"

Mason handed him a rough outline and the first couple of one-sheets. George looked them over, saying things like, "Uh-huh" and, "How about that?"

"I've never heard of this author," he said. "Eileen Jarman, isn't that your sister?"

"Yes."

"Does she have an agent?"

"I think the agent is waiting to hear if you're on board," said Sophia.

"I never take unsolicited projects from no names," he said. "No offense to your sister or anything. That's just how this business works."

"Tell us again about these stories that are stuck in production and could use character closers like us," said Sophia.

George nodded. "How about that?" he said. "I recognize hardball when I see it." He looked down at the outline. "It's not a bad story." He perused it some more and then sighed heavily. "Give me the agent's name. I'll see what I can work out."

Mason and Sophia smiled. She gave him the card that Eileen had given her, and he recognized it immediately as Lewis' agent. George told Mason and Sophia to wait outside while he made some calls. After a long discussion with the agent and several other calls to character placement agencies, George pulled all the strings within his reach.

Once everything fell into place, he invited his guests back into his office. Before they went home that day, Mason and Sophia joined Union Local 2557, Characters Guild West and the project *Begging the Question* was well on its way to receiving a green light through Lewis' agent and Beforehand Character Placement. They rushed home to tell Eileen the news.

Chapter 31

Production began shortly after the contracts were signed. Eileen, Mason, and Sophia all campaigned heavily to make their apartment the setting, but those plans were nixed when Beforehand rented a smaller apartment just down the street—a decision the producers at the character placement agency told them they'd come to appreciate if the line between their lives and the fictional versions of the characters they were playing started to blur.

The story commenced with Chloe—Sophia's character— riding the light rail home from the Auraria Campus where she worked as a part-time college professor of history at Metropolitan State University. As she clutched a briefcase between her legs to make room for other passengers to sit, her phone vibrated. It was a notification of an email sent to the account Chloe used to solicit questions for her sex and relationship advice column, *Begging the Question*. She opened it.

I've been reading your column now for a few months and this is my first time writing in. A lot of letters started that way. The writer of this letter was a woman who wanted nothing more than for a man to give her anilingus and enjoy it. She wondered how it felt and where to meet a man who was interested in such things.

When she made it home, her boyfriend Jack—played by Mason—was noodling around on his guitar while he watched television.

"Did you take out the trash?" Chloe asked.

"It's out," said Jack. "It was the highlight of my day."

"I'm sure," she said as she placed her briefcase on the floor and rifled through the mail. "Are you making dinner tonight?"

"I could," he said. "Green chile and tortilla chips."

"That's what we had last night."

"Don't you like it?"

"I liked it last night."

"I could do baked potatoes. It'd take an hour."

Chloe sighed. "You know, I have to do research for my column tonight and your lack of motivation is not making it easy. Could you at least think of something sexy to say?"

Chloe also worked for an alternative weekly newspaper in Denver. They needed to find a replacement when the syndicated sex and relationship advice column they ran for years became too expensive for the publication. And since she had a quirky, female-friendly, kink-positive sex and relationship advice blog, they reached out to her. She accepted the job immediately. But since her kinks were very specific—lots of dressing up, role playing, and exhibitionism—she felt compelled to research questions from time to time.

"What now?" Jack asked. When she first landed the job, he was excited for her, assuming it would increase her sex drive. While it certainly multiplied the frequency of sexual congress, it also made it weirder as she grew more curious about the letters she was receiving. And Jack was pretty vanilla when it came to his sexual proclivities.

"I need you to go down on me, but from the other side,"

she said.

He shook his head. "I can't do that."

"Can you at least try? I want to see what it feels like."

He glanced at her, then over towards the fridge, then back at her. "Get a few beers in me and maybe. But you have to shower first."

Chloe met all his demands and even wore his favorite lingerie. She also made a concerted effort to employ her best moves before she asked him to do the thing. But his attempt to fulfill the fantasy of the curious columnist was lackluster at best. He lasted thirty seconds, tops, and then passed out from the beer.

She stayed up in bed for hours that night. She could hear the couple in the apartment next door having ear-piercing, window-rattling sex and she grew envious. They were engaged in extraordinary passion as her unemployed boyfriend snored next to her, filling the room with the scent of exhaled beer.

After she took care of her needs, she responded to the writer who emailed her. While she elucidated at length about technique and the importance of hygiene, the essence of her advice was contained in a few sentences: "Find an employed poet who looks eccentric and comfortable in his own skin, offer him a vodka tonic, and seduce him with a vengeance. If it sounds like such a man doesn't exist, it's because he probably doesn't. There's always Craigslist and/or porn and masturbation."

Once her anger at her boyfriend faded a bit, she erased the sentence about the man not existing. He had to be out there somewhere, right?

. . . .

When Mason and Sophia finished the scene, they ran into Eileen in the hallway, fiercely typing away at her laptop.

"Hey Eileen," said Sophia.

"Hey," she said distractedly. After typing several sentences, she added, "That was great."

"So," said Mason awkwardly. "Was the sex scene weird? You know, because…"

"That's why I stayed out here," she said. "But no, I've heard you have sex before. Besides, that was the only sex scene between you two."

"Really?" said Mason.

"At least for the time being—and besides, right now you're Jack to me."

"But isn't there a lot more sex in the story?" he said to Sophia.

"I was wondering when you'd figure that out," said Sophia. "You didn't read the character development on the synopsis sheet, did you?"

When they arrived back at the apartment, Mason read the sheet, and as he did, he sulked more and more until he got to the end. "You screw other guys in this."

"Yes, I do," said Sophia. "Most of it is standard character sex where there's no feelings involved. We don't even have to have real sex if we don't want to. We could just, you know, dry-hump and stuff like that."

"Still."

"Still what? Listen, I think it's time we set some parameters on what we do with other people."

He scoffed. "How about the parameters just be other people?"

She sighed. "I can't be in a relationship like that," she said. "I told you that about me."

"I know," he said.

Reluctantly Mason agreed as Sophia identified situations where it was okay to partake in sexual offerings and those where it wasn't. For example, sex with people outside their standard social scene was acceptable, as long as it was clearly understood by all affected parties that no strings were attached. Unprotected sex was strictly prohibited in all circumstances, obviously. Siblings or other family members were likewise off the table—a condition that only applied to Sophia's potential suitors, since all her family resided in Kansas and were virtually inaccessible to Mason. And if they started out the evening with each other, they would have to end it that way—so no bailing on dates.

Several hours later, Eileen came home with her laptop under her arm. She looked exhausted. Mason accosted her before she had a chance to make it to her room.

"Eileen, I've been thinking about this. Can my character Jack go to a gender-bending alien rave in the book?" he asked.

"I don't see how that really fits with the story," she said.

"You're the author. You can make it fit."

"No, I'm telling you, it would mess up the story. And besides, it would be a huge production. Lewis told me arranging sci-fi sets can cost thousands."

"Okay, okay," he said. "How about this? Can I befriend a talking dog?"

"An animal that only talks to you? That only you can understand? That's kind of trite, don't you think?"

"How so?" he wondered.

"What, are you serious? *Calvin and Hobbes, Mister Ed, Unhappily Ever After*..."

"*Unhappily Ever After*... Wasn't that the *Married with Children* knockoff where the guy talks to a stuffed puppy?"

"It's a toy rabbit, actually," she said. "He was voiced by

Bobcat Goldthwait. We used to watch it together, remember?"

"That's right," he said. "That was years ago... What a terrible show."

"That's why, no, you can't have a talking animal that only you can understand."

Mason thought about it. He didn't want to perpetuate hackneyed premises. He wanted the novel to succeed.

"How about a talking dog that everyone hears?" Mason said.

"Like the dog in *Family Guy*?"

He sighed. "I get the point you're trying to make, but it's like my high school music teacher said, 'There's nothing new under the sun.' You can't really have a story that's not derivative of something else. Besides, my character's dog will be a beagle named Herman who charms everyone he meets."

"Oh, Herman," she said.

As children, their grandma procured a small runt of a dog named Herman who was one of the tamest, most well-behaved beagles of all time. They always narrated his life with what they imagined he was saying in a voice they imagined he possessed—a low, dopey elocution that loosely mimicked his howl.

In light of her fond reminiscence, Eileen reconsidered it. "That could work, I suppose," she said. "I already emailed them the one-sheet for tomorrow. Let me see if I can add to it."

Mason thanked her as she exasperatedly excused herself to her room so she could work. She kicked off her shoes and leaned back on the bed, resting a few wonderful minutes before firing up her laptop again. She was deep in the throes of a marathon writing spree when she heard a knock at her door.

"Mason, go away!" she screamed.

"It's Sophia."

"What do you want?"

Sophia let herself in. Much like Mason and Eileen, she had almost always lived with a lot of roommates and didn't hold privacy in very high esteem.

"I know you're working, but I have a request for the story," Sophia said. Defeated, Eileen looked at her expectantly in a don't-just-stand-there-hit-me-with-what-you-got kind of way. "Okay, hear me out on this. Jack needs to have a sexual experience with someone else. As a character he needs to be more excited about dating an overly curious sex and relationship advice columnist and being in an open relationship."

"Is that what's best for the character in the story, or is that what's best for your personal life?"

"Can't it be both?"

"Sophia, we are not supposed to discuss the story. I'm the author, you're the character. It's unprofessional."

When representatives from Beforehand had met with Eileen and her agent, they were concerned about a possible conflict of interest due to the close proximity of all involved parties. Both Eileen and George—the latter of which was there on behalf of his characters—assured them that they would refrain from any and all discussions of the story. They had all signed a contract to that effect.

Eileen promised to consider Sophia's proposal, if for no other reason than to get her out of the room so she could focus. The more she typed, though, the more she realized its potential. Perhaps both of their bullshit suggestions were crazy enough to work.

Chapter 32

Jack found Herman the next day when he went to take out the recycling. A stray for weeks, the dog had been rummaging in the neighbor's trash when he heard Jack dumping a load of glass into the recycling bin. Jack had a sneaking suspicion he was the target of wandering eyes, but he shrugged it off, attributing the feeling to the nosey neighbor at the end of the block.

"Psst."

Jack quickly turned around as he manically scanned the alley, his suspicions of being watched seemingly more plausible.

"Psst."

There it was again. He responded randomly to the direction he was facing and said, "What?"

A 20 pound runt of a beagle bounded towards him, as he sang under his breath, "Doot da doot da doot di do."

Jack expected to see the beagle's owner, but the dog didn't appear to have one.

"Hey mister," the beagle said.

Jack stared at the tiny, tri-colored beast. "Are you talking to me?"

It certainly appeared as though Herman was actually speaking. The people at Beforehand must have strapped a tiny speaker around the dog's neck—though it wasn't visible—and perhaps another character provided the voiceover. He sounded nearly identical to the Herman impression Mason and Eileen used to do. It was uncanny.

"Yes, I'm talking to you," said the beagle. "I could use some assistance."

Jack wondered what a small stray could ever possibly need help with. "Um, okay," he said.

"There's a trash can back there that smells like it has taco leftovers in it and I can't quite tip it over. Could you do me a solid and knock it down for me?"

"I don't think so," said Jack.

"Why not?" asked Herman. "I'd do it for you."

"You don't know me."

"If I knew you."

Jack smirked. "Why don't you come inside, and I'll make you tacos?" he said.

"You'd do that for ol' Herman?" asked the dog with an upward inflection at the end of the sentence.

"Yes Herman, I would do that for you," he said with a smile.

"Alright, snack time," said Herman. And as he walked up the stairs to Jack's apartment, he began singing. "Doot da doo..."

"Chloe, we have a talking dog now," yelled Jack as he and Herman walked from the front door to the kitchen.

Chloe didn't acknowledge his proclamation. When she was sitting in her bed and checking her email, she had learned to effectively ignore the sound of his voice. In fact, her brain interpreted his words as, "We're taking a dog out." That didn't make sense and it didn't matter. All of her mental capacity was intently focused on a message from someone that frequently sent her mail from the day she started her column.

Some of these messages were playful, some were cryptic. They never solicited advice, though, so she never felt compelled to answer or publish them. The email she found in her inbox today, however, struck her in a way that none of the others had. It said, *When you tire of the advice seekers, you won't have far to turn.*

Before now she never felt compelled to respond, but she had been in an inquisitive mood all day and couldn't help herself. She hit the "Reply" button and typed the word, *What?* She decided to forego her professional signature for the less formal listing of her name following a dash. She sent it off without considering the potential ramifications.

It wasn't until she logged out of her account that she immediately regretted her decision. Fearing she had just torn the lid off a Pandora's Box of potential madness, she imagined a scenario where she gave an obsessed fan the tiniest bit of attention, and he tracked her down and stalked her. It miffed her enough to sign back into her account so she could send an email to her boss questioning the wisdom of her actions and asking for advice.

She heard the notification vibration on her phone the second she saw the email on her computer. Whoever she sent it to had returned it in less than a minute.

Waves of panic overwhelmed her. Was this going to be one of those situations she read about in horror novels where a deranged lunatic played increasingly cruel mind games with her as she slowly built up enough resolve to overtake him in a fiery, mind-bending denouement? She hoped not. She hated those novels.

Her brow furrowed as she hovered the cursor over the email. She could picture the intensity of an imaginary theatrical score, increasing in volume and tension as she agonized about the message. She knew she wouldn't sleep unless she read it, so she clicked the mouse.

Never mind, the email read.

Chloe was aggrieved, as if someone was deliberately playing with her emotions for some sinister end. She also felt the unmistakable feeling she would get after a bad sexual experience—a lot of emotional investment and needless buildup for nothing other than the disappointment of extreme brevity.

She stared at those two words for a few minutes, trying to extract even a semblance of another meaning that wasn't immediately apparent. But this wasn't a poem. It wasn't open to interpretation. It demanded that Chloe completely forget about the earlier cryptic email—the one that was only open to interpretation.

Her fervent concentration on the matter was violently interrupted by the sudden clatter of C&C Music Factory in the living room. The volume of the stereo practically begged the neighbors to complain. Chloe slammed the screen down on her laptop and left her room with the intention of turning it down and scolding the perpetrator. She had some frustration she needed to unload and any asshole who played "Gonna Make You Sweat" at full volume was a deserving target.

Once she made it to the living room, however, she perked up a bit when she saw Herman and Jack gyrating wildly. Herman's head bobbed up and down, his long ears fluttering around the room, as if he was sitting in the sidecar of a motorcycle going 55 miles an hour. Jack appeared as though he was power walking in place with his thumbs extended. His eyes were closed and he grinned from ear to ear.

Chloe yelled. "Hey!"

But the music was too loud and they just kept dancing. Herman ran over to the lamp on the end table and tried to put the lampshade on his head, but the hole was too big and it dropped around his neck. He twisted his front legs through the opening in the top and it fell around his torso. He laughed uproariously at himself and yelled, "Hey Jack! Hey Jack! Look, I'm a hula dancer!" He balanced himself on his hind legs and wiggled his torso, swaying his front legs to the left and right.

Upon witnessing such a spectacle, Chloe couldn't help but grin. She had never met this strange talking, hula dancing dog and she was enthralled by him. She walked over to the music and gently turned it down.

"Awww," said Jack and Herman.

"Awww, nothing," said Chloe. "You're going to piss off the neighbors."

"Neighbors shmeighbors," said Herman. "We were just getting our groove on."

"Who the fuck are you?" said Chloe.

He puffed out his chest. "I'm Herman, of course."

She looked over to Jack. "Where did you find this guy?"

"In the alley," he said. "He was a stray."

"I was free!" sang Herman.

Chloe laughed. "Herman, you are quite the character."

Herman ran across the floor and stopped just short of her feet. He stared at her longingly in the eyes and said, "I would like for you to pet me now."

She smiled, crouched down, and began petting him as he mumbled, "Oh yeah, that's the stuff right there." Then he rolled on his back and politely suggested she pet his belly.

As she serviced the needs of the beagle, she looked up towards Jack and said, "I got this really weird email."

"Oh no," he said. "You're not going to make me dress in latex and tickle my underbrush with feathers again, are you?"

"Underbrush?" she laughed. "No, nothing like that."

"That just feels so good," muttered Herman.

"Then what?" he said.

"Just come look at it."

Much to Herman's chagrin, they left him alone on the floor as Jack followed Chloe into her room. She opened the conversation thread and watched his face for a reaction as he read it.

"That's pretty vague," said Jack. He reread the words out loud as he furrowed his brow. "Maybe it's just some lonely hippy college kid who's into crystals and thinks he's being clever. You know the type. He probably listens to the Dead and practices alternative medicine."

She shrugged. "I guess that seems feasible."

"It seems likely. Can you imagine anyone else typing something so meaningless?"

"I guess not." Chloe felt much better about the situation.

They were both still sitting in front of her computer when another email popped into her account. Since Jack was at the helm, he instinctively opened it. The message was straightforward: "I'm a 20-something female and my deepest desire is to have sex with a random stranger in public. Do you have any advice for making this happen?"

After Jack read it, he deflated. "Damn it," he said.

"Damn what?"

"You're going to go fuck some random stranger now, aren't you?"

"No, I'm not," she said, though she and Jack knew it was a damned lie. Hell, even Herman knew it was a lie and he was still in the other room.

"Being your boyfriend kind of sucks sometimes. No offense."

"None taken," she said. "Why don't you hook up with someone else? I wouldn't care."

He shrugged. He couldn't imagine where he'd even begin. When he was in college, he knew a guy who was in an open relationship and all it meant was his girlfriend had all the sex she could handle while he awkwardly hit on women and never slept with anyone else. He got the short end of the stick.

"Think about it," she said.

He didn't respond, he just pouted in an attempt to make her feel guilty. But it didn't work; it never worked. The only reason she ever felt bad in those situations was because his behavior made her realize she was dating a manipulative asshole. And assholes always make people feel bad.

But just as the silent tension in the room began to thicken, the beagle bounded in and said, "Who's taking me for a walk?"

Jack immediately turned off the pout and agreed to take him. Chloe was relieved. She was beginning to really like Herman.

Chapter 33

Jack and Herman had been gone for a really long time, so Chloe texted them. Jack replied half an hour later with a selfie of him and Herman at the B-Street Bar. She used the opportunity to head straight to the Cherry Creek Tavern—a bar in which Jack would never deign to set foot. Every weekday, they hosted happy hours where status-seeking social-climbers would drink martinis and compare smart phone photos of their chicly decorated condo interiors. On the weekends, the same patrons engaged in severely out-of-key karaoke renditions of Neil Diamond and Jimmy Buffett songs. The place might as well have been called No Jacks.

There were slim pickings among the men at the tavern that night. Chloe had taken a seat at the far end of bar so she could survey the scene, but most of the seats were occupied by couples and a few groups of cackling women. About halfway through her first drink, she remembered one of her coworkers on the faculty once referred to this place as a "cougar bar," and she spoke the truth. Most of the female clientele were forty-somethings with low-cut dresses and hordes of jewelry.

And of the handful of men in attendance, only one had any sexual appeal and he was a blonde who wore sunglasses inside and a shirt with an arrow pointing to his crotch and the words, "Free Lollipop."

She drained one glass of white wine and was about to head back home when in sauntered a man with slicked back hair, tattoos, and a Social Distortion T-shirt. He moved around the bar with purpose and ease, as though he was gliding. He ordered a whiskey in a glass and then took a seat right next to Chloe.

"Oh, hello," said Chloe.

"Hello," said the sexy stranger.

They sat in silence for several awkward seconds before Chloe said, "Not much of a talker, huh?"

He shook his head. When Chloe asked him his name, he simply said, "Don."

Chloe felt a chill. She remembered something about a strange horror story set in the Colorado mountains where a man named Don saved the protagonist from the ghost of a miner.

"Have you ever heard of *Wrong Turn in Susurrant*?"

Don smiled. "I don't think it's out yet."

"Oh right," said Chloe. "I'm hoping to get a promo copy. I'm a journalist."

"I know. I've read your work. It's quite spectacular."

"Spectacular? Oh my! Well, thank you."

"And now that I met you, might I add that you're spectacular as well?"

"Oh."

"And your eyes..."

"Spectacular?"

"Indeed."

"Okay. You know you really need to come up with another adjective. You're not making much of an impact here."

He apologized and drank some of his whiskey. "Your eyes

are striking," he said after he cleared his throat. "And your tattoo intriguing."

"Thank you," she said flatly. "So Don, where are you from?"

"Well..." The pauses between his sentences were excruciating. He was very deliberate with every word, carefully constructing responses as to not waste a syllable. "It's not where I'm from... It's where I am."

"That's very deep."

"Hmm," he grunted and then slowly drank his whiskey. "We've communicated before."

"We have, huh?"

"I sent an email. When you tire of advice seekers…"

"…You won't have far to turn," said Chloe. "What does that mean?"

He stroked his chin in contemplation before he answered. "People who seek answers come to you."

"Well yeah, it's kind of my job."

"Being a wise soul grows stale and boring."

"Hmm," said Chloe. "I guess I can see that happening at some point."

"It will happen… Just don't forget to dance."

She smiled. "Fair enough."

He smiled at her alluringly. Chloe wanted to jump on him and take him right there at the bar, but social mores and years of slut shaming prevented her from this course of action. So she found herself in the position of sweet-talking a man for sex—a situation with which she had had little experience.

"So what do you like to do, Don?" she said.

"Dance, and have sex," he said.

Maybe it wouldn't be so difficult.

"Boy are you in luck..." she said.

The bathrooms at the Cherry Creek Tavern were much cleaner than standard bar facilities. They didn't reek of urine or contain trash cans overflowing with wet paper towels. And the fact that they were single occupancy really benefited both sex fiends and coke heads.

Chloe didn't have any drugs, but she was standing in the bathroom with the clear intent of making passionate love. She felt sheer ecstasy when she tore Don's T-shirt off his body. In all her years of exhibitionism, she had taken off a lot of clothes in public restrooms (generally with long-term boyfriends), but this was the first time she had disrobed a complete stranger.

She discovered quickly that Don was a man without inhibitions. He explored every curiosity Chloe mentioned with passion and without shame. She climaxed on three separate occasions and brought Don to orgasm—at the height of which he screamed, "I haven't felt this good in 250 years!" Although she had no idea what that meant, she was glad he didn't say, "Spectacular."

Once they gathered their clothes and unlocked the door, they were greeted by the disapproving stares of the bar staff and customers. Apparently the house stereo receiver blew a fuse at the exact moment Chloe had her first orgasm, so she treated everyone in the establishment to earfuls of orgasmic delight.

"We were just leaving," said Chloe.

"Yeah you were," said the bartender. "I better not have to clean up a mess in there."

"We were careful," she said.

They picked up the pace and got the hell out of there. Once they were outside and a block or so away, Chloe kissed Don passionately.

"I will see you again," said Don.

"Oh," she said. "I don't think so."

He nodded, hugged her one last time, and turned to walk away. She said goodbye to his back and he raised his left hand in the air without uttering a word. When he thought he was out of sight, he jumped up, clicked his heels, and shouted, "Hooray!" Chloe saw the whole thing and laughed to herself. She considered jumping and clicking her heels, but decided against it due to the likelihood she would hurt herself. She imagined trying to explain any injuries she might sustain from such an action and carefully walked in the other direction.

. . . .

Herman and Jack also fared pretty well. The second they took stools at the bar, a flock of admirers gathered around the handsome-looking, wise-cracking beagle. When the bartender tried to take his order, he claimed his drinking days were behind him, but he did take a few slurps of spilt beer from the bar. He wasn't drunk, per se, but he displayed the smile of a dog with a mighty buzz. He was telling old jokes and borrowing hair ties so he could put his ears in a ponytail. At one point he even moonwalked on the bar. (Although, technically he didn't actually moonwalk, he awkwardly stumbled backwards on his hind legs, knocking over drinks and menus in the process. Everyone loved it all the same.) He also taught everyone the words to "Hooka Tooka" so they could have a drunken sing-along.

After a few hours of carousing and cavorting, they ordered waters and journeyed to the patio. Once outside, a swarm of Herman's fans trickled out, and he continued to regale them with tales from when he was a stray up until a few days ago. If he could hold a pen, he'd be signing autographs.

"Your dog is amazing," said a young twenty-something woman wearing a Tortured Metaphor t-shirt. She had short, curly hair that was dyed red, cut-off black jean shorts, and a lot of very colorful tattoos of '50s pinup girls, birds, and dragons.

Jack saw what she was wearing and smirked. "That's a cool shirt."

"Thanks," she said. "Have you heard of these guys? They were a local band."

"Yeah I've heard of 'em," he said.

"You kind of look like the lead singer."

He let out exactly one laugh. "Ha," he said. "No, I was never in Tortured Metaphor. I was in another band."

"Oh yeah? Would I have heard of them?"

"Maybe. We were called Deadly Optimism."

"Hmm, never heard of it."

"We were huge in Eastern Europe."

"Oh, yeah, I've never been there."

"It's beautiful."

"Is it?"

"Yes," he said. "Especially this time of year."

"Okay okay, who wants to rub my belly next?" Herman asked of his sycophants who eagerly complied with his request.

The woman with the colorful tattoos practically melted as she smiled. "My name is Bonnie," she said, extending her hand towards Jack's.

"Hey Bonnie, I'm Jack," he said as he shook her hand.

"Oh yeah, your hands are like magic," the beagle muttered.

"Do you want to get a drink at my place?" Bonnie asked. "My roommate and her dog are camping and she has a waterbed. I think Herman might like it. Spike—that's her dog—he loves it."

"Hey Herman!" Jack shouted.

"Mmm, are you a masseuse?" Herman said to a woman petting him.

"Herman!"

"I'm busy, Jack."

"Ever been on a waterbed?"

Herman thought about it. He knew the words "water" and "bed," but he never heard them together. He pictured a small pool in a bedroom with a floating mattress on top. It sounded relaxing.

"Ever been petted by two people on a waterbed?" Bonnie said.

"No, I have not," said Herman. "If you'll excuse me, ma'am. I appreciate the superior petting you've been treating me to, but I must be leaving now. Apparently there is a bed made of water that I must experience." He bounced over towards Jack and said, "Alright! Waterbed party!"

When they arrived at her house, they were greeted by a large trash bag leaning on the wall next to the front door. Bonnie cursed her roommate, who was supposed to take it out to the curb before she left. She invited them in before excusing herself momentarily to drag the bag out before the city trucks collected the trash in the morning.

Herman ran straight for the waterbed and promptly hopped onto it. Jack petted him deeply and told him how handsome he was as his eyelids grew heavier and heavier. By the time Bonnie made it back into the house, he was fast asleep.

Bonnie petted him for a few moments before whispering to Jack. "Come on, let's let him sleep."

She took Jack's hand and led him out of the room, closing the door behind her. She didn't latch it in case Herman needed access to the water or dog door in the middle of the night.

"Do you want to watch a movie?" Bonnie asked. Of course, the invitation was merely a ploy to get close enough to one another without any undue awkwardness so they could commence making out and heavy petting.

Jack agreed and sat on the couch as Bonnie rattled off potential films to watch. She chose *Howard the Duck* because Jack admitted he had never seen it. They didn't even make it through the opening credits before they began caressing, osculating, and no-strings-attached fornication—the specifics of which dared not appear in print due to the author's tendency to get squicked out when broaching such topics.

A half hour or so later—maybe longer, because who was keeping track?—everyone in the house was fast asleep. Herman made gentle waves in the waterbed with his snoring and Bonnie and Jack nestled like spoons in her regular bed.

Chapter 34

Jack and Herman didn't make it home until the next afternoon. When they walked through the front door, Chloe was typing out advice on sex with strangers in public places. *Choose a bar or restaurant with a clean, single-occupancy bathroom,* she wrote. *And try not to climax too loudly—especially if the establishment's sound system isn't in good working order.*

Even though Jack knew he had permission to sleep with other people, he still slouched under the crushing weight of guilt. He couldn't bring himself to face his primary lover—in fact he would have been home a few hours sooner if he hadn't procrastinated by taking Herman to a dog park after he left Bonnie's.

He didn't make eye contact with Chloe as he attempted to walk briskly past while she sat with her laptop at the dining room table. Of course, Chloe wasn't about to let him slink by without any explanation.

"So," she said, "You guys were out pretty late, huh?"

There was a twinge of jealousy in her voice, because even people in open relationships experience irrational insecurities.

"Yeah, we went to a house party after the bar," he said. "Herman and I passed out on the floor."

"Hmm," she said.

"I have to go to the bathroom," said Jack, who made a beeline straight for the only room in the apartment with a locking door. He must have sat in there for half an hour.

"So Herman tells me he slept on a waterbed last night," said Chloe the second Jack emerged from hiding.

"Herman said that, did he?" he asked. She nodded. He looked over at Herman.

"Don't you remember?" Herman said. "At Bonnie's place, she let me sleep on a waterbed and I made waves."

"Thanks Herman. I almost forgot."

"I got your back, Jack," said the dog.

She looked at Jack, wide eyed and incredulous. "Who's Bonnie?"

"She's...uh..." He stared at the ground wishing there were some kind of explanation down there waiting to be discovered. "She's this girl I slept with last night."

Chloe smiled. All she wanted was the truth, and now that she had it, her rational thought-process kicked in again. She reached out and lovingly held both his hands as she gently told him to follow her to the couch where they could sit down to talk.

"Why did you lie to me and hide in the bathroom?" she said as Herman leapt next to her on the couch, demanding her affection.

"Because..." He couldn't think of a good answer. "Well, because I don't want to hurt you."

"We have an arrangement. You know it isn't going to hurt me."

"I know, but it still felt like—I don't know—like I was wronging you somehow."

"Well, get over it.

Simultaneously, Jack felt like a weight had been lifted from his being as another weight fell on his lap. The former was a figurative mass that would no longer burden him, while the latter was a literal Herman who grew tired of Chloe's love and needed a welcoming lap on which to nod off.

"Okay," said Jack with a shrug as he affectionately stroked the beagle's back.

Chloe hugged Jack and Herman at the same time. Herman made a low level humming sound and then said, "Alright, Herman sandwich!" The humans laughed while the dog appreciated life, as he was wont to do.

"Let me ask you something," she said after resuming her position on the couch. "Do you love me any less, you know, now that you've slept with someone else?"

It was an absurd question. Of course he still loved her. He shook his head. "No, not at all."

"And I still love you," she said.

"I know. And I get it. What you're trying to say—I get it."

"Good."

· · · ·

Mason and Sophia walked back to his house together. They were both exhausted from the grueling hours of character work and needed some time to unwind mentally and physically.

Of course when they arrived at the apartment, they found Eileen typing furiously on the couch with her laptop balanced on her lap. She was drinking black tea and had dark circles under her eyes. It looked as though she hadn't slept in days.

"Eileen," Mason said, "you okay? You look...uh..." He considered the most tactful way to phrase it. "You look not good."

She hardly paid him any attention as she kept writing.

"Eileen!" Mason said louder.

"What?"

"Maybe you should take a break."

She glared at him, said the word "no," and took a long drink of tea.

"Well she sure told you, buddy," said Sophia. "Come on." She took Mason by the hand and led him to his bedroom.

He knew Sophia wanted to talk about the big picture and whether or not he had learned any lessons from their character placement adventures. But all he was in the mood for was sex and sleep—not necessarily in that order.

So once they made it behind the closed doors of his room, she surprised him by immediately initiating sex. She cradled his crotch with her hands and told him to get naked—a request he wasted no time fulfilling. She disrobed and treated him to some of the best fellatio of his life. He couldn't remember his name while she went to town down there. Then she stopped, leaned up, and kissed him fervently before taking the dominant role in wildly passionate intercourse.

Fortunately for Eileen, she remained overly invested in her writing and only noticed the hyperactive amorous carnality when Mason shouted, "Are you prepared to accept the seed of Jarman?" At first she cringed at the thought, but then she remembered it was a line Mason once hypothetically attributed to Henry Rollins right before he came—substituting "Rollins" for "Jarman," of course. She smiled at the thought, feeling grateful to have something kicking around that brain of hers to make the current situation less weird.

The brief distraction made her realize she really needed to use the bathroom, so she set the laptop next to her on the couch and ran across the apartment. When she returned, her phone was vibrating on the coffee table, but by the time she picked it up, it was too late to answer. It was Lewis, so she hurriedly called him back.

They exchanged pleasantries; he inquired about her progress on the story. She didn't have any idea whether or not it was any good, she admitted, and that filled her with uncertainty.

"You're always going to feel inadequate that your prose doesn't stack up against Harper Lee's or Jane Austen's, and that's okay," said Lewis. "Even if you tried to write like them, you'd be a sorry knockoff of a writer—a poseur, if you will. And you know I hate that word, but in this instance it works." There was silence on the line and he could almost hear her insecurity. "You know how I told you about my brother, the drummer?" he continued. "He always says, 'I'm not Gene Krupa or Neil Peart, but I always leave a distinctive mark on whatever band I'm in.' And what that means is that he has his own style, one that he developed. You don't have to be Harriet Beecher Stowe. You don't have to be Louisa May Alcott. You just have to be good at being you."

"'You just have to be good at being you?'" she asked incredulously. "You know, that just doesn't help. Not even a little."

"Yeah, it's the same line of shit one of my buddies told me when I started freelancing after I dropped out of high school. It didn't work then and it doesn't work now."

"So why did you bother trying to use it on me?"

"I don't know," he admitted. "I suppose it's fortunate I'm not a motivational speaker."

Eileen agreed.

"Anyway, the point is to keep writing through the doubt. You'll have moments where you think you're brilliant and moments where you think you're shit. It's all part of it. If it was easy, fucking everyone would do it."

"How do you know what parts to write about?" she said.

"Well, for one thing, the characters are there for your benefit, so you choose the parts of the story you want to present to the reader. It's what a good writer does. And the other thing you have to think about—did you ever read any Howard Zinn?"

"Oh yeah, I love that guy."

"He wrote nonfiction, of course. But his whole thing was to present history from the perspective of those who got the short end of the historical stick—like the discovery of America through the eyes of Native Americans and not Europeans, or the Constitution through the eyes of slaves and not property-owning white males…"

"Yeah," she said. "I remember when I read *People's History of the United States*. It was the first time I realized that history even had a perspective. In high school, it was always just presented as a bunch of facts."

"Right," he said excitedly. "That's what you have to do, present your narrative from a perspective that no one's presented before. Pretend that you're the only one on the face of the earth who can tell this story."

Eileen mulled it over. She was fairly certain she had been taking his advice from the beginning, but that still didn't settle her insecurity. Perhaps no one could judge whether or not her work was adequate until it was published. And by then, the critics and online armchair reviewers would be tearing it apart and it would be too late.

"Am I even getting through to you at all?" he wondered.

"A little, I guess," she said.

"Promise me one thing: Just don't stop. You have a lot of people pulling a lot of strings to open this opportunity for you, and if you quit now, the door to this industry will close."

"Not to put the pressure on or anything."

"Pressure is good. It lights a fire under your ass."

"My ass is already hot," she said. She couldn't hear him nodding.

· · · ·

The story resumed a week later with Jack taking the light rail to the campus where she worked to surprise Chloe on her lunch break. She had left her meal container on the counter that morning and Jack felt bad enough to bring it to her.

By the time he arrived at the lounge in the Tivoli where she generally took her meals, she had already procured her lunch—a ham and cheese sub from a fast food chain—and was dining next to a muscular man with blonde hair and a dark tan. Judging by the look of confusion and borderline dread on her face, she wasn't exactly ecstatic to see him.

"Jack," she said, "what are you doing here?"

"I brought you your lunch," he said. "But it looks like you already got another one."

"Uh, yeah," she said.

She attempted to hide her sandwich from him by shielding it with her hands. Since he was a lifelong vegetarian (vegan for the last ten years), he was extremely disapproving of the very sight and smell of meat. He was like Morrissey in that regard.

Mostly, Chloe didn't mind the diet she dated into. But every now and again she would either accidentally forget her lunch or deliberately leave it behind so she could enjoy the convenience and deliciousness of nutritionally devoid cuisine that was so prevalent in the American diet.

And while she savored her forbidden meals without the glaring eyes of Jack, she also made it a point to flirt with young twenty-somethings who sported tans and rock hard bodies, because why not? If Jack had a job working in such close proximity with so many young, good looking people—in fact, if he had a job at all—he'd take full advantage of opportunities such as this. Or at least, that was what Chloe had convinced herself in order to alleviate any potential feelings of guilt about the situation.

The other aspect of her very informal lunch dates that she appreciated was the lack of both bitterness and misanthropy of her dining partners. Unlike Jack, these young adults were fresh faced and wide-eyed. They assumed they could bring the world to its knees and live luxurious lives where they would never have to settle for anything. Their futures were only bounded by the limitations of their imaginations. The cruelty of reality hadn't crushed their dreams into a fine powder and swept it under the rug the way it had to a majority of thirty-somethings. It was a nice change of pace.

Jack dropped the container on the table. "I guess I'll see you later," he said.

As he began to walk away, Chloe said, "Wait."

He turned around expectantly, but she couldn't think of anything to add.

"What?" he said.

"Hmm," she said. "You... You look good."

His eyes narrowed. He desperately fought the urge to tell her to fuck off as he grimaced at her incredulously. Balling his fists by his side, he turned and angrily strode away.

"Well, that dude was pissed," said the young, dashing man.

"Yes," said his professor. "He certainly was."

Jack walked through the campus as thoughts of fury permeated his brain. He couldn't determine whether he was more upset about Chloe's meat eating or her fresh-faced companion. Since he was trying to find peace with the concept of an open relationship, he attributed his white-hot frustrations to her ham and cheese sub, which was an egregious affront to decency and everything in which Jack believed, he told himself. Of course, somewhere deep within his being, he knew that it wasn't true, but at the moment he was filled with rage, so he let his brain fire off mental accusations as fast as he could think of them.

His indignation didn't last long, however. Since it was nearing the end of May, a large portion of the female students celebrated the warmer weather with more revealing attire, and Jack couldn't help but notice the tans and rock hard bodies of the young women walking past. In fact, he treated himself to a seat on a bench so he could concentrate on the view at hand.

In keeping with his own inner-narrative that he was a decent guy—and not some old creepy pervert—he only spectated for a few minutes before continuing on his way home. But after a few steps, he was detoured once again by a spectacular view of a man and woman walking together, both of whom seemed to be chiseled out of stone.

He followed the couple into the Arts building where they quickly disappeared behind throngs of other students. With absolutely nothing else on his agenda for the day, he wandered around the building, reading announcements for art shows and flyers for concerts.

And then he came across a handwritten notice that intrigued him. It read: "Needed: singer/guitarist for post-hardcore band. Think: Fugazi, Mclusky/Future of the Left, Nomeansno, Alice Donut, and Minutemen. You: Sing and play guitar with delicate fury (or ferocious delicacy), write songs, and believe firmly in the power of absurdity. We: Play bass and drums, write songs, briefly considered a two-piece, cancelled those plans, and are now looking for you." It listed both a number and an email address. Jack ripped the notice off the wall in order to quell any potential competitors.

Ordinarily he would've emailed the creators of the flyer, but for whatever reason he felt a nagging sense of urgency, so he pulled out his phone and called. No one answered so he left a message and crossed his fingers for a response.

The thought of Chloe with her young man friend and meat-filled sandwich long behind him, Jack raced home and played his guitar until his fingers were sore. Then he picked up a pen and a notebook and wrote two new songs in a matter of hours. It was the best he'd felt in nearly seven years.

Chapter 35

When Chloe didn't make it home for dinner that night, Jack assumed she was making sweet love to the strapping blonde man she was sitting with at lunch. Instead of wasting his time and energy analyzing and agonizing about it, he texted Bonnie with a question that was seemingly innocuous yet loaded with innuendo: "What are you up to?" She texted back the equally ambiguous, "Nothing. How about you?"

After several non-committal texts, they both eased their way down to brass tacks, culminating in Bonnie's invitation to bring Herman over so they could all watch movies together. Jack quickly equipped Herman with his leash, lured him with promises of a waterbed (his response: "Alright waterbed!"), and ran out the door.

When they arrived, Herman instantly bounded to her roommate's room to make some waves. Bonnie and Jack followed him so they could offer their petting services. Once again, the beagle succumbed to superior relaxation and fell asleep within a few minutes.

"Your roommate won't mind Herman sleeping here?" whispered Jack.

"She's gone again," Bonnie said. "She and Spike and her boyfriend took a road trip to the west coast. They won't be back for a week."

"They sure go out of town a lot," said Jack.

"She's a trustfunder… Come here." Bonnie led Jack over to her coffee table where three DVDs were laid out.

"Are we going to watch all of these?" said Jack.

"No, this time I'm going to let you pick the movie," she said.

Before them were the following titles: *Ghostbusters*, *Titanic*, and *So I Married an Axe Murderer*. Jack weighed the pros and cons of each. "How about this," he said, as he picked up *So I Married an Axe Murderer*. "If we skip the scene where they're at the butcher shop."

"Are you vegetarian?" she said.

"Yes. Well, I'm vegan actually."

"I'm vegan too. Well, mostly vegan. I'm 100% vegetarian and 99% vegan."

"That's cool. What makes you only 99% vegan?"

"Don't laugh when I say this, but white cheddar popcorn."

Jack laughed. "Seriously? White cheddar popcorn?"

"Yes, I love it, but I only eat it, like, once a month."

"They make vegan versions of that, you know?"

"I know, but they don't taste as good as the original."

Jack smirked and immediately felt a pang of guilt. He could tell he was falling deep in like with this woman and it scared him. He shook his head.

"What?" said Bonnie. "It doesn't taste as good. I promise."

"No, I was shaking my head for a different reason."

Bonnie pressed him for more information, and Jack was as forthcoming as he felt he needed to be. He told her about Chloe and their relationship status and she explained her situation, which was similar—though her boyfriend lived in another time zone. For practical reasons, Jack failed to mention the nascent crush he was developing on her.

It didn't take long for them to drop the subject all to-gether. Sensitive to the conversational pitfalls they were navigating, Jack picked up the movie and suggested they watch it. They never made it to the scene in butcher shop, however, since she initiated physical contact shortly after the opening credits. What began on the couch soon ended in her bedroom, and they lay in each other's arms for what seemed hours.

Eventually they decided to get dressed so they could take Herman for a walk and swing by the corner liquor store for some booze. When they returned to the house, the beagle took up residence on the water bed, and the couple drank and watched almost the entirety of the movie they started earlier, sans the scene of contention. They tried to be inti-mate one last time before bed, but ended up passing out cold before anything exciting happened.

Around eight the next morning, Jack awoke to use the restroom. On his way back to bed, he went to check on Her-man, but couldn't find him. Although Jack wasn't initially concerned, he felt compelled enough to keep looking, if for nothing else than peace of mind. He checked every room of the house, but Herman wasn't in any of them. His concern grew and he began calling the dog's name as his search became more frantic. He scanned the house, and as his glance passed the front door, he realized it was open and the screen door had a Herman-sized hole in it.

He bolted out of the house wearing nothing but his box-er shorts. He looked up and down the street, but nothing caught his eye. He yelled the dog's name, but there was no answer. Just as he was on the verge of running back up to Bonnie's room for his clothes and shoes—so he could con-vene a proper search party—he heard a choking sound emanating from a trash bag.

"Herman," said Jack as he ran towards the pile of trash bags on the curb.

He began tearing at the plastic as trash and debris flew everywhere. On the last bag he ripped open, he felt the dog's torso and pulled it free, but it was lifeless and limp. Herman wasn't breathing.

"Oh shit, oh shit," said Jack. "Herman! No Herman, don't die." He was shaking the animal as Bonnie came running out.

"What's happening?" Bonnie said.

"Herman's suffocating."

"Oh fuck."

"What should we do?"

"I don't know!"

They were both paralyzed with fear. Jack was afraid they were going to lose the beagle and he couldn't imagine that was how the story was supposed to go. Something was genuinely wrong. Herman's gums were a greyish white and his eyes were rolled back in his head.

At that moment, a woman came running down the street. She had dyed jet black hair and two full sleeves of tattoos. It looked an awful lot like the author of the story.

Bonnie gently patted Herman's face in the hope that he would respond, but he was lifeless.

"Give me the dog," the running woman said when she made it to Jack and Bonnie.

"Eileen," said Jack, "what are you doing here?"

She didn't answer the question. She just snatched Herman, checked for his pulse and to see if he was breathing. She laid the dog on the sidewalk and began giving him mouth-to-nose CPR—one breath every two to three seconds. After a half minute that seemed like a century, Herman started coughing and convulsing.

276

A human voice was coming from his throat now. "Aaaaah," it said. "Shit."

Herman's head shook back and forth and began spasming uncontrollably. Then he momentarily stood as still as a rock before levitating several feet off the ground. In flash of blinding light, the beagle contorted and a man took shape through the dog's back. With a loud snapping noise, the two split and launched to separate sides of the yard.

Jack ran over to Herman to check on his well being. He shook the dog and asked if he was okay, and although he appeared unscathed, he didn't say anything.

"Herman?" Jack said, cradling the dog in his arms.

"He's not going to respond," said the man.

Jack knew that voice. His brow furrowed as he slowly moved his head in its direction. "Uncle Ernest?"

"Hey Mason," Ernest said. "Or should I say 'Jack?'"

"I don't know," said Jack. "Eileen, do you have any idea what to do here?"

"I have no idea," she said. "I just wrote myself into my own story so I could save Herman and Unkie Ernest."

"How did you even know how to do CPR on a dog?" said Mason.

"I saw it on a reality show about veterinarians," Eileen said.

"That's unreal," said Ernest.

"Ernest, what the hell were you doing in the garbage bag anyway?" Jack yelled.

"Eileen brought me back as Herman," he said. "I was just getting into character. Besides, it's her fault." He pointed at Bonnie.

"Don't look at me," she said. "How was I supposed to know they were going to suffocate in the garbage?" She pointed at Herman with one hand and Ernest with the other.

"You threw away taco leftovers," said Ernest. "They're our favorite."

"You got carried away," said Eileen. "You weren't supposed to go inside the bag."

"But I found the motherload! There was a whole thing of refried black beans in there."

"You threw away a whole thing of refried black beans?" shouted Jack. "Well, no shit then. Hell I would have risked my life for a whole thing of refried black beans."

"See?" said Ernest to Bonnie.

"The one-sheet said to throw away beans and there weren't any other kinds of beans on set," said Bonnie. "So yeah, I threw away the beans they gave me."

"I guess it's Beforehand's fault then," said Eileen.

"This is all so confusing," said Jack. "Are we even still in the story."

"We have to be," said Eileen. "Uncle Ernest is still here and he can only live in fiction. Don't worry, I'll write it all down later. That's why it's in past tense."

"Really?" Jack wondered. "That's how writers decide on which tense to use?"

"No, no. It's not like authors who can write really fast use present tense. It's more complicated than that."

"I see," said Jack, whose tone reflected his waning interest in the subject.

"You asked," she said.

Jack shrugged and then turned to Ernest. "That was a very good portrayal of Herman, by the way," he said.

"Thank you," he replied.

"That's the exact voice we used to give him," said Eileen.

"I know," said Ernest. "I remember that dog. He was something else."

"He sure was," said Jack longingly.

Eileen, Jack, and Ernest all beamed at the thought of their former canine companion. Jack still had the other Herman in his hands.

"What do we do with this dog?" he said. "Can we keep him?"

"The Front Range Beagle Rescue Fund loaned him to Beforehand as a foster dog," Eileen said. "He's been living with his foster mom in between the action."

"I'm giving him to Mason," said Jack.

"That's fine," said Eileen. "We can figure out all the details."

"Well shit," said Jack. "It's early in the morning. As long as we're still on the clock, why don't we go get a drink? Eileen, you can make the next scene at the bar, right?"

"Yeah sure."

"And Beforehand picks up the tab, right?" Jack asked.

Eileen explained how any expenses incurred by the characters had to be recouped by her royalties.

"Yeah, but this book's going to sell a million copies, so…" said Jack.

She smirked. "Maybe," she said. Like any writer, she consistently imagined the kind of lifestyle and universal admiration a bestselling book would afford her. "But don't worry about any of that now. I think we could all use a drink."

Chapter 36

"Chloe says she'll meet us here," said Eileen, reading a text message from her phone.

They were seated at a table in the back of the B-Street Bar. Everyone had a drink, including Herman, who sat in a chair at the table with a bowl of water in front of him. Jack loaded up the jukebox with ten dollars worth of punk and indie tunes so no one could play music he deemed substandard—a ritual he performed nearly every time he went drinking.

"So what's it like being dead?" Jack asked Ernest.

"Kind of unexciting," he said. "Definitely anticlimactic. All that angst you were feeling about life, it's laughable to think anyone could feel that way."

"Why?" asked Jack.

"Because you die eventually. After that, it doesn't matter."

Jack laughed. "So you're telling me not to worry about anything because one day I'll be dead?"

"Exactly."

"I think it'd be hard to keep that perspective all the time, you know? Especially as someone who still has a few decades ahead of him," said Jack.

"I understand that," said Ernest. "But you were desperate for advice when I was alive. Now that I'm dead, I can officially say,

'Don't worry about it.' All this worrying you do, you're going to feel silly about it when you die. It's a tacky way to live." He took a long pull from his drink.

Jack thought "tacky" was a tacky word to use, but he didn't want to disrespect the spirit of his uncle, so he kept mum. "Since when can dead people drink?" he asked instead.

"Since they began appearing in novels," he replied. "This is the only time I get to really let loose."

"So being dead is boring?" Bonnie said.

"It is, in a way. It's not like there's shuffleboard or anything."

"I could write some shuffleboard playing into the story if you want," said Eileen.

The cocktail server interrupted the conversation to inquire about the status of their drinks. Everyone ordered another one.

As she went back to the bar to fill the order, Ernest explained that he didn't even know how to play shuffleboard. He just thought of a stereotypical activity of retirees for the sake of conversational merriment.

"Do you talk to other dead people?" asked Kate.

"Sometimes. I spoke with one of your friends, Ma-, I mean, Jack. An interesting soul named Don."

"Don!" said Jack with a smile. "How's he doing?"

"Good. Did you know he plays the banjo?"

"No," he said. "That never came up."

"When I spoke with him, he was getting ready to appear in your story," Ernest pointed at Eileen. "He was happy that he was about to make love again after a couple centuries, or however long it's been."

Jack's brow furrowed. He suspected he didn't want to know the answer to the question he was about to ask, but he knew it would torment him if it didn't say anything. "Who did he have sex with?"

"Uh," said Ernest.

No one said anything for several excruciating seconds. "Well?" Jack said.

"Well what?" Eileen said. "He had sex with Chloe."

Jack looked defeated. "That's...um..." He couldn't finish the sentence.

"We'll talk about it later," said Eileen.

"Talk about what later?" said Chloe, who had just arrived.

"Nothing!" Eileen and Ernest shouted.

"Oh-kay," she said. She scanned the faces of those present and focused on Bonnie. "Hello, I'm Chloe." She extended her hand.

Bonnie reached out and shook it. "I'm Bonnie," she said.

"Oh, *you're* Bonnie. Very nice to meet you."

"Likewise."

With Chloe so outwardly eager to meet his mistress, Jack knew he didn't have much of a right to his feelings of betrayal. He downed the rest of his drink and flagged the server for another.

"Get me one, too," said Chloe. Her eyes were swollen and she carried an aura of exhaustion.

"What's wrong, Chloe?" asked Ernest.

"Oh, I just got fired from my advice column. They're going to replace me with a pot columnist."

"Advice on how to smoke grass?" said Ernest. "Hell, I could write that."

"I think it's going to focus on the industry. They really just need relevant content to draw readers to their pot advertisements."

"Well shit," Jack said.

"Let's not worry about me," she said. "We're all together again. Let's drink to us and I'll worry about my shit later."

Since it was a creative setback and not necessarily

a financial one (she was only paid $50 a column), the atmosphere improved when Chloe got her drink. After that, it didn't take long before the conversation devolved into a round table of stand-up comedy, with each participant trying his or her best to one-up the last. Even Herman had a great time. Although he couldn't talk anymore, he still charmed the wait staff, who petted him extensively and gave him half the dog treats from a basket behind the bar.

Around three in the afternoon, Jack received a call from the number listed on the flyer he found on campus. He excused himself and answered it outside.

The jubilation of hope joined forces with the alcohol coursing through his system, and Jack returned to the bar with his face lit up. His cohorts hadn't seen him smile like that for a long time. He was almost laughing when he got to the table.

"What are you so smiley about?" said Chloe.

"I'm going to be in a band again," he said.

"Really?" asked Ernest. "Just like that?"

"Just like that," he said. "They've heard of Deadly Optimism and I was hired without an audition. I mean, they did say, 'Let's see if it clicks obviously.' But I think I'm in. We all really like the same bands."

"Congratulations Jack," said Ernest. "Now I'm not going to have to haunt you."

Jack laughed. "Can you really haunt people?" he said.

"Oh, I don't know. I've heard of it happening, but I don't have the kind of temperament to go in for it."

"Who would you haunt if you could haunt anyone?" Jack asked. He was feeling euphoric and playful. It was like the world had shifted its weight and all of a sudden Jack wasn't burdened by it anymore.

Ernest pondered his question. "Historically or people alive

now?" he said.

"People alive now," Jack insisted. "It doesn't make sense to haunt dead people."

"I was assuming we might have access to a time machine in this hypothetical situation," he said.

Jack sighed in mock exasperation. "You can actually haunt people, Uncle Ernest. And unless death destroys our sense of time and you can travel freely into the past, then no, you do not have access to a time machine." He banged his hands on the table as he spoke. Everyone in attendance was laughing—including his uncle.

"Okay, no I can't travel back in time, so I guess I can't haunt Hitler or Reagan... Oh, how about George W. Bush? I could pretend to be the ghost of Saddam Hussein."

"Good answer," said Eileen.

They all came up with their own answers of who they would haunt. From beyond the grave, Jack would go after Rupert Murdoch, writing passages of the *Communist Manifesto* (or the Sermon on the Mount) in the steam of his bathroom mirror. Eileen would vex the grand wizard of the KKK, taking a Bic lighter to a tiny cross over his bed as he and his wife slept. Chloe would scare Bill Cosby with even more accusations. And Bonnie would appear in the presence of Dave Grohl—not to exact revenge, but to hang out.

As mid-afternoon grew into early evening, Eileen informed the group that the chapter was nearing its end. Although they hated the idea of this scene ever concluding, they agreed that after several hours of drinking, they should probably get some food.

Jack turned to Earnest. "So what's going to happen to you?"

"I go back," he said.

"Are you just going to disappear?"

"Something like that. I think I'll hit the john and do it in there so I don't freak anyone out."

"Are we going to see you tomorrow?" he said. Ernest shrugged. "Eileen, what's the production schedule for tomorrow?"

"I don't know yet," she said. "I need to make new one-sheets for the rest of the week. I've screwed up everything by making an appearance in my story."

Ernest went to the bathroom and didn't come out. And then the scene was over.

. . . .

On their way out of the bar, and once Sophia was out of earshot, Mason asked Bonnie—whose real name was Molly—if she wanted to hang out sometime, maybe get some vegan food. She was less than ecstatic about the proposal.

"I'm sorry, but no," she said.

"Oh," Mason said, visually taken aback. "I thought there was something between us there."

She smirked "You know we're just playing characters here," she said. "I'm not even vegan and I hate cheddar popcorn."

The afternoon had gone so well for Mason's character, so he wasn't expecting such a crushing real-life defeat. "Hmm," he sort of said.

"You seem charming and everything; I mean, if the character you're playing is anything like you. I just try not to get involved with people from work."

"I see."

"Don't get me wrong, the sex was great, and everything. I love being sensual with characters. It's very artistic and all.

And thanks for being open minded about the sex toys and everything. But, well, you know…"

Mason let out another half-audible sound that wasn't positive or negative. She leaned over, kissed him on the cheek, and said goodbye.

When Sophia returned from the bathroom, he was extremely happy to see her. Once he discovered his new crush had no interest in him, he felt relieved to be able to fall back on his old girlfriend.

"Where's Bonnie?" Sophia asked.

"Her name's Molly," said Mason. "She went home."

"Oh, I figured you'd try to wrangle her into a three way."

"I was going to, but she was not into it."

"That happens," she said.

Mason shrugged, picked up Herman, and they all headed home.

When they made it back, Eileen immediately went to her room to type. Mason told Sophia they needed to talk, and she felt her stomach clench the way it did when anyone heard those words. He led her to his room.

"I just wanted to ask you something," he said. "What happens if, during this open relationship, one of us falls in love with someone else?"

"Oh, I don't know. Can we cross that bridge when—if—we get there?"

"I need some reassurances here. It's not like this is just common jealousy. You plan on having sex with other people. That's a really intimate connection. What if you met someone who has more in common with you than me? And what if he's, you know, more endowed? What happens if you start to fall in love with him?"

She tried not to laugh at his penile insecurity. Why did every male she had ever dated worry about size? Still, he brought up a lot of valid concerns, so she seriously mulled it over.

"The same thing that would happen if you fell in love with someone else while you were in a monogamous relationship, I guess," she said.

"What happens in monogamous relationships?" he said.

"What happened when you cheated on your girlfriend when you were on tour?"

Mason thought about the consequences surrounding that event, but there were none. "I never told my girlfriend," he said.

"And what happened when you got back?"

"You mean, did I still love her?" he said as she nodded.

"And did you still stay with her?" she said.

Mason sighed. And then he thought about how he had fallen out of love with all the girls he had dated previously. And all of them were in monogamous relationships with him at the time of the respective break ups. The world didn't end, he realized.

And then he realized she had out-argued him once again.

Chapter 37

"I need to talk to you, Mason." It was the first thing Eileen said when she returned home the next day. Since she sent text messages to her brother and all the other characters instructing them to take the day off, she was the only one who worked.

"Okay," he said. Sophia sat next to him on the couch. She was as curious as him.

"In the other room. Sorry Sophia. I need some alone time with my brother."

Sophia nodded in understanding as Mason followed Eileen.

"Okay, so I spoke with the woman playing Bonnie last night about the details... You know, the sex details."

"Okay," said Mason warily.

"She told me everything, even showed me the sex toys," she said. He felt a total wave of embarrassment and awkwardness. He felt as though he was talking to his grandma about sex. "I just wanted you to know that I'm using all the steamy details. Of course it'll all be in the name of Jack, but I wanted to tell you in case people start connecting you to your character work."

He shrugged. "I'm not embarrassed by any of that," he said.

"Good, because it works so well with the plot. The Jack character needs this experience to help him out of his shell. He's the prude. Part of his character transformation is the re- alization that he needs to adopt more of a carefree lifestyle. That's the only thing that will cure him of his anxiety and angst. Well, that and playing in a new band."

Mason considered his reputation, and the likelihood it would survive his association with sexual experiences that he hadn't considered until recently. He didn't see himself as a sexually hip kind of guy, but maybe she was right. Maybe that was part of the problem.

"I guess that makes sense," he said. "I'm sure I'll be fine. Someone like grandma's not going to read it, anyway."

"And who cares if she does?"

He nodded. "You know, as far as the band part of the story is concerned, the reason I was able to play that happiness so convincingly is because I lost myself in the character. I imagined it happening to me and it made me feel really good—like so good that I wanted to start another band…"

"That's the other thing I need to discuss with you. That flyer from the band was a real flyer. The only difference was that they just had Fugazi, Mclusky, and Minutemen as their influences, so I added Future of the Left, Alice Donut, and Nomeansno just so you'd be more stoked."

"I don't get it," said Mason. "When I talked to them on the phone, I told them I was in Deadly Optimism and they said they heard of it. Deadly Optimism was never a band."

"I called them before I redesigned the flyer and wrote the one-sheet for that day. I told them about the character placement we were doing and that you were going to tell them you were in a fake band. Then I told them about you and Tortured Metaphor and they were super stoked. When you set up a practice for next week, that was real. You have band practice next week."

"So you put flyers up all over campus?" he said.

"They did at first. I redesigned it and rehung it everywhere."

"Hmm," he said. "What if I didn't find one? It was just by chance that I went into the Arts building."

"Chloe would have brought one home," she said.

Mason grinned. "You're really killing it with this story, Eileen."

She thanked him and told him to follow her back into the next room. She had more news that involved Sophia.

"So I got you an actual sex and relationship advice column in a publication called *Deadlocked Magazine*," Eileen told Sophia. "They're going to pay you and everything."

"You mean for Chloe?" Sophia said.

"No, for you. When you wrote the responses as Chloe, I showed them to the editor of *Deadlocked* and he loved them."

"Isn't the editor that guy who used to run *Proclamation Indignation*? Eli, is that his name?"

"Yeah, that's him," said Eileen.

"So am I writing them as Chloe or as me?"

"As you," said Eileen. "If you want, you can use Chloe as a nom de plume, or just call yourself by your name."

"Is it still going to be called *Begging the Question*?"

"I'll have to talk to my agent and the publishers about copyright issues, but I think it will still work. I have a different title for the book now anyway."

They asked Eileen what she was going to call it, but she wouldn't tell them. "The cat's in the bag," she said.

· · · ·

Since Eileen broke the fourth wall and inserted herself into the story, she used the opportunity to create two diverging plots lines. One involved her uncle and all the things she wanted to say and do with him since he had died. The other focused on Jack and Chloe's struggles—which so closely mimicked those of Mason and Sophia that she didn't bother convening character enactments. Once she rewrote one-sheets and revised character developments, she was able to convince Beforehand she could finish the novel by observing the events unfolding in her own apartment. All the placement agency needed to do was provide minimal settings for her and Uncle Ernest. Since it went a long way in minimizing costs, the arrangement satisfied everyone invested in the endeavor.

Eileen spent her mornings with Ernest—who walked with her through Denver and told her stories—and her nights at the apartment, incessantly typing in her bedroom with the door open. She didn't tell Mason or Sophia about the arrangement. She wanted the circumstances to occur organically.

Late one afternoon, she ran into Sophia who was also heading back to the apartment. After exchanging pleasantries and hugs, they walked together.

"Have you gotten a lot of sexy questions to answer for *Begging the Question?*" asked Eileen.

"I did," said Sophia. "I already turned in my first column—two days early, I might add."

"Alright," she said. "How much are they paying you?"

"They said $50 a column, but they're adding a weekly feature on the website where I pretty much do the same thing for $25 a pop."

"That's not terrible."

"No, I can't quit character placement just yet, but it's a

start."

During the walk, they could appreciate the first truly hot days of late spring. The green leaves, the late sunset. They both felt grateful, not just for the weather, but for all the excitement unfolding in their lives.

"You and Mason doing anything tonight?" Eileen said.

"Yeah," she said shyly. "But take my word when I tell you that you don't want to know about it."

"Sexy time, huh?"

Sophia laughed. "Something like that."

"Don't worry. Whenever I hear you two going at it, I think of him as Jack."

"That's very clever of you. Writers—you're all just so smart."

When they walked through the door of the apartment, they were greeted with a picture-perfect, social media-worthy image of Herman stretched out on Mason, who was sprawled across the couch. They were both snoring loudly.

"Aww," the girls said in near unison as they pulled out their phones to document the situation. The commotion awoke Herman, who glared at them as though they were ruining Christmas. His stirring jostled Mason, who took one look at the beagle and started laughing.

"You're ruining his life," said Mason.

"Come on, you have to get up," said Sophia. "We have to get moving." She dropped her purse on the coffee table and headed for the bathroom.

"What're you up to tonight?" asked Eileen.

"We've got a double-date thing with this other couple," he said.

"Sounds interesting," she said.

Sophia met the other couple through her column. A woman wrote in with a question about where to find another down-to-earth couple to experiment with light swinging. She and her boyfriend were curious, but they didn't want to dive into the Olympic-sized swimming pool of swapping romantic partners without dipping their toes in the water first.

Instead of responding to the question in her column, Sophia personally replied to the email by volunteering her and Mason as the other couple. She was witnessing her lover's slow transformation from outright rejection of an open relationship to well-nigh curiosity—maybe even slight acceptance.

The date began simply enough at a restaurant mutually chosen by representatives from both parties through email. Sophia and Kaitlyn conducted an extensive correspondence detailing not only the eatery in which they would be dining, but boundaries and limitations to which they would adhere. It was a double date where they would be testing the waters of controlled, small-scale swinging. There would be no sex or intimacy of any kind sans kissing. That was the established rule for the evening.

"Y'all are by far the most interesting folks I ever met," said Kaitlyn's husband Jay, a delivery truck driver from Alabama with blonde hair, high cheekbones and an extremely healthy physique. He had no visible tattoos and wore a baby blue golf shirt. "Character placement? I never heard of such a thing."

"I just kind of fell into it," said Mason. "It's a fun enough job." Mason never mentioned he joined the union for fear of alienating Jay and what he presumed was his southern anti-union heritage—which was hilarious, considering he was a driver for UPS and a teamster.

"What do you do, Kaitlyn?" asked Sophia.

"I'm a personal assistant," she said. She was skinny,

blonde, and had donned extremely short blue jean shorts and a shirt with what Mason assumed was the state flag of Alabama emblazoned on it.

"Anyone famous?" said Mason.

"No, just someone who's extremely rich and too lazy to go to the cleaners or to shop for groceries," she said.

"Now, now," said Jay. "She ain't that bad. And the checks are always on time."

"That's true," she said.

While the couples didn't have much in common, they certainly shared a mutual attraction. Jay and Kaitlyn each secretly yearned to engage in sexual exploration with severely eccentric people—even though they'd never want to bring someone like that home to meet the family. And Mason and Sophia always desired the radiance of magazine-ready model doppelgangers—even if they'd never want to accompany one to a punk show. Each couple held an air of mystique to the other.

After dinner and a few drinks, Mason invited everyone over to his house. The other couple remained apprehensive, but once Sophia reminded them of their kissing-only agreement, they consented. In the cab ride over, they rearranged the seating order so Jay sat next to Sophia and Mason next to Kaitlyn. While no romantic touching occurred, they were comfortable near each other.

More drinks commenced when they returned to the apartment. Eileen briefly introduced herself before disappearing back into her room.

"So I can't help but notice, no one's kissed yet," said Sophia upon finishing her fourth drink.

"That's true," said Jay. He met eyes with Kaitlyn and then shifted his gaze to Sophia. "I just have two questions. Who's going first and how do we keep it from getting awkward?"

"Jay, why don't you sit over here?" Sophia patted the couch cushion next to her.

"Ma'am, you don't have to twist my arm."

He sat down and waited for her to make the first move, which took approximately three seconds. The two kissed passionately as Mason and Kaitlyn watched—the latter of which was much more turned on than the former.

By his standards, Mason allowed a generous amount of time to pass, so he turned to Kaitlyn and said, "Okay, I think it's our turn."

She agreed and wasted no time sliding comfortably into first base. Although the parameters had been firmly set prior to the occasion, Kaitlyn placed Mason's hand on her breast. Without thinking he reflexively jerked it away, but she whispered in his ear that it was okay. As she pulled away to gently kiss his neck, he stole a glance at Sophia and noticed both of Jay's hands on her breasts. Much to Kaitlyn's delight, Mason followed suit.

Once they made it to the point where kissing either became something more or ceased altogether, Sophia pulled away from Jay and said, "Okay, we should figure out what we're doing here. Do we go forward with this tonight and take it to the bedroom, or do we take what we've done here and sleep on it?"

The excitement in the room slowly dwindled to nil as rational thought began to overwhelm the heightened passion. Collectively, they decided to discuss the events of the evening with their partners when sobriety returned with all of its insecure over-analyzing.

Sophia made tea and Jay and Kaitlyn called for a cab. As they sipped the hot beverages, the couples sat in traditional seating arrangements, adhering to an important rule of the open relationship: If you start the evening with your partner, end it that way. There's no bailing on dates.

Before Jay and Kaitlyn left, they conducted a four-way make out session that all involved parties would keep in the memory bank for lonely evenings for many moons to come. Sophia assured Kaitlyn they would be in contact soon enough.

Once the door closed behind the departing couple, Sophia literally jumped into the arms of Mason, who nearly dropped her on the hardwood floor. "I'm going to ravage you," she said.

Mason awkwardly yet swiftly carried her into the bedroom, shut the door, then became Jack in the imagination of his sister.

Chapter 38

"So what do you think?" asked Sophia the morning after the big date.

"About what?" said Mason.

"Don't play coy with me."

"They seemed nice."

"Sure, they did. But like, what did you think when you saw me and Jay kissing?"

It was complicated and Mason didn't know how to articulate the wellspring of emotion rollicking through his brain. Part of him found the experience enticing and thrilling in a way he never thought possible. Another part of him was almost physically repulsed by the sight of his girlfriend with another man. One emotion gave way to the other in a manner of seconds and neither held his sway long enough to establish its dominance. He was confused and at a loss for words.

"I don't know," he explained.

"You don't know how you feel?"

"No, I really don't."

"Are you upset? Did it turn you on?"

"A little of both."

Her brow furrowed. She knew these experiences conjured up a flurry of reactions, but she was hoping he would eventually recognize that he emerged from them emotionally unscathed. But last night when Mason, seemingly jealous and frustrated, told Kaitlyn it was their turn to kiss, Sophia felt a pang of regret. Perhaps, she conceded to herself, Mason wasn't on the cusp of a "eureka moment" after all. As much as she wanted him to experience the joy of an open relationship, she didn't want to bully him into it.

"You know, I've been thinking," she said. "We don't have to keep doing this. If you just want to be monogamous, we can just be monogamous. I don't want to force you into anything you don't want to do."

"Seriously? You seriously mean that?"

"Yes, of course I do."

"So you're saying I get to be jealous and mean and petty and irrational whenever you talk about wanting to be with other men?" he wondered.

"Um…"

"You said it."

"That's definitely *not* what I said," she said. "It's not what I meant either."

"Okay, okay," he said. "I'm just joking."

Sophia raised an eyebrow. "Joking about what?"

"About being mean and petty. I don't want to be an asshole. I do want to make everything work. I want us to be happy together."

"That's all I ever wanted."

Mason smiled. For the first time since they began dating, he didn't feel pressure to be anything he didn't want to be. And once she gave him the luxury of his own destiny, he could finally stop defending himself and try to see the world from her perspective. Maybe non-monogamy wasn't just about what she wanted to do. Obviously he played an integral part in her romantic plans.

"You know," he said, "when we first started dating, I thought you were enlightened or something. Or like, you lived in some alternate universe where there was no jealousy. You were very intimidating. But I mean, I understand more about where you're coming from. I get that overcoming jealousy is something that would bring me a lot of happiness and a lot less guilt. But you have to understand it's going to take time."

"Of course," she said. "That's why I was glad to meet Jay and Kaitlyn."

Mason smirked.

"What?" said Sophia.

"Do you think they call each other Jay and Kay?" he said.

They shared a laugh that drained the tension from the discussion.

"As long as we keep it at a glacial pace," continued Mason, "it's—I don't know—tempting enough to keep going."

Sophia smiled. "Okay," she said. "Thank you for placating me and my sexuality."

"You're welcome." He glared at the ceiling in deep concentration. "You know what else is weird about this whole thing? The way society handles it, you know? It's like, because we're not in a monogamous relationship, I shouldn't look the way I do."

"What do you mean?"

"I mean, I should have a horrible goatee and greasy hair and always keep the top of my shirt unbuttoned so my chest hair can stick out. And I should be sleazy and untrustworthy and maybe smell like stale donuts and cheap cologne. And I should probably drive a hot pink car with a horn that plays 'Get Down Tonight.'"

Sophia guffawed. "I really don't think all that's necessary," she said.

"Of course I know that. But assuming the worst about people who are promiscuous is like being impressed with fame and fortune—it's an American reaction. Because that's the culture we were raised with, and whether you accept it without question or you reject it all, it's still there. And it's deeply ingrained."

While Sophia recognized the truth in what he was saying as it applied to him, the perspective he espoused simply didn't pertain to her in the least. She was proudly independent because she had to be. Pretending there was any truth to the twisted sexual mores of this culture only caused confusion, guilt, and harm.

"It is ingrained," she said. "But you can overcome it. The old fashioned, puritanical views of sex don't have to define you as a person."

"Yeah… What you're saying makes sense intellectually. But I feel like the way culture defines you affects you in this weird emotional way. Every time I think I'm capable of being open minded about my sexuality, I think about what my grandma would think."

"Why?" Sophia shouted. "Do you honestly think your grandma has your best interests at heart?"

"She would say she does because she wants me to go to heaven."

"And what if she's wrong? What if there is no heaven? You can't possibly think she's right. You don't even believe in god!"

"No…"

"No, you don't! Look at her god, anyway. He hates everyone who wasn't born straight. He hates everyone who isn't at constant war with her sexuality. He hates everyone who enjoys life in any genuine capacity. That's total bullshit. You're not hurting anyone. Why the fuck would any god waste his time on you? He should be more concerned about the Waltons and Koch brothers of the world. Talk about people who are fucking shit up."

Rationally speaking he couldn't refute any of her arguments. Yet, he still had a nagging sensation he felt in his gut that society's opinion of him mattered somehow. And that was the biggest obstacle to overcome in embracing non-traditional lifestyles like open relationships. Mason even admitted he found the romantic interaction between Jay and his primary lover alluring, among other things. Accepting this attraction as a component of his personality meant rejecting thousands of years of unquestionable sexual virtue—at least as far as western values were concerned. He didn't quite have the gumption to pull it off.

"Yeah," he said. "By the way, it's *Koch* brothers—pronounced like the soda, not like cock."

"You say potato..." she said. She was glad to inject humor into the discussion. It lifted their spirits and allowed them some empathy and breathing room in a conversation with such high stakes. "But you're right. I shouldn't insult cock like that."

"I know where you're coming from," he said. "And I don't want to let my grandma's twisted worldview prevent me from, I don't know what to call it..."

"Self-actualization?" she said.

"Yeah, that sounds right."

"You know Mason, I had to deal with all this shit too. I wasn't born confident and emotionally reasonable, you know? I was sexually active at a young age and people were terrible to me. I can't count how many times they called me a slut. But it doesn't matter, because those people never even cared about me. It wasn't about me anyway. It was about them yelling hateful bullshit so they felt better about their shitty, boring lives and the shitty, boring choices they were making."

Sophia did have it more together than a lot of people Mason knew, including himself. There was an air about her that seemed unflappable. She never apologized for being herself—indeed the concept would have never occurred to her.

Her self-reliance manifested itself in myriad ways: She didn't wear a lot of makeup. She cut her own hair, poorly, and wore the results with pride. And although she wasn't fashion forward by anyone's standards, she cultivated her own distinct style.

But most of all, she had no angst. She crafted a unique lifestyle and maintained an unwavering devotion to it. She was amazingly self-assured.

"Don't get me wrong," he said. "I want to live without doubt and self-pity. I want to tell myself there's nothing wrong with me, but I'm not there yet. I'm going to need time and I'm going to need your patience. I love you though, I really do."

"Oh Mason, I love you too."

They embraced passionately, and would have escalated into heated intercourse if it weren't for Eileen's interruption from the living room.

"That's perfect!" she shouted.

Sophia and Mason looked at each other and laughed.

"What's perfect?" Mason shouted into the other room.

Eileen didn't answer. They could hear her typing. Again Mason shouted, and again there was no response. He stood from the bed and began getting dressed. Sophia followed his cue and reluctantly started getting ready as well.

He sauntered into the other room and stood directly behind Eileen's computer screen. "How's the story going?" he asked.

It took him a couple of tries before she acknowledged his presence. "The story?" she said. "It's writing itself. It's amazing. It's like someone else is channeling words through me."

"Good for you," he said.

"Thank you," she said. "Though I do have to say that your character is kind of weird to write."

"Why?" said Mason.

"Because it's amazing how happy he is," she said. "A few months ago, I never would have written your character like this."

"Well it is a character," he said.

"I mean sure, Jack is an exaggerated version of you, but this version of you doesn't dread everything like a character based off of you a few months ago would have. Plus you have a job, a girlfriend, a dog. You're going to start playing music again."

Mason didn't want to entertain the notion that he was content with life. He didn't want to jinx any stroke of good fortune by dwelling on it.

"I guess that's something," he said dismissively. "What about you?"

"Well yeah. But unlike you, I can admit when things are going my way," she said. Mason laughed in derision. "You know how long it's been since I felt any kind of anything?" she continued. "I spent years doing nothing when I was living with Paul. You know how shitty it feels to do nothing? To have no goals? To float through life with nothing to show for it?"

"Who the fuck do you think you're talking to?" Mason said. "Of course I know how that feels."

"Sorry," she said. "It's just, I don't mind being all roses and rainbows when my life is finally out of the crapper. I get to be thankful that I'm smiling more. Not like you—you think every smile is an invitation to eventual sadness, like you're tempting fate."

Mason derived a certain level of comfort from sadness and disappointment. With despondence, there was nothing on the line, no risk.

"Yeah, well," he said.

She shook her head. "You're happy right now. Just fucking admit it."

"Come on, let's not get all sentimental," he said. "No one likes happy people."

Eileen sighed. "No one likes happy people? You're so damaged," she said, shaking her head. "You know, if you don't mind, I need to get back to work."

"Speaking of," he said, "do you still need us to do any character placement?"

Sophia quickly emerged from Mason's room when the subject of work came up.

"The setting's been scrapped," Eileen said. "The story's been evolving as a character-driven retrospective piece between me and Uncle Ernest."

"Are we in it anymore or did we just set up the story between you and Ernest?" wondered Sophia as she sat next to her on the couch.

"You're kind of in it and you kind of aren't," said Eileen. "And I have to leave it at that."

"Hmm," said Mason. "How's Uncle Ernest doing?"

"He's great," said Eileen. "We're working through a plot now and we're having a fucking blast."

"What's the plot about?" said Sophia. "Or are we allowed to know?"

"I can tell you about that part," she said, "as long as it stays between us."

The story was from the perspective of Eileen chronicling events from her uncle's past, though the narration was in his voice. She merely asked him to expound his experience of hitchhiking to San Francisco in the spring of 1966 to see Andy Warhol's *Exploding Plastic Inevitable* with the Velvet Underground and Nico after his first marriage failed. She said the one-sheet was extremely concise for those scenes: "Head to Ernest's favorite bars. Take extensive notes." It was kind of like a loophole in the laws of fiction, she explained. She had the distinct pleasure of bringing back her deceased uncle for the purposes of novelizing his life. It was the most fulfilling endeavor she had ever experienced.

She detailed the vicissitudes of his trip to California, like when he found himself on of the receiving end of a shake down from backwoods cops 60 miles west of Salt Lake City, or when he got stranded outside of Reno for an extra day, nearly missing the first night of the two day Warhol residency. On his second night in San Francisco, he met a woman who eventually hitchhiked with him to L.A., where he saw The Doors and Them multiple times at the Whisky a Go Go. It was quite the summer.

"He told me a little bit about that trip," said Mason. "Can you even imagine seeing The Velvet Underground and The Doors in their prime? That would be 'unreal,' as Uncle Ernest would say."

"That's funny," said Eileen. "He keeps using that word when he's telling me the story. 'That was unreal, man.' You know, there's a reason those bands were his favorite."

"Other than the fact that they were unreal?"

"Other than that," she said. "You don't say that word as well as he does, by the way."

"I know, I know. It's not very becoming of me."

"Anyway, he's sentimental about them because of this

girl named Starla Moonstone that he met during one of the *Exploding Plastic Inevitable* shows. They fell madly in love on their first night together and after a few days of hanging out in the Bay Area they went back to West Hollywood where she lived in a cramped one-bedroom apartment with two other eccentric artists. This was Los Angeles in the '60s, so of course they were all having sex with each other and with other people. It was hard for Uncle Ernest because he had just fallen in love with this girl and now he had to share her with another guy and girl. He had never done that before."

"Hmm," Sophia said. "That sounds familiar."

"There are parallels to your story arc," she said. "The past has a funny way of repeating itself."

"Do we get to see Uncle Ernest again?" Mason wondered.

"Maybe not during this story," said Eileen.

"But maybe during the next one?" Mason said. "Is there going to be another one?"

"Let's hope so, right? Uncle Ernest and I have already been talking about other stories we could make together. I can make characters for you and Sophia."

"We'd love that," said Sophia.

"Yes, we would," said Mason. "So can you tell us what you're going to call this one yet?"

"No," said Eileen. "But I guarantee you'll like it."

"I'm sure we will," said Sophia.

Herman, who had been sleeping at the other end of the couch this whole time, opened his eyes and stared at Mason. He emitted a low humming noise, which Mason had come to learn meant the beagle expected him to scratch his belly. He rolled over on his back and lifted his front and hind legs in the air.

"I'm being summoned," Mason said as he sat on the couch

and fulfilled his obligations to Herman.

Eileen saved her work, closed her computer screen, and joined him. Sophia was right behind her. All three of them began petting Herman. The dog was having the time of his life, melting into the couch.

"You think anyone could be happier than this dog is right now?" said Sophia.

Mason and Eileen locked eyes.

"I can think of at least one," Eileen said as she smiled at him.

"He's definitely happier," said Mason. "But I get what you're trying to say."

Epilogue

"You're late," said Eileen.

"I know," he said. "I just had to pick up my flyers." He handed one out to everyone at the table.

"What's this?" Ernest said.

"It's a flyer for my band's first show."

"You're called Inoperable Kitten?" Ernest asked.

"I know," said Sophia. "Tell him it sucks!"

"Jack, it sucks," he said.

"They needed a name for the flyer, and that's all we could come up with. We'll change it before we release anything."

"Sorry, I have to call you Jack one last time for the story," said Ernest.

"That's okay."

"So is your band any good?" asked Ernest.

"Well," he said. "It's starting to come together, I think. But I have to say, don't expect too much from the first show."

"Starting the band is the most important thing," he said.

"I guess," said Mason. "The whole thing is starting to make me realize there's no finish line. I mean, I thought I'd be happy just starting a band, but it only made me want something else. Now that I started it, I just want us to be good. So I'll just keep going, you know? Once we're good, I'll probably want to be better. Then when we're better, I'll wish we could transform our talent into money. And then if we ever got any money, I'd wish for more. There's no end…"

"Until you die," said Ernest.

"I guess that's it," Mason said.

Ernest stared blankly at his grand nephew for a few moments, then he said, "You know, you're never really going to be happy. I wanted you to start playing music again so you had something to make you miserable. You see, right before my death, you had allowed yourself become miserable for no reason, and that's the most miserable thing you can do. You just can't languish in ennui."

"So I'm always going to be unhappy?" said Mason.

"Yes, it's in the striving for success that makes you unhappy, but it's a good kind of unhappy," he said. "Eventually you'll have a sense of accomplishment, and that's what fulfills you."

"But even that's fleeting," Mason said.

"Life is fleeting," he said. "That's why you have to celebrate the victories, no matter how small they seem to be. A life wallowing in all the small defeats is a life wasted in a personal hell of your own making."

Mason thought about it. "That's really good advice," he said. "Why did you wait for the epilogue to tell me that? You could have told me that when you were alive."

"Well, you have to save some your best material for the end. You can't just blow your wad."

"Yeah, but…" He trailed off. He couldn't think of anything good to say.

Ernest changed the subject. "Anyway," he said, "originally I wasn't supposed to be in the epilogue, but I told Eileen I had one more thing to tell you."

Mason's tardiness had allowed Ernest, Eileen, and Sophia to get a couple rounds of drinks. They ordered one for him, but Ernest drank it when the ice started to melt.

Mason excused himself momentarily to get another drink and ended up buying the entire table a round since he was never sensible when he fell into expendable income. Not only would he eventually receive his inheritance, but Beforehand had over-paid him for his character work—even at his union rates.

"So what's up?" he said when he returned from the bar. "What do you need to tell me?"

"Two things actually," Ernest said. "First, I ran into a soul I knew from life on the other side. He was super rich and had a bunch of kids from a couple different wives. And he was dead just like me."

"So?"

"So he's dead."

Mason laughed. "So you're saying that even people who have it all end up dead too?"

"Indeed I am," he said. "And the second thing I get to tell you because Eileen let me." He looked over at his grand niece. "Ready, Eileen?" She nodded. "You've been had!" he yelled. "She tricked you into the potential you had all along, you nitwits!" He laughed uncontrollably.

Mason and Sophia exchanged bemused glances. "Do you have any idea what he's talking about?" Mason said. Sophia shook her head.

"I'm going to let Eileen explain it," he said. "I have to get going. Eileen, thanks for the drinks. Soon enough my inheritance will work its way through the proper channels and I'll pay you back." He guffawed. "I love you all so much it's unreal. I'll see you next novel."

Ernest hugged each of them for a long time. He had a lot of love to give. And for whatever reason, this goodbye wasn't sad for anyone.

"I think this time I'll leave out the back door," he continued.

"It's slightly classier." He began whistling the Doors' verson of "Back Door Man" as he walked.

Once he was gone, Mason asked Eileen to explain his cryptic remarks.

She told them it all began when Lewis stayed with her at the apartment. He told her how writers of fiction can bring spirits back to life through character placement.

"Could I bring back my uncle after he's gone?" Eileen asked.

"Only if you're a writer," Lewis said.

"How do I become a writer?"

"You write."

Then when she stayed with Ernest in the days before he passed, he confessed his anxiety about Eileen and Mason wasting their potential. He was most concerned with Mason, however, because he seemed to be in desperate need of guidance, since he was so directionless and alienated by life.

"What if there's a way I could force Mason, Sophia, and me to live up to our potential and you can even come back and check on us?" she asked.

"How would you do that?"

"I would write."

She once again elucidated the fiction loophole that allowed disembodied spirits to return to earth. Then she explained the plan she and Lewis devised. It involved Eileen writing a novel in which Mason joined a band and Sophia started a sex and relationship advice column. Through Lewis, she would have an agent; through George, she would have characters (and procure jobs for her brother and his girlfriend); through the laws of fiction, Ernest could actually witness the results.

"It was almost too perfect," Eileen said. "The genius of

it was getting you to do the things you were too busy or scared to do on your own, and making it seem like it was just a part of character work."

"Yeah, but you stopped using us halfway through," said Sophia.

"No, you were still in the novel. I was fictionalizing your interactions with Jay and Kailyn. By the way, who do you think connected you with them?"

"You did that?" Sophia said.

"Yep, found them on Craigslist and invited them to send you an email for the advice column."

It had been several months since that first double date and since then, they had interacted a half dozen times with pleasing results for all involved parties.

"Were you listening to our sexual experimentation?" said Mason.

"Yes," she admitted. "But don't worry. You were Jack during all that, so it wasn't gross."

"Oh, well good."

Silence settled in around the table as Mason and Sophia contemplated their reaction to the ruse. Never had they felt such a sense of betrayal with such beneficial results. It was a confusing set of feelings.

"And one more thing," said Eileen. "Beforehand was paying you the entire time I was writing about you."

"Oh," said Mason. He looked over at Sophia. "We figured they overpaid us because they made a mistake or George threatened them or something."

"No, you actually earned that," she said. "I got Jay and Kaitlyn some money for their appearances as well; though it's pretty minimal since they're not union."

"I hope they don't think they were tricked into being prostitutes or anything," said Sophia.

"No, no," Eileen assured her. "I already talked to them. They understand what went down and they signed releases, no problem."

Mason and Sophia stared at one another in amused bewilderment.

"I'm going to go to the bathroom and then grab another drink while you sort this all out for yourselves," Eileen said as she stood up to leave. "You guys want anything? I'm thinking about getting something to eat."

"No, we ate at Citizen Café earlier," said Sophia.

"Is he tricking you into being vegan?" asked Eileen.

"Kind of," she said. "I'm tricking him into being more open sexually and he's tricking me into eating better."

"Well, isn't that nice?" Eileen said. "Alright, I'm going. Talk amongst yourselves."

"Well," said Mason after downing a large portion of his drink, "it appears as though we've been duped."

"Yeah," said Sophia. "I definitely didn't see it coming."

"How could you see something like that coming?"

"You mean this real life fiction where your disembodied great uncle and your sister use literary devices to trick us into changing our lives in ways they approve of?"

"Yeah."

"Yeah," she said. "I guess part of me is pissed, because how dare they decide what's best for us. But another part of me..."

"...is glad they did it?"

"Exactly," she said. "And of course... I might be guilty of the same thing."

"What do you mean?"

"I may have told Eileen to include Bonnie in the story."

"Really?" said Mason. "So I would know what it's like to be with someone else?"

"Yes," she said sheepishly. "So you would realize it was no big deal."

"That's… a bit manipulative," he said. "But whatever. I had her write Herman into the story. So I got a beagle out of it."

"See, everyone is guilty."

"I suppose so," he said as he mulled it over. "You know, I can also say I'm in a better place because of it. So I guess that's cool."

"Well, you did get a sexy live-in girlfriend."

In the intervening months, Sophia had moved out of her house and into the Jarman's apartment so she could be closer to her lover, his sister, and his dog—in that order. All of a sudden everyone's rent was super cheap.

"Of course," he said.

"And I got a column and a sexy live-in boyfriend, who's the singer of an unfortunately named, and possibly shitty band," said Sophia.

And soon she would have a functional website and podcast if all went according to plan.

When Eileen returned to the table, she asked how they were reacting to the situation. Although they admitted hurt feelings associated with being duped without their consent, they were in the mood to forgive such slight indiscretions—especially since they were made with more or less benign intentions.

"So you have to tell us," said Mason. "What are you going to call your book?"

"*The Dog's Out of the Bag*," she said.

Mason nodded. "Okay," he said. "I'm into that."

They ordered another round of drinks and Mason raised his glass. "Here's to selling a million copies of *The Dog's Out of the Bag*."

"Cheers," they said.

After they drank, Mason said, "You know what the weirdest part about this whole thing is?"

Eileen and Sophia shook their heads.

"Our lives were written into a book for months and we didn't know," he said. "It kind of makes you wonder, doesn't it?"

Sophia nodded. "I guess you have to be careful what you say around writers."

Eileen smirked and said, "Yeah, who knows when you're going to end up in someone else's story."

Acknowledgements

First and foremost, I would like to thank the Once Upon a Time Character Placement Agency for supplying all the characters for this book. I certainly appreciate their team for being much more adept and easygoing than a certain other agency I utilized for my first novel (an unscrupulous, cut rate corporation that preys upon first-time, self-publishing novelists and will remain nameless because I can take the high road like that). I am indebted to A.C. Coben, Victoria Fisher, and Zoe Gosselin for their outstanding performances as Mason, Eileen, and Sophia respectively. Thank you for bringing such warmth and passion to the project. My dog Herman was very gracious for appearing in the story and allowing his body to become possessed by a discarnate spirit. He definitely enjoyed all the biscuits and affection everyone bestowed upon him. And finally, I'd like to express my gratitude to all the other characters who made appearances. This story would not have been the same without you.